THE AWAKENING

BOOK ONE OF THE JAGUAR OF THE BACKWARD GLANCE

ANDREW J. PETERS

THE JAGUAR OF THE BACKWARD GLANCE SERIES

The Awakening
The Sim Ru Prophecy

This second edition is a reworked and reformatted version of the acclaimed *Werecat* saga.

ONE

March 15, 2012

IT WAS THE Friday before Spring Break, Jacks's last semester, his senior year at Calverton University. Most students were heading home for the week, and the ones whose parents had money were taking off to places like Mexico and Florida's Gulf Coast. Jacks could have gone home on a Greyhound bus to the papermill town in Pennsylvania where he grew up. But since he told his parents he was gay, his father pretended he didn't exist, and his mother followed him around with the full force of maternal martyrdom, begging him to come with her to church or at least sit down with her to read The Bible.

Late that afternoon, Jacks's housemates, Jonathan and Gabe, announced a profound decision. They were ditching their plans to go home and booking bus tickets to Montréal. They found a motel room they could share for eighty dollars a night. They wouldn't be returning to school with tans after a weekend in Montréal in late March, but the drinking age was eighteen, and Gabe hadn't turned twenty-one yet. Plus, Jonathan said they had clubs where the go-go boys stripped down all the way and danced on the bar. Jacks jumped at an invitation to go along. They made it to the campus bookstore just before closing to sell back their textbooks, and they scrounged up a few hundred dollars for the weekend.

For the bus ride, Jonathan mixed up a ridiculous concoction of orange soda and vodka, and they shared swigs from a metal thermos. Their motel was predictably a dump, and Jonathan and Gabe threw down their backpacks on one of the room's twin beds, signaling to Jacks they'd be hooking up if nothing better turned up that night.

Montréal was a fantastical metropolis to Jacks. When they hit the streets to dive into the city, it was hard for him to not stare up at the skyscrapers like an idiotic tourist. The sidewalks were crowded with people. He had a smile slapped on his face taking in so many things. The European architecture, which signaled to Jacks a sense of proud sophistication. The endless retail shops. The high-shouldered handsome men in well-made trench coats and scarves, talking on their phones in French.

They made it to the city's Village, the gay neighborhood, and hopped from club to club, downing shots between drafts of Canadian beer. That's when memories got murkier for Jacks. They danced. They caught a drag show that was wall-to-wall people, and then he wandered off on his own. He'd probably had a petty fight with his friends. It made no sense, but Jacks felt lonelier when he was out drinking with people. His solitude bit at him, and he got mean and did self-destructive things.

He remembered walking the streets, the world careening, blurred cars speeding by him. The main part of the city was built on a slope, and he was determined to keep heading steeply uphill like the labor of a mythological god. Then he was in some kind of park. Mount Royal, he would later piece together.

He must have been drawn there by the thought of climbing the mountain, maybe as a drunken lark to show the world he could do it, or maybe it was a wild idea to jump off from the top. Jagged emotions came back to him—laughing, screeching, and then heaving with tears. If a cop had caught him, he could bet he would've tried to fight him.

The unrailed concrete stairways were in serious need of repair, and at some point, he must have lost his balance and tumbled into a forested ditch. That was when he got so dizzy he threw up and passed out in the leaves and dirt. He vaguely recalled the sensation of being dragged along the forest floor and having no will to stop it.

Jacks woke up shivering beneath cheap blankets. Sunlight, filtered through unwashed windows, showed he was in a park building, hollowed out, strewn with leaves, long ago abandoned.

A stranger stooped down in front of him, offering a paper cup of steaming coffee, light and sweet.

Jacks shrunk up against a wall. The guy had long black hair. His jawline and upper lip had a few days growth of beard, and he looked to be, perhaps, ten years older than Jacks. He wore a vintage trench coat, and at first Jacks figured he must be some crazy homeless man. But his eyes were a stunningly bright shade of green, like some gorgeous print model, and he seemed sober and well-groomed. Jacks was cold and thirsty and pretty damn hungover. He took the cup and sipped the sweet coffee. It was delicious and warming.

After a few sips, however, the strangeness of the circumstances came back to him. What was he doing holed up with some guy who could be a lunatic? Had they slept together?

Jacks set down the cup and stood up from the blankets, grateful his clothes were intact. He smelled like dirt and the seat of his jeans was black with it.

"I've got to get going."

The man was oddly casual about everything. He cocked his head. "Where will you go?"

"I'm staying in town with friends. They'll be worried about me."

A merry look passed over the man's rugged face. Jacks didn't know what to make of it. Did he think he was lying?

"You probably saved my life or something. I was pretty far gone last night." Jacks rooted in his pocket. All he had was a pair of five dollar bills, but he offered them to the guy. "Here. Thanks."

The man glanced at the cash and coughed out a chuckle. "I don't want your ten dollars."

What do you want? Jacks wondered, spooked.

"Stay with me for a while. It's early. You'll have plenty of time to catch up with your friends."

"Nah, I've gotta go." He replaced the bills in his pocket and stepped around the man. Their shoulders brushed together, and a warm sensation spread like tentacles through his body. The man caught his arm.

Jacks pulled away, telling him, forcibly, "Don't touch me."

"If I was going to hurt you, I would have done it while you were passed out last night."

"Yeah, I guess you would. Look, I'm cool. Whatever your reasons for getting me out of the cold last night, I'm grateful, okay? I just don't make a habit of meeting people this way."

The man fixed on Jacks challengingly. "Do you think you're better than me? You came into my territory, drunk and helpless. I could have let you freeze to death." His voice softened slightly. "Surely, you can spare some time."

Jacks hadn't meant to offend the guy. The word "territory" lingered in his head. As far as he could figure, they had both been trespassing in the park, and squatted in some long-

forgotten cabin. He looked at the man again. Was he danger-
ously psychotic? The guy seemed too calm for that. They stood
an arm's length from each other while Jacks deliberated. It was
bonkers hanging out with some stranger, who had to be a
vagrant, but Jacks couldn't dismiss the feeling that he owed
the guy.

"Sorry. I'm not trying to be rude."

"Then maybe we can start again." The man reached out his
hand. "Benoit." His hand fit over Jacks's like a warm, luxurious
glove.

"Jackson. Well, everyone calls me Jacks."

THEY COVERED UP together beneath blankets in the
abandoned cabin, sharing the warmth and drinking the coffee
Benoit had bought. Perhaps, precisely because they were
strangers to each other, Jacks turned confessional and
explained how his life had come to this. He told Benoit about
his disastrous night in the Village, which had led him to
roaming in the park. He unloaded about the sense of alienation
that had haunted him for years and was recently made worse
when he came out to his parents. Jacks hadn't shared such
things with Jonathan and Gabe, at least so deeply, but somehow
telling them to Benoit felt natural. He never showed the
faintest distraction nor rushed to reassure him. Though Benoit
didn't share much of his own story, just vague fragments of
growing up in Québec City and taking some time to travel the
country since his father's death, Jacks felt he understood and
cared, maybe more than any one he'd ever met.

Benoit suggested they take a walk around the park, and he
toured Jacks through many amazing things. They saw the
granite disks of La Montagne des Jours. Benoit translated the
etched words that encircled them. They were strange verses by

past visitors to the park, which evoked an unexpected sentimentality.

*You're going to write me often? Sometimes I close my eyes,
and I guess I'm there. You smile. You should have brought me
here before. The wind in the trees. Light tasks.*

They came to a toboggan run, and Benoit found a
discarded plastic sled. Though a recent rain had washed away
most of the snow, and they were too big for it, he coaxed Jacks
to climb in with him, and they slid a few yards and got stuck in
the grass. Benoit pulled Jacks out, and they went bounding and
tumbling down the hill. They landed in a muddy jumble, sore
but laughing.

The park filled up with joggers, older couples on walks, and
young people on racing bikes. Benoit led Jacks to secluded
places on their walk. They wove through monolithic Inuit
sculptures—primitive, hulking icons of polar bears and statues
of creatures that were half man and half bird. When they
stopped at the Belvedere to look out on the panorama of Beaver
Lake, Jacks could picture what it looked like in winter from
Benoit's vivid description: the throngs of ice skaters, horse-led
sleighs on snowy trails along the shore, the lakeside meadow
filled with people sculpting blocks of ice. He spoke so
eloquently and knew so many details about the world.

Jacks's cell phone groaned with missed calls and text
messages from Jonathan and Gabe. He ignored them for a
while, but then his conscience gained up on him. While Benoit
stopped in a public bathroom, Jacks wrote back to his friends:
"Met someone. Tell you all about it later."

At the Kondiaronk Lookout, where they could see downtown Montréal in the hazy morning and the gray St. Lawrence
River in the distance, Benoit stood close behind Jacks and
crossed his arms over Jacks's stomach. That felt good, but Jacks
was suddenly aware of his dirty clothes and his unwashed

body. He worried Benoit might try to kiss him. He had thrown up last night, and the taste of it, mixed with coffee, lingered in his mouth. But Benoit just nuzzled against his neck, and nibbled on his ear, which tickled and made him laugh.

Benoit opened his trench coat so that Jacks was enveloped with him. "I have a room in town. You can get cleaned up. A change of clothes. Some breakfast?" He chomped playfully on Jacks' neck.

Jacks took Benoit's hand, and they headed down the slope into town. He thought it was strange Benoit had slept in the park when he had a place to stay, but his rational mind was several steps behind how Benoit made him feel. Safe. Desirable. Normal.

BENOIT'S ROOM WAS at a hostel near the park. They had strict rules against guests bringing in people, but Benoit improvised a plan. He kept the front door clerk distracted with a sightseeing question so Jacks could slip past the entry lounge with Benoit's key and hold open the locked door to the dormitories.

Inside, Benoit gave him a towel and showed him to the men's bathroom, which was a dingy, tan, tiled facility. Jacks peeled off his clothes and stepped into a curtained shower stall. Hot water washing away the grime from his body felt luxurious. He stood beneath the showerhead and closed his eyes.

A presence filled up the space behind him. Jacks turned and jolted, covering his mouth with his hand. Benoit had undressed and slipped into the stall noiselessly. As Jacks took in his bare, rangy body, it was all at once a welcome intrusion. Benoit's green irises sparkled, somehow more brilliant in the darkened stall, and then he kissed Jacks forcefully and backed him up against the shower wall.

Jacks clenched his eyes shut as Benoit devoured all parts of his body. He felt weightless, beyond himself, as though feeling the effects of a drug. When Benoit stooped to his waist, Jacks raked his hair. He teetered with exquisite tension, inhaled by Benoit, their bodies joined, the world stripped away. He raked Benoit's hair harder. A strange vision filled his head: hands morphing into claws and reaching out to gouge the wall. Benoit clasped Jacks's back and scored lines down his skin. Jacks shuddered with a desperate groan. Breathing heavy, he squinted down at Benoit. His emerald eyes flared, still hungry.

TWO

FOR DAYS, THEY holed up in Benoit's room, fucking endlessly and briefly tending to their basic needs until they were inspired to go at it again. It was like their bodies were made for each other, and Benoit knew precisely where Jacks needed to be touched and how firm or teasingly gentle and when he craved a slap on the bottom or a bite to turn him on even more.

Once that week, Jacks caught his reflection in the mirror and stared at himself with a mixture of amusement and horror. His neck was stained with bruises. His complexion was as pale as a corpse, and his eye sockets were hollow and darkened. He looked like he'd been chained up as a sex slave, which was not far from the truth, though Jacks was an entirely willing participant. He was badass. Jacks washed up hurriedly to return to Benoit.

More texts from his friends went unanswered. Jacks had found a spectacular sex partner, and looming larger in his head, he had found a connection with another man. The L word dangled in his head, though he thought it best to wait for Benoit to say it first.

Benoit had his mysteries, but at the time, they just seemed quirky. He never ate anything but meat and milk, pushing aside the vegetables in his Chinese takeout dinners with his chopsticks, which he had mastered perfectly, and pulling apart his fast food cheeseburger to discard the bun. Benoit slept deeply in the afternoon and stayed up all night. When Jacks surrendered to sleep around three or four in the morning, he woke a few hours later to find Benoit opening the door with coffees and chocolate croissants from an early morning bakery. Benoit said he liked to go there when the pastries were fresh. He also only drank the coffee, which was nearly white with cream.

In fact, Jacks's fascination with Benoit made the oddest things about him the easiest to dismiss as aspects of his character that showed an appealing, rebellious streak. He clearly didn't have a job, and he never complained about money nor asked Jacks to split the cost of their meals. He never had a place to be, whether to keep up with family or friends, and he told Jacks he didn't own a cell phone. As far as Jacks could tell, everything Benoit owned fit into his vintage traveler's bag, and it included unusual items like an embossed, antique pocket watch and a leather motorcycle jacket that looked like it went back to the 1950s. He was unlike any person Jacks had ever met, and somehow, he found Jacks interesting too.

A couple of times when Jacks watched the evening news on Benoit's tiny TV set, he caught a few seconds of a story about an early morning jogger in Mount Royal Park being gored by some wild animal like a wolf. Benoit always took the TV remote and switched to another channel, complaining about sensationalized journalism.

As the days crept closer to the Sunday when Jacks was to return to Calverton, a weight fell over him. He could tell

Benoit felt it as well. Benoit drew into himself, and whenever their eyes met in his little room, he looked away, holding something in. On Saturday afternoon, after making love, they sat apart for several hours: Jacks on the bed, Benoit on the room's only chair, with the TV on and neither one watching it. Anxiety pressed in on Jacks, and he had to break the silence.

"You could come back with me."

Benoit looked at him with cold incredulousness. "You want to take me to your college?"

Jacks tried an easy smile to lighten the mood. "I mean, to visit for a while. I've got my own room. Jonathan and Gabe won't mind. They've both had boyfriends stay over before."

"Boyfriends?" Benoit sneered.

Jacks drew into himself for a moment. "I guess I shouldn't have assumed. I've never been in this situation before."

"What situation is that?"

Benoit's words scalded Jacks. "I don't know. We never talked about it."

Benoit stood and paced around the bed. "I'm fully grown, Jackson. I'm not someone's boyfriend, and I'm not interested in having a casual affair when it's convenient for you."

"That's not what I'm saying. I would stay if it was possible. There's seven weeks left in the semester. I can come up weekends—"

Benoit halted and glared at Jacks. "You belong here."

The corners of Jacks' eyes burned. He was so confused. Benoit's anger scared him. Everything was so much better when they were holding each other.

"What am I supposed to say?" Jacks wiped his teary eyes with the bedsheet. "I think I'm falling in love with you, Ben." His voice turned fragile. "Do you feel the same way about me?"

Benoit stormed toward him. "Why else would I have saved

you in the park? And now you want to walk out like it meant nothing?"

Jacks tried to process things, but it was like a dream had turned into a nightmare. "Can't we try to make this work, like in a normal way?" He cringed from using that word. "I don't mean normal. I mean, I know we live in different countries, but we can still see each other, can't we? We're not so far away. It'll be hard at first, but it's not so long. I graduate in May."

Benoit smiled at him, cruelly. "Yes, that would work well for you. You'll be fucking the first man who gives you the tiniest bit of attention."

Jacks threw off the bedsheet, pulled on his briefs and stood. "You know what? Go fuck yourself." He grabbed his jeans from the floor, but Benoit held his arm to stop him from putting them on. He looked briefly placating.

"Is it so bad that I want you to myself?"

"You make me feel like scum. Why do you do that? I blew off my friends all week to spend time with you." He shrugged. "But I guess you don't care. You just pegged me as an easy lay. I've been there before. I thought you were different, but obviously I was wrong."

Benoit gripped his arm tighter. "Spare me the adolescent dramatics." He released Jacks and stepped away. "If you leave tonight, it's over. If you try to come back, you won't enjoy it. I promise you."

Jacks had his pride, but it was overpowered by something visceral he had only just discovered about himself that week. He staggered to Benoit and wrapped his arms around him. "I want you to have me to yourself." He took Benoit's hand and placed it on his chest. "You'll be right here."

Benoit pushed him away. He crossed the room and sat back down in his chair. He draped one leg over the other, and his dangling foot swayed back and forth.

"If you want to be with me, come back tonight to where we met. After the park closes. With only what you wore the night I found you. Do it, if you want to be with me."

He stood, grabbed his trench coat, and strode out of the room.

JACKS HOPED Benoit said that out of raw emotion, which would abate with time. It was crazy dramatic, but Jacks couldn't really say Benoit's behavior was so far out of the norm. He'd never gotten so deep in a relationship. They'd been in bed together all week, sharing every physical intimacy known to man, and clearly, Benoit wanted him as his partner or boyfriend or whatever. Maybe Benoit had reasons for reacting so intensely. He might have been burned before in a long-distance relationship, or maybe there was a problem with him crossing the border. Based on his lifestyle, it wouldn't be surprising if he had a troubled past. Jacks wouldn't judge him for that. They just needed to talk and be honest with each other.

But Benoit didn't return an hour later, nor two, nor three. At that point, Jacks realized he was way over his head. He didn't know what to do, so he called the one person he felt he could confide in: Jonathan.

Jonathan picked up immediately. He said he and Gabe had been mad worried about him, and Jacks eased into an explanation.

Jonathan wanted to know how Jacks had met this "mystery guy." Jacks knew the situation would sound sketchy, and Jonathan didn't hold back his skepticism.

"You met him in the park after storming out of a bar, wasted?"

Jacks hadn't even mentioned that he actually passed out in

the park and met Benoit in some decaying outbuilding the next morning. "Ye-ah. It was kind of random."

"Dude, do you even remember the fight you had with me and Gabe?"

Jacks said nothing. That night had been a blur, and it felt like it had happened ages ago.

"You basically called us a couple of hypocrites and said our friendship was bullshit."

Jacks covered his face in his hand.

"Oh, and then you made up some shit about Gabe making out with some guy in the bathroom."

That part brought back a fuzzy memory. Jacks did see Gabe fooling around with a stranger in a stall when he went to the bathroom that night. "I'm really sorry. I honestly don't even remember much about it. I was pretty fucked."

"Yeah. Well. I can't believe you stayed up there. Who is this guy?"

"His name's Benoit."

Jonathan wanted more details, which embarrassed Jacks even more. The fact was, he didn't know much about Benoit. Jacks hadn't planned on doing it, but he lied. He said Benoit was thirty years old, and his family was from Québec City. The last part was the only concrete detail Benoit had given him, and then he added that Benoit was on vacation in Montréal.

"I'm glad you met someone, I guess," Jonathan said. "It all sounds a little sus, if you want to know the truth. So, are you coming back tomorrow?"

Jacks stood up from the bed and bit his lip. "I don't know. He asked me to stay with him." Jacks tousled his hair. "It's been a crazy week."

"Wait. He asked you to stay up there, and you're seriously considering it? What are you going to do? Drop out of school so you can move in with him?" Jonathan didn't let Jacks answer.

"That's like really smart. You met some guy on vacation, and now you're staying in Canada without a visa to see where that goes?"

Jacks knew it sounded insane, but his relationship with Benoit hadn't been some random hook-up. He thought he could explain that to Jonathan and get some real advice on what he should do, but he found himself stumbling over words and feeling like Jonathan didn't understand at all.

"You do you, Jacks. But our rent's due Monday. Are you going to send me your share or are you blowing that off too?"

Jacks said he'd send his portion of the rent from his banking app. If his work-study check had gone through last Thursday, he should have enough to cover it since he'd barely spent any money all week. He stepped away from the conversation feeling even worse than before the call. Jacks didn't remember the fight, but he could imagine he was drunk and acting like an asshole. He'd tried to apologize, and now Jonathan sounded like they weren't even friends anymore. He didn't care Jacks had a guy who might be "the one" and was torn over what to do. Maybe he didn't even believe it. Jonathan just thought he was being a flake and skipping out on rent.

Hours ticked toward midnight, and Jacks hedged on what to do. On his cell phone browser, he found a bus at five thirty in the morning that would take him back to Calverton. He could head down to the station and wait for it. Pretend that Spring Break had been a dream. He would re-emerge in the real world, forgetting everything. He cried thinking about it, and he ached for Benoit. Maybe he should have asked more questions about the guy he was sleeping with, but nobody had ever wanted him like Benoit.

He owed Benoit the respect of hearing him out. Near midnight, he left the hostel and started walking to Mount Royal Park.

It was just across the street—a boundless, darkened slope of land. He crossed the park-side street, Avenue des Pins, talking to himself. What're you doing, Jacks? Meeting some guy you know practically nothing about, in a park, in a foreign country, in the middle of the night?

He grinned wryly to himself. Yeah, that's exactly what you're doing. Because you fucking can. You're twenty-two years old, and you've got no ties and nobody to disappoint. So, let's do it.

He took the path he and Benoit had come down that first day. Signs were posted about the park closing at dusk, but the place was much too big to keep people out in any practical way. Soon into his trek, Jacks was disoriented. Nothing looked familiar as he climbed up stairwells and followed meandering trails. He took guesses at turns and pushed along briskly, with his shoulders tight and his eyes and ears attuned to his surroundings. The news stories about people being killed by wild animals lingered in his head.

Miraculously, he stumbled on a sign for Montagne des Jours, where Benoit had read him French poetry from engraved stone disks. It pointed up a paved road that disappeared under the darkness of trees. The abandoned cabin had to be in that direction. He sped up to a jog, keeping to the middle of the pavement.

Headlights glared on a bend of the road ahead of him. Jacks ducked onto the tree-lined shoulder. He watched a police car roll down the road toward him. Searchlights played out the window on the forested brush as Jacks flattened himself on the cold ground.

The police car passed. Jacks stood and dusted himself off. This was fucking insanity. When he found Benoit, he was going to provide answers, no half responses or dramatic diversions. Jacks jogged back onto the road.

The road inclined, and as Jacks looked to one side, something struck him as familiar. There was a drop off, and a broad, forested expanse below. He wasn't one hundred percent sure, but it looked like the vicinity of the remote cabin. He carefully descended a steep escarpment, watching his steps over slippery leaves and mud.

He couldn't find any trails at the bottom, so he was pretty much walking blind. But an instinct pulled at him. He wandered a little, stumbled down a slope, and his sneakers scuffed an asphalt path. It had to lead to something. He decided to take the path heading to his left.

Crowning an incline, he saw light in the forest. He sprinted toward it. The cabin was at the end of the path, and it looked like it was burning from the inside out.

Frightening thoughts rushed through Jacks's head. Had an accident happened or a suicide, arranged in spite? Nearing the cabin, things came into focus. It wasn't a raging fire. The windows of the cabin were aglow, but that burning light inside was contained.

Jacks swung open the door. The cabin's gutted interior had been decked out with hundreds upon hundreds of candles. He saw blankets mounted in one corner, approximating a bed. The spicy scents of sandalwood and patchouli hung in the air. Jacks looked around the space. Where was Benoit?

Warm, humid breath grazed his ear. "You came."

Benoit had snuck up on him. He sealed his mouth over Jacks's and he surrounded him in his arms. Jacks nudged Benoit away—a moment of refusal—but his body caved to Benoit's proximity and the arousal of surprise.

They pulled each other's clothes off. Benoit bullied Jacks on his heels, through the room, until the blankets bunched up at Jacks's feet, and he toppled backward, braced by Benoit's arms, the nest of blankets beneath him.

Benoit shucked the sneakers and socks from Jacks's feet, and he took off his boots. Then Benoit was upon him, and Jacks ceded sight to sensation. They molded into one another, and Benoit rubbed his stubbly beard against Jacks's chest, burning him like a brush fire, sending his head swooning. Benoit leaned back, and Jacks looked down at his chest. It was scored pink and dotted with tiny domes of blood.

That was rougher play than Jacks was used to, and before he could process what was going on, Benoit clasped Jacks's open palm to his heart.

"Will you be mine, Jackson?"

Benoit's intensity confused Jacks.

Benoit kissed the tips of each of his fingers, and then, with a sudden forceful grip, he curled them like a claw and raked them down his chest. Jacks hadn't cut his fingernails in over a week, and horribly, he felt them scraping into Benoit's flesh. Benoit was planted on top of him. Jacks threw his weight from one side to the other and managed to tug his hand away. But Benoit's thighs clamped solidly around his sides, and he captured his hand again.

"It must be done."

"I don't want to hurt you."

"I promise you, you're not."

Jacks freed his hand and twisted his body to get out from under Benoit, but Benoit held him tight. The spark in his eyes made Jacks think he was turned on by the struggle. The dark room, dappled in candlelight, suddenly felt like a scene from a satanic ritual rather than a romantic retreat.

"Stop. You're freaking me out."

"It's the only way. Blood to blood. We'll be mated forever."

"I don't understand. Please, you're scaring me."

You know, Jackson.

That voice hadn't come out of Benoit's mouth. But it was

Benoit's, and it was somehow in Jacks's head. Benoit hovered over him, and in a blink, Jacks saw a black panther head glaring down at him. In another blink, the feline phantom was gone.

Jacks fought for his life to get away. He freed his hand and tried to push up from the floor. Benoit slashed Jacks's exposed chest with his nails, gouging a bloody tear. On reflex, Jacks shoved Benoit's shoulder, and a fingernail caught Benoit's flesh below the collarbone.

Benoit pinned Jacks's hands above his head. Blood seeped from his wound. The room spun while Jacks was paralyzed with terror. Benoit sealed himself on top of Jacks, chest to chest, with his feet hooking his ankles.

Jacks fought and cried out, but Benoit held him like an iron apron. He imagined their blood commingling and understood it was some sort of occult rite. Two heartbeats drummed in his body: his quickening, Benoit's calm and steady. Gradually, the rapid contractions of his heart slowed down as Benoit's pulsing chest lulled him into a steady meter. He felt lightheaded and weak. A feline purr reverberated through his body, and then he blacked out.

THREE

JACKS WOKE WITH a violent start. Based on his last memories, he expected to be in severe pain and fighting for his life. But he felt no trace of his struggle with Benoit. He wondered, hopefully, if it had been a terrible dream.

The abandoned cabin spread around him, however. It was still nighttime, and the house was lit with a multitude of candles. Had Benoit left him? Jacks couldn't say if he had passed out for a couple of minutes or several hours. He lay flat in the bedding where Benoit had attacked him and didn't move. If Benoit noticed he was awake, still alive, he would probably try to hurt him again.

In a shadowy corner opposite him, he glimpsed the terrifying silhouette of an enormous black cat with fearsome, iridescent green eyes. It was half a man's height at its shoulders and easily six feet long.

The wild beast swayed toward him. His lungs shrunk up, and he held himself completely still. Should he make a break for it or play dead in the hope it would lose interest and go away? He watched the dangerous animal, trying to judge its intention. Its eyes were fastened on him, though he couldn't say if it took him for a mild curiosity or dinner. He heard a voice.

It's me, Jackson.

Jacks couldn't help from pushing up from the bed and swinging around, searching for Benoit. He sounded so near.

It's me.

The cat came up an arm's length from Jacks and sat on its haunches with its big forelegs pitted in front of him. Though his eyes were still wide with terror, instinctively, Jacks felt it. Benoit was in there, however that was possible.

As he gazed into the cat's big, glassy eyes, he saw a feline head reflecting back at him with pointed ears tucked back defensively. Jacks looked down at his hands and saw bushy paws. He only then realized he hadn't stood. He'd gotten up on fours. A scream rose up from his chest, and a bestial howl came out. He stood and turned around himself. He had a tail. He could see his balls, but his penis had receded beneath the fur and skin between his hind legs. He was a golden mountain lion.

Benoit gazed at him steadily. *You're beautiful.*

The ritual flooded back to Jacks: the slashing of skin, Benoit's weight pressing down on him, the mixture of their blood. He thought the words and heard his own disbelieving voice in his head.

What did you do to me?

I made you better.

You made *me*— A wave of desperation came over him. *I want to go back to what I was. Change me back. I didn't want this.*

You'll be able to change in time. You'll be able to go back and forth. It's a gift, Jackson. You should be thanking me.

A gift? It was a diabolism, or maybe he had completely lost his mind. Jacks couldn't get enough air into his chest. He was panting with a big tongue lolling out of his mouth. Everything about his new self was horrifying and foreign.

Benoit nudged Jacks with his muzzle. Jacks shirked away.

There's nothing to be afraid of. We are nature at its finest. A superior state of being.

Jacks stepped around himself again, confirming what he had become. Though what *had* he become? *What am I?*

You're my mate. You're the creature you were always meant to be.

Jacks lurched away from him. Benoit's affectionate tone only made the situation more frighteningly bizarre.

The change is never easy at first. But you will learn and come to appreciate that I reared you. Yes, look at yourself. You've never been so powerful. Think about the abilities you possess, Jackson.

Reared me? What does that even mean? Jacks was practically whimpering.

The Rearing. I awakened your feline soul.

You think I should be grateful for this? Is this a fucking joke? What are *you?*

Benoit's voice rose in an impatient complaint. *Yes, I am a monster. We are monsters. But only in the eyes of humans. You knew this. Do you regret now answering my command?*

He sounded so sure of what Jacks knew, so sure he'd had the potential of *this*, Jacks cracked open a bit to the possibility. Their relationship had been a seduction all along. They'd spent all week in bed, which felt now more like an imperative, a primitive need, rather than a fast-burn romance. Jacks turned coyly shy, remembering the sensuous thrall of Benoit's lovemaking, his dominance, the aggressive edges that aroused Jacks. He was bonded to Benoit. Maybe it was wrong. Maybe the sane thing to do was to snap out of it, but he couldn't deny something inside him wanted to follow Benoit wherever he would lead him. Unless it was all a deception on Benoit's part.

He laid down in the blankets with his head tucked between his forelegs. *I don't understand any of this. Did you do it because this is how you want me?*

Benoit strode over. *I did it because your feline soul needed to be released. We are the same, Jackson. You felt it, too. You just didn't have a name for it.*

Benoit clawed up a spot in the blankets next to Jacks and lay down, leaning his back into Jacks's underbelly. *We have so many experiences ahead of us. The world is ours, Jackson. I have so much to tell you, but that can wait. The ritual has been exhausting for both of us. Just know you'll never be alone now, and I will always protect you.*

Jacks was suddenly aware of that exhaustion. His feline body was shutting down, demanding sleep. It was cozy, lying with Benoit as they were, and his brain was too tired to think anymore.

WHEN JACKS WOKE the next morning, he was tangled in the bedding with Benoit. They were both back to their human selves, though Jacks couldn't deny what had happened the night before. Gold and black fur clung to the blankets. Benoit was tucked against him with his eyes shut, looking blissful. Jacks gently rustled out of Benoit's embrace and stood.

He found his phone and was alarmed to discover it was one thirty in the afternoon. He glanced at Benoit. He was in a deep slumber, as he always was during the day. He never woke before five, maybe four thirty at the earliest. Jacks eyed the cabin door. He could quietly step into his clothes and walk out. Call an Uber to take him to the bus station. Go back to his normal life and pray that it would stay normal.

What if it didn't stay normal? If that monstrous change came over him again, he'd have to hide himself deep in a forest or something like that. He might never be able to have contact with human beings again. Jacks examined his naked body. His fair, lightly freckled skin didn't look any different. He didn't see anything about his anatomy that had changed. He didn't feel supernatural, however that should feel. But he'd been a mountain lion just a few hours ago.

He was suddenly restless, and his hollow stomach ached. Jacks threw on his jeans, his hoodie, and his sneakers, and he ventured out of the cabin for coffee and food. Then, he would decide what to do.

It was a gray and drizzly day, which meant not many people in the park who he could follow to a commercial area with food vendors. As he looked to the top of a wooded escarpment, a railing to a trail caught his eye. Jacks hiked briskly toward it, not breaking a sweat nor breathing harder while tackling the steep incline. At the top, he felt fresh enough to hurdle the three-foot high rail rather than take it one leg at a time. He landed on the paved trail, perfectly grounded and wanting to take that leap a few more times. Jacks had never been athletic, but now he felt like he could hike all day through rough terrain. He took the sloping trail at a jog and sped up to a run, exhilarated by his long, powerful strides. He could see his breath, but the cold, damp air didn't penetrate his body. His lungs seemed to have an infinite capacity as did his muscles. Jacks was strong, unstoppable.

A tempting scent wafted to his nostrils, and Jacks followed its invisible stream, charging off the trail to climb a bank of wilderness which was a faster route to food. He emerged at the plateau of the mountain with a plaza and a chalet, and he slackened his pace a bit because of the people. Inside the cafeteria, he scanned the overhead menu, stepped up to the counter, and ordered five chicken sandwiches, four sandwiches with ham, three bags of peanuts, potato chips, a grand chocolate chaud with whipped cream, and a latte for Benoit. Mercifully, his ATM card worked at the cash register. That last work-study check had gone through. When he picked up his order, Jacks wolfed down three of the sandwiches right where he was standing. He washed it down with long gulps of his hot chocolate until he finished.

He headed back to the cabin with the rest of the food, eating peanuts and chips along the way. Food had never tasted so good. Especially the protein, which his body craved voraciously. His mouth watered from the scent of the chicken and ham in his bags, but he fought against being so gluttonous. Benoit needed to eat, too, and bringing him food would hopefully put him in a good mood. He had said his transformation—an awakening, he'd called it—was a gift. Jacks was starting to feel that, and he needed to understand more.

He entered the cabin undisguised, and he watched Benoit respond to the scent of food. He stirred a little but kept his eyes shut.

"Come back to bed. It's early."

"I was hungry. You're lucky there's anything left." He sat down at Benoit's feet with his bag from the cafeteria, hoping to entice him to have one of the sandwiches.

Benoit made a grouchy face. "You shouldn't be going out by yourself. It's not safe. Were you tempted to run away?"

"I needed to eat. I got you a latte with extra cream." Jacks could dodge through parks now like a military commando. It built his confidence. He found Benoit's bare knee under the blankets and gave it a jostle. "C'mon. It's nearly three in the afternoon."

He watched a quiet smile pass over Benoit's face. Then Benoit yawned and rustled up to a seated position. He looked at the takeout bag that reeked of greasy meat. Jacks stretched it toward him, and Benoit grabbed it. He pulled out two of the grilled ham sandwiches, set them on his lap, and ate the meat.

"Do you ever eat anything besides meat and dairy?"

Benoit eyed Jacks grumpily.

"I'm genuinely asking. I want to know about these things."

Benoit wiped his mouth and fingers with the napkins Jacks had brought. "You only need meat now." He stifled a belch with his fist and made a sour face. "The fresher the better. This scavenged food is like eating from a dumpster."

Jacks stood. His limbs were so restless, and the cabin felt too confining. He stepped around. "I want to *do things*." He couldn't help himself from ranting. "I ran all the way to the chalet. Didn't break a sweat. It was mostly uphill. How far you think that is? A mile? Two? At least one mile. I felt like I could do it ten times. You want to go for a run? It'll be dark soon." Jacks broke out in a smile. He was lightheaded, practically manic. "I want to try out some shit. Climbing trees. Seeing what's out there in the forest, y'know?"

"You're in limerence. It happens after the change."

"What do you mean?"

"The first stage after the transformation is a period of hyperacuity. You'll be restless for a while, but it will pass as your body adjusts." Benoit fixed on him severely. "Stay close to me. It's easy to overestimate your abilities."

Jacks snorted a laugh. His body was definitely hopped up on something, but he loved it. "I don't know. I need to stretch my legs." He glanced at Benoit, and he was overcome by a different enticement. Jacks crawled over next to him and leaned his thigh against Benoit's. "After, we could come back here, and y'know, do all the things you like." He cleared his dry throat. "I bet it'll be even hotter than before."

Benoit looked him over dispassionately.

"Okay." Jacks sprang up to his feet. "You don't want to go anywhere and you don't want to fool around. So, what are we doing?"

"Keeping you safe. Teaching you how to keep a low profile."

Jacks rolled his eyes. "I don't know how I could have a lower profile. We're in a forest in a foreign country."

"You need to stay out of sight."

"Why?"

"You left your friends while on vacation. You're expected back at college." Benoit studied Jacks. "Did you tell anyone where you are?"

"Yeah. I called Jonathan earlier, but it's no big deal." His body was buzzing like he'd just done two lines of pharmaceutical cocaine. "I'm not thinking about going back to school if that's what you're worried about. I obviously can't, being like this."

"That's not what I'm worried about. People will be looking for you. They could report you as a missing person. That's what happens when people disappear."

Disappear. That struck Jacks as brilliant. He was craving adventure. He could barely fathom all the things he could do with his new abilities.

His heart rate accelerated, and a pinpoint of pressure grew in his gut. He bore into that sensation, tensing his abdominal muscles like bracing for a punch, and he exploded into his cougar form. That surprised Jacks for a moment, and then he had a playful urge to pounce on Benoit. Benoit was too quick, however. He morphed into a jaguar and growled and gnashed his teeth to bully Jacks back.

This isn't the time to play around.

FOUR

BENOIT TAUGHT JACKS how to return to human form. It was basically the same way he'd reared into a mountain lion, squeezing up his gut like he was pulling his feline half inside him and reemerging through that spot as his biped self. Then he pushed Jacks along to his room at the hostel. Benoit said they were traveling. He had a place for them in New York City where they could stay for a while. Benoit packed his bag, and they took a taxi to Gare Centrale. They caught a 5:55 p.m. train to New York. Benoit wasn't wasting time.

Jacks was happy to be on the move. He'd always wanted to visit New York City to see what it was all about. He'd be seeing it with his enhanced senses and abilities. There had to be a billion things to explore, and they could do everything with no fear. They had the strength of big cats. They could walk Manhattan from one end to the other in the middle of the night and fucking own the streets.

His brain was still buzzing from the effects of his transformation, but when the conductor announced they were approaching the stop for Calverton, his thoughts slowed down enough to consider some practicalities. He told Benoit they were getting off. He had some things at his apartment he wanted to get. He couldn't keep wearing the same clothes, and he had an iPod and a laptop that had cost some money. Along with his comfy gray cotton sweater and a pair of designer Western jeans, which he had blown his biweekly work-study paycheck on and fit him goddamn perfectly.

Benoit looked at Jacks like he was insane. "We can get you clothes in New York."

"I want my stuff." Jacks stood and went over to the exit doors. Benoit was pissed, but he followed Jacks off the train when they got to the station.

Jacks knew they had to avoid sightings or confrontations with his housemates. They needed to get into his room, get out, and go on their way. He led Benoit off the country highway to Calverton and through the fields of farmland and wooded stretches that surrounded the college town.

It was a long trek under a nearly pitch-black sky, but the new attunement of his senses laid bare what had once been totally obscure. His eyes could penetrate the night. The familiar smells and sounds of campus pointed him in the right direction—the furnace-heated dormitories, the frat houses redolent with beer, a faint teenaged commotion here and there, the scent of people.

They skulked through the backyards of the houses on his block and drew up by some bushes behind his home.

There was light in the first floor bay window of the firetrap Colonial, and pop music and a television blared from inside. A Sunday night. The guys were home, probably with some friends over.

Benoit looked at Jacks impatiently. Jacks ignored him and studied the house. He had never considered it before, but there was a clear climb from the back porch railing to the porch roof and around the corner of the house to his second floor bedroom window. His slumlord had never installed a storm panel or fixed the double-hung window guard.

"Just stay here," he told Benoit.

Jacks approached the house, weaving through the shadowy parts of the yard, on some sort of autopilot. His body knew to distribute its weight so his steps were soundless, to halt and wait out sounds of movement from the kitchen adjoining the porch, to scamper quickly behind the railing. His arms and legs were supercharged with catlike agility. He scaled the porch and kept a light step on its creaky roof. He reached for the window ledge to his bedroom, raised his upper body to its height, and found a foothold with the toes of his sneakers lodged at an angle on the house's wood siding. The height of his perch—twelve feet or more—barely registered as a danger.

He peered through the window into the darkened room. A familiar scene spread out in front of him: his cluttered computer desk where he had left his laptop charging, his over-flowing laundry bag, his faded, wood-paneled chest of drawers, and—as luck would have it—the duffle bag he had taken on the trip to Montréal, where he had left his iPod. Jonathan and Gabe must have brought it back and put it in his room.

He glanced at his bed and redoubled on it. Some sort of shadowy, muted movement was going on there, and as he zoned in, he saw two figures shuddering together, joined from buttocks to hips. Jacks recognized Gabe's long neck and buzzed head in the driver's position. Gabe was fucking some guy in *his* bed?

Jacks wanted to pounce inside and menace both guys out of his room, but his better sense stopped him. How was he going to get his stuff while *this* was going on?

As he rescanned the room, a plan occurred to him. He wasn't going to let some rude housemate drama ruin his plans—

Gabe seizing the opportunity to bag some dude in a place where Jonathan wouldn't catch him, or whatever. Jacks didn't understand their on again/off again relationship, and he supposed, it wasn't his place to understand it. Jonathan had accused him of making things up. He could figure things out at his own pace.

Jacks felt along the bottom edge of the window, and carefully, patiently slid up the pane until the top of it caught on the warped window frame. That created an opening of two feet or so for him to duck inside. He pulled half of his body through the window.

Raunchy odors and stale marijuana smoke assailed his nose. The guys were caught up with what they were doing and unaware of the open window. Jacks wriggled the rest of his body over the window ledge and landed in a contorted position on the floor, overestimating just how stealthy he could be. Gabe turned to the window, and his fuckbuddy glanced over too.

Jacks could only think of one thing to do before someone hit the lights. He bore down on the achy spot below his diaphragm to summon his cat self. In the span of heartbeats, his skull and skeleton lengthened, bent, and curved. His musculature broadened, and he was crouched on four paws with fur rustling through his back threateningly. He fixed on the two young men and raised his voice into a snarl.

They scrambled to the far side of the bed and bolted out the nearby door. Jacks grabbed the strap of his duffle bag with his mouth and looked at his laptop. There was no way to pack it quickly with just his mouth and unopposable paws. Nor did he have time to sort through his dresser for the clothes he wanted. The duffle bag had some going-out clothes, a few changes of underwear, his toiletries, and his iPod. It would have to do.

Beyond the bedroom, the music cut off, replaced by a frenzied conversation from the first floor.

"A goddamn mountain lion came through the window."

"Whoa—you're freakin' out."

"We both saw it. In Jacks's room. We've gotta call the cops or animal control or something."

"Why are you guys naked?"

Jacks didn't stay to hear the rest. He secured the pack in his jaws, climbed out the window, and jumped down to the ground. He galloped back to Benoit's hiding spot.

A quiet grin showed on Benoit's face, betraying a hint of pride.

Let's go, Jacks telepathized.

Benoit reared into a panther, and they stampeded through the backwoods toward the train station.

THEY GOT BACK to the Calverton train station just after midnight and discovered the next train to New York City was at 8:15 in the morning. With nowhere else to go in the meantime, Jacks and Benoit tucked up together on the platform to stay warm and shared a can of salmon Benoit had brought along.

Jacks was bursting with questions about being a werecat. While they had privacy and time to kill, Benoit filled in some blanks.

"Our ancestry goes back to the ancient world, when cults in Africa, Asia, and Central America knew of the father god. Werejaguars trace our origins to an Olmec king. He was the first to endeavor to possess the jaguar soul. To please his god, he made ritual sacrifices of young warriors to no avail, but he was so determined to gain the god's power, he killed his favorite jaguar cub, laid it at the god's totem and plunged a dagger into his own heart to die beside it. He was said to have been reborn with the soul-shifting magic. Little was recorded about what happened to him, but some centuries later, in the same region, the Aztecs had an unstoppable army of jaguar-warriors."

That was interesting to Jacks, but he wanted to know about Benoit more personally. "How did you become a werejaguar?"

"My father was French, but we traveled the Americas during my childhood. He had a hand in a little of everything, running goods from Guyane through the Caribbean Islands and all the way up the Atlantic to Québec. When I was sixteen, we were staying at a sugar plantation near Cayenne on the same night the Portuguese and British landed to take the city. Everyone ran off into the countryside to escape the bloodshed. It was nighttime. It was chaos. They were burning everything in town. I got separated from my father, and I wandered into the jungle looking for him."

Jacks was a poli-sci major, but history was his second favorite subject. He knew a conflict between France, Portugal, and Great Britain placed Benoit's story something like two hundred years ago. "You're talking about colonial times."

Benoit nodded. The space inside his head expanded. How could Benoit have lived so long? He had some fine wrinkles in the corner of his eyes, but if they indicated something like a lifeline, he had one groove for every fifty years.

"While I looked for my father in the jungle that night, a she-jaguar stalked me, though I didn't know it at the time. She must have been very old, from the glory days of the Aztecs. Near daybreak, she showed herself to me when I was cornered on the bank of a river. Her spotted muzzle was big enough to wrap around my head, and she was so close she could have been on me in seconds. I couldn't move. I had never seen such a powerful animal.

"She must have known enough to sort me out from the foreign men who would kill her for her pelt. Maybe she needed to pass along the gift to somebody before she died, or maybe she felt something more for me. I'll never know. After she attacked me and slashed her chest, my father and a group of men gained up on us, following my screams. They shot her, and then stood around in disbelief as her feline body transformed into a dark-skinned native woman. They buried her by the river. We never spoke about what we saw."

"How did you survive all this time?"

"My father offered his knowledge of trade routes to the Portuguese and managed to get us on a ship to Québec where he had some friends. After what happened to me, he vowed to never return to South America. He settled into the fur trade, which was very profitable. We had a house and a shop on Rue du Petit Champlain, among the wealthiest residents of Québec City." He chuckled mildly. "The first time I transformed, I hid myself in the cellar overnight. I was certain my father would shoot me." He dug his fingers into the scruff of Jacks's neck. "Unlike you, I had no one to teach me what I was going through. Over the years, I came to know my feline soul, and my father turned a blind eye to it. I think he blamed himself for losing track of me in Cayenne, and I don't think he could bear to face what happened to me."

"What about your mother?"

"I never knew her. My father told people who asked she died of fever shortly after I was born, when they were living in Bourdeaux. When I was older, he confessed to me he'd never married, and I was the result of an affair he'd had with a native girl in Puerto Columbia. Her family offered him a dowry to marry her, but he couldn't bring himself to live the rest of his days in a 'backward country.' After I was born, my mother disappeared. My father feared that she'd been killed for the shame she'd brought on her family, and he feared what would happen to me. So he bought me from her father with nearly his entire savings and sailed back to Bordeaux so that his mother

and sisters could help raise me. I don't remember much of it."
Benoit's brow furrowed. "My grandmother with her wooden
peel bringing loaves out of the oven. The pigeons that flew into
the attic where I slept. Playing with the painted Santons at the
crèche they set up for Noël. Before my father told me the truth,
I thought they were memories of the home he had with my
mother."

He broke out of that reminiscence. "My father took me
along on his trading adventures as soon as I could wash and
dress myself, so most of my childhood was aboard a galley and
at rowdy stayovers in Caribbean and South American ports.
People loved him. He had a charm about him and fell into
opportunities that were always profitable. After he told me
about my mother, he made me swear to always say she was
French to avoid people's prejudices. I was his only son. He
wanted to make certain there would be no issue with his holdings passing to me. The inheritance came sooner than either of
us imagined. Our fourth winter in Québec, he died of
pneumonia."

Benoit's face was hard. Jacks let a moment pass in silence.
But he couldn't keep the questions inside him contained for
long. "What did you do? You were what? Twenty years old?"

"I'd been helping my father with his trade since I was
twelve. He was insistent about the business staying in the
family. So, I kept his fur company going, but while the
employees and clients grew older, I didn't. Questions would be
raised. I had to leave Québec. I sold off everything to a British
firm and placed funds in foreign bank accounts." Benoit
stretched out a bit. "I traveled the world, never staying in one
place for more than ten years. Europe. Africa. Southeast Asia.
Polynesia. Central America. It was exciting for a time, but I
became bored eventually, which is why I returned to Québec.
It was the closest thing to home for me."

Jacks interlaced his hand with Benoit's as he thought about his remarkable past, and the profound accident of the two of them meeting in Mount Royal Park.

"How did you figure out all this history and what it means to be a werecat?"

"The information is out there if you weed through all the nonsense about witches and demonic possession. I visited Aztec ruins in Mexico and spoke with Zapotec mystics. I lived with the Ashanti people, who worship the leopard in West Africa. In Masharata, India, some villagers have knowledge of the magic through the cult of Waghia, the Lord of Tigers."

"So, you've met others like us?"

Benoit nodded quietly. "That's a story for another time."

"Why?"

"It's scarcely been twenty-four hours since your awakening. Some things about our kind are best left for later."

Jacks didn't like being treated like a child. He wasn't sure if Benoit thought he was protecting him from darker truths or if he just enjoyed withholding knowledge from him.

Benoit gave him a little squeeze. "I'm telling you all this because it made me realize what that she-jaguar did to me wasn't a curse. It was the greatest gift anyone could have given me."

"Why did you choose to give it to me?"

Benoit shifted slightly. "I sensed in you someone who could be my mate."

"What...how?"

"Werejaguars are solitary, but even we need companionship. Especially as we grow older, and we see that a life without connection is empty. Jackson, I wasn't looking for a mate, but I found you in the park that night, and I felt your link to our ancestry, a miracle really. Very few are suited for the transformation."

Jacks glossed over his last words, unsure of what he was saying. "Were there others you...converted?"

Benoit's eyes glimmered. "There was one, many years ago." Jacks gazed at him expectantly.

"I had a lover in Vietnam."

Jacks squeezed Benoit's ribs, trying to tease out more information.

Benoit glared at him in reproach. "You're already showing your feline jealousy."

Jacks laughed. "I want to know about your Vietnamese lover."

"He was handsome and graceful, and when he reared, he became the most magnificent orange-and-black striped tiger."

Jacks drew into himself. How did he measure up to a tiger? Benoit nuzzled against his neck.

"But he wasn't loyal to me."

"Why are you a jaguar and I'm a mountain lion?"

"My maternal ancestors have roots in the Amazon people who knew of jaguar mysticism. Chavin or Arawak, as best as I can say. Yours must descend from North America. Many of the continent's first peoples held the cougar with great esteem. They knew of dual souls. From the Hopi in the West to the Ho-Chunk and the Cherokee of the Mississippi Valley."

That unearthed a buried memory. Jacks had always been told he was a mutt of German and Welsh heritage, but he had once seen in his mother's box of old photographs an old-fashioned portrait of his great-grandmother. She had long, straight hair, high cheekbones, and a dark complexion. She wore many beaded necklaces and a pleated robe. His mother kept the photo at the very bottom of her scrapbook box. She told Jacks it had passed down to her when her mother died, and she had never met her grandmother. She said she'd been told Jacks's great-grandmother was from the South, and perhaps she had some Spanish or Portuguese heritage. As a boy, that hadn't seemed absurd, but now, Jacks knew it had to be a lie to cover up the "shame" of his Native great-grandmother. He could feel her tribal roots in his bones and even name them. Cherokee.

Jacks had never felt like he was part of any religion or group. In fact, something inside him had always resisted the idea of being part of a community, and he wondered at that moment if it could be some restless spirit within him, refusing convention, searching for something real that would explain where he belonged in the world. Just as coming out had made him crave connection, he'd felt something else separating him from other people. He carried the wild cougar soul. It was a rare gift, like Benoit had said.

In a moment, Jacks was rearing. His feline eyes stared up at the star-speckled sky. At first, he could barely trace the lines of the constellations, and then they gradually came into focus as an expansive plane of images he had never seen before in the stars. A soaring falcon, a rattlesnake, the round head of a bear. There among them was a proud cougar standing on its hind legs, looking down on him.

The springtime night was fresh and crisp. Jacks leapt down to the train tracks. His muscular limbs propelled him forward at an unbreakable pace. He slackened his jaw, the air filling up his lungs, feeling free.

FIVE

Six weeks later

THE BODEGA'S FLUORESCENT lights scalded Jacks's eyes. He'd come in from the darkened street, and his vision always took a moment to adjust, though he'd been to the all-night store enough times to feel at ease amid its compact layout and moldering aromas. The white throb behind his eyes abated, and he gave the place a scan while quietly drawing air under the roof of his mouth. No sign of customers. The cashier, Farzan, was hidden behind the lottery case at the counter, likely immersed in a medical textbook. Jacks snuck past the counter and into a narrow aisle, which was flanked by tall metal shelves filled with boxed dry goods. He wanted to see if he could surprise Farzan.

Dirt scored the linoleum floor. Above, the tiles of the drop ceiling were water stained and warped in places. It was a dismal store, but its peculiar odors had assumed a sense of pleasant familiarity. Traces of industrial cleaning products and roach spray. Mold and mildew. Earthy scents tramped in by customers that pulled at Jacks' curiosity and would lead him on an endless investigation if he didn't ward against his impulse to snoop.

He skulked toward the humming refrigerator cabinets, and then his reflection in the backlit glass halted him. Jacks had told himself he was working a grunge look, but he was crossing into vagrant territory. Thick, unwashed hair framed his scruffy face. His black wool cap made him look destitute and dangerous, not hip and counterculture. Did he stink? He'd all but forgotten how to discern such things, though he'd left out in a long sleeve, hooded T-shirt and jeans washed at the laundromat and only worn twice since.

Jacks opened a cabinet door and grabbed some items. He wasn't going to play a prank on Farzan when he looked like such a mess. He headed to the canned food aisle to grab a few more things, and then he set down his armful of groceries on the checkout counter with careful courtesy.

Farzan wedged a pen in his bulky, soft cover textbook and stepped over.

"I *saw* you come in." His tone was dismissive, but his bronze complexion had darkened shyly. They'd only known each other for a couple of weeks, but Farzan was fun to talk to, and they'd established something of a camaraderie through Jacks's late night visits. Farzan was just one year older than Jacks: twenty-three. His dad owned the shop, and Farzan worked the overnight shift while he was going to medical school at NYU. He had struck up conversations about superhero movies and rock bands, and it turned out they liked a lot of the same music. The guy was mad cool, but Jacks felt too embarrassed to have a long conversation that night. Besides, he had to get back to Benoit.

Farzan looked at the items on the counter as though they were a personal affront: five packages of hot dogs, two cartons of milk, a graying plastic envelope of assorted cold cuts, and a half dozen cans of Vienna sausages.

"Stocking up on proteins again?"

Jacks's face tensed in a tight grin. "Ye-ah." He dug into his jeans pocket for cash.

Farzan took his time scanning the items at his old, computerized register. He was probably starved for company. The crooked Bud Light clock on the wall behind the register showed two twenty-five in the morning.

"This is no good," Farzan said. "You need a complex diet. Do you want to develop a vitamin deficiency? Overconsumption of animal products has been linked to cancer. Particularly processed foods like these."

"You sound like a doctor already."

While ringing up the items, Farzan glanced at the snug fit of Jacks's light cotton hoodie around his chest and shoulders. "It's also a myth that a diet rich in meat leads to muscle development."

"I buy other stuff at the market down the street." Jacks's eyebrow twitched.

Farzan waved the package of cold cuts at Jacks pointedly. "I can't sell you this. They're past the expiration date." He threw the package into the garbage can behind the counter with a thud.

"I'll get another one." Jacks started toward the refrigerated cabinets.

"Don't bother," Farzan called after him. "They're all the same. We only restock on Tuesdays."

Jacks stepped back to the register. Farzan was scavenging around for something behind the counter. When he came back to Jacks, he had a plastic tub in his hand that smelled flowery, like saffron. "My maman made this for me. It's Adas Polo.

Basmati rice with lentils and raisins." He looked at Jacks instructively. "Very healthy."

Jacks nodded along, though he had no idea why Farzan was showing him the stuff.

"As usual, she gave me enough to feed a family of refugees. I can't possibly eat it all." Farzan brought out a large Styrofoam coffee cup and shoveled the rice into it with a plastic spoon.

"Oh, you don't have to do that."

Farzan didn't seem to hear him. He packed the cup to the rim, sealed it tight with a white lid, and set it on the counter with finality.

"Thanks." Jacks scrounged out a wad of bills from his jeans pocket. "Um, how much?"

"For the Adas Polo, no charge." He emphasized, desperately, "So long as you promise to eat it." He glanced at the register screen. "For the rest, thirty-four dollars and eighty-nine cents."

Jacks fished out a twenty and two tens from the bundle in his hand. Farzan took the money. "Frankly, with your diet, I don't know how you're still alive." He fit the bills into his register drawer and peeked at Jacks. "You said you were going to share that bootleg recording of the Death Cab for Cutie concert."

Jacks's insides sank. He'd been meaning to bring Farzan his memory stick of music downloads. "Sorry, I keep forgetting."

"Another reason for you to eat more healthy. You need omega fatty acids for good brain health, like in beans and legumes and fresh vegetables and fruits." He crossed his arms in front of him, putting on something of a paternalistic air, though it came across as more maternal. "It's okay that you forgot the download. I know you'll be back."

Jacks quirked his mouth playfully. "Thanks."

Farzan gave Jacks his change and his bagged groceries.

ON THE STREET, Jacks's vision sharpened like a photographic lens. He scanned the row of curtain-walled storefronts ahead of him and peered into the dark, recessed spots along the street. Everything was still. Farzan's bodega was an oasis in a desolate world of concrete and aluminum.

That didn't mean the neighborhood was safe. People got jumped by gangs, and fights between drug addicts broke out at all hours. The police only seemed to pay attention *after* someone got beat up or stabbed. Jacks had been living in the neighborhood for a couple of months, and he heard violent outbursts on the street more nights than not. The sounds of strife pulled at him, and he watched whatever was happening on the street from a darkened perch, hungering to get involved. For the first time in his life, he could do something to protect people from getting hurt. Except he couldn't. Benoit always reminded him of that. So, Jacks just looked on until the cops showed up and treated everyone on the street like a criminal. That was just as unsettling as the original incident. People had a right to be out at night. It wasn't their fault they lived in a shitty neighborhood.

Jacks turned off the main strip onto a side street.

He heard voices from somewhere up ahead, cloaked in darkness. They were one and a half, maybe two blocks down the street: young men, talking in Spanish. Jacks had only taken two semesters of Spanish, but he could pick up that the conversation was animated and drunk. The guys would probably heckle him or try something worse. Not that Jacks couldn't handle himself. He was actually thirsting to try out his abilities. But he could hear Benoit's admonition in his head. *We don't get involved.*

There were other routes home. He fast-tracked down an alley between a pair of slummy apartment buildings. He watched the shadowy borders: rows of garbage cans, an abandoned car picked over to its frame and axles, and one of the resident heroin-addicted homeless slouched against a building by the laundry room vents. The rats rooting around the garbage cans were the only life stirring in the alley.

After weaving through concrete backyards, his path ended at a tall fence topped with barbed wire. It enclosed an old loft that was once a furniture factory. Jacks surveyed the shadowy space behind him, and then he secured his grocery bag around one shoulder. He climbed the chain-link fence deftly, making little noise. At the top, he angled and stretched his body around the sharp coils as easily as a cinematic jewel thief. His feet hit the ground on the other side, sure and steady. The back door to the factory was straight ahead.

The bolt to the door was broken, and he slipped inside. A vast space, pitch black, opened up in front of him. Besides the high-lofted bed where he and Benoit slept, the factory had been gutted. The sour smell of sawdust and unfinished wood still lingered, though the furniture and most of the machinery had been cleared out years ago. Jacks saw nothing unusual. He unhitched the grocery bag from his shoulder.

A phantom force tackled him from the side.

The bag flew out of Jacks's hand, and he landed on the concrete floor, stunned breathless by the smacking pain in his back. His invisible attacker pinned him by the shoulders with an insuperable weight. He heard a feline growl, and the meaty breath of it fanned his face. Black as the shuttered factory, Benoit lorded over him. The elliptical pupils of his green, iridescent eyes were wide, enlivened by the capture of prey.

Jacks gently massaged the back of his head. Then he remembered the groceries and glanced around. They were strewn across the floor, and the milk cartons had burst into a puddle.

"Nice, Ben. How're we supposed to eat when you do stuff like this?"

You're too careless. You never enter a space making so much noise.

"I didn't think that applied when I'm just trying to bring groceries home."

Benoit curled his claws into Jacks's shirt. *You need to be prepared for any situation.* He lapped Jacks's neck and face with his rough tongue. It felt like an examination, picking up scents, rather than an affectionate gesture. Jacks pushed him away, and Benoit came back at him more forcefully, pinning Jacks to the floor again so he could scour him like he wanted to. Jacks tensed up, and his mind shuttered in a blur of heat.

His breastbone buckled, and his chest expanded in a feline curve. Hot bursts of pressure raced down his back as his spine extenuated and arched, sprouting an appendage from his tailbone. His shoulder blades flexed backward impossibly while his hips realigned, and the muscles of his shortened limbs broadened and knit together, taut. His nails grew and thickened while his fingers and toes retracted, and the balls of his hands and feet bulged into fist-sized roughened pads. As his skin drew up tight around his muscles, thick fur burst through his body. He could feel the complex transformation of his head —skull elongating, jaws receding, mouth and nose molding together into a muzzle. Fine shoots of whiskers prickled out of him. Though his feline senses worked in his human form, they were now multiplied times ten. His surroundings came into newfound focus, the unveiling of a hidden world.

A lazy breeze blew through a shattered pane in one of the factory's high, whitewashed windows. He could hear and feel a subway car approaching distantly downtown. Benoit gazed at him proudly and a little warily. Then Jacks noticed a trace of exotic spice in the air.

Jacks cocked his eyes reflexively to the groceries. The home-cooked food Farzan gave him had spilled out of its container. Benoit's tail swung back and forth. *What have we here? Flirting with the kid from the bodega again?*

His defenses rose, though he kept them to himself. He liked Farzan. He was kind, and it was frickin' impressive that he was going to medical school and holding down his family's business every night. And yes, Jacks thought he was cute, but he wasn't flirting. Benoit only let him go out on his own in the middle of the night. He missed having contact with people. Wasn't that normal?

Benoit circled him with a superior glare. *You're still so young. Fraternizing with humans as though you belong with them.*

We need to eat, don't we? I told you where I was going.

Benoit pounced on his back, and he gathered the folds of Jacks's neck in his jaws. *You need to learn your place.* His hypnotizing purr rocked through Jacks's body, and his hindquarters molded around Jacks's rump.

Jacks threw himself over to one side and thrust his hind paws into Benoit's belly. He managed to twist him onto his back. Benoit's thick limbs found an advantage, and they tumbled over one another, fighting to clamp down for a pin. Jacks could hold his own for a while, but Benoit was stockier, and he had jaws that could pulverize a crocodile.

Benoit got Jacks's neck in a visor grip and grappled him onto his belly. Before he could press his full weight on top of Jacks, Jacks wrangled away and scampered up to the loft bed. He settled in a pile of scavenged mattresses and blankets and licked his paws to clean his face.

Benoit climbed up to the perch and circled around Jacks in a dance of reconciliation. A willful gaze. Tentative nudges of his head that Jacks rebuffed with growls. Eventually, Benoit lay down with his heft leaning into Jacks's side. He turned to lick Jacks's face, and Jacks shook fussily away. Benoit curled his paw around Jacks's head to pull him close, and he groomed him. They lay curled together looking out at the empty factory.

A runty, tiger-striped stray had found the groceries and was lapping up the milk from the floor. She was just a cat, not a soul shifter, and they had taken her in from the streets as their own. Jacks had named her Bella.

At least someone is getting some supper, Jacks telepathized to Benoit.

Benoit glared at Bella in regal fashion. Her ears perked up, and she scurried up the scaffolding to the loft and nestled between the two big cats.

Benoit groomed Bella with wide laps of his scratchy tongue. While Jacks was still struggling to understand and accept his nature, Benoit was entirely at home with his. He spent less and less time in his human form whereas Jacks could only sustain the change for a couple of hours. Benoit said it would get easier with time.

Jacks stared into the depths of the gutted factory. *What are we doing? I'm starving. Are we going to live like this forever?*

Where would you like to go?

At first, coming to New York had felt like an adventure, but in two months, Jacks had barely ventured beyond a few blocks of the factory. Benoit wouldn't allow it. He kept saying Jacks wasn't ready for it, that he couldn't take chances being recognized if his parents had opened a missing persons investigation. Jacks respected that Benoit knew far more about living as a fugitive, not to mention a soul shifter, but he was being a bit extreme about things, wasn't he? He wasn't really teaching Jacks anything. They were just hiding from the world, and Jacks was feeling like he'd been kidnapped rather than liberated as Benoit described it.

I don't know. Someplace with indoor plumbing? A kitchen?

You'd like a suite at the Waldorf Astoria? You need to learn how to survive as a cougar first. Then we'll see if you're ready to navigate both worlds.

Then show me something. This isn't even existing. I'm bored, Ben. Bored out of my mind.

Jacks's heartbeat fluttered. That had come out hot.

Alright. Benoit raised himself, arched his back, and started toward the edge of the loft. *C'mon. I'm taking you hunting.*

BENOIT HAD NEVER taken Jacks hunting before, and though he was feeling a little apprehensive about what it might entail, he'd asked Benoit to show him something. It was the first time they'd gone out at night together. He followed Benoit up through the factory's heating shaft to the roof, and they traveled from one building rooftop to the next, heading crosstown.

At night, the tightly packed apartment buildings formed something of a canopy that they could traverse with ease while keeping potential dangers in sight below. The streets were barren. Windows were dark. Only once, a dog broke out in a vicious bark from the top apartment of a six-floor brownstone they passed over, and Benoit sprung ahead and leapt onto the next rooftop. Jacks followed, leaving that little drama behind.

Benoit halted on the roof of a Fifth Avenue apartment building, and Jacks drew up beside him. Below, Central Park was a dark lake banked by the high rises of 110th Street and distant Central Park West. Not far from their perch, Jacks could make out the elongated silhouette of the Harlem Meer. When they first arrived in the city, Benoit had taken him through the park, and Jacks remembered that swampy lake where they had paddle boats, and old retired men fished during the day. A trickle of taxicabs glided around the park's borders.

Benoit climbed stealthily down the fire escape facing the avenue, and Jacks followed. If they were spotted, making a getaway wasn't much of a worry, unless the terrified onlooker was a thug with a gun. But they didn't need a SWAT team scouring the neighborhood because of a report of two big cats loose in the city. Benoit was expert at staying camouflaged. Jacks mirrored his pace, his noiseless steps on metal rungs, the lithe turns of his body as he wove down the contraption.

On the street, they slunk behind a parked car and scanned up and down the avenue. A livery cab swooshed by, leaving a trail of high-pitched Indian pop music. In its wake, everything was still. Benoit looked at Jacks, and then he sprung across the street. Jacks galloping after him, they jumped a wall and landed under the cover of trees.

Damp earth and sweet maples trees filled his nostrils. Nocturnal chatter tantalized his ears. A million things lived here, some as tiny as crickets, others more curious, nesting in the trees or scrounging about the brush. Benoit scowled at a flutter of birds overhead. As sly as they were, some creatures had noticed their entrance to the park. Jacks wondered what Benoit was hunting. A rabbit? Bloodthirsty instincts swarmed inside him. He wanted to stalk prey not just because he was hungry, but because he could do it.

Benoit led them along the marshy bank of Harlem Meer. He had a swagger in his stride, and he stopped at a tree here and there to sniff the bark of a trunk and rub his neck against it. At the meer's southeastern end, they neared the Conservatory Gardens, a circular expanse of walkways and shallow hedges, and they gave the open area a wide berth. They clipped through a little clearing, and Jacks raced after Benoit as he bounded up a rocky escarpment overlooking the pitch black meer.

Benoit crept up the bald pinnacle, steady and deliberate,

his jaw hanging to vent in the night air. He had picked up the scent of something. Jacks tried to pinpoint it, but he was still getting used to focusing his feline senses. The thick stench of a skunk overwhelmed him.

He followed Benoit as he wandered around the spot, and the night air currents pushed the foul smell away. Jacks honed in on something familiar. Waterfowl nested below on the margins of the meer. His tail swung in anticipation. Jacks had never killed an animal. The thought had been abhorrent to him as a human, but cougars needed to kill to survive. It kept the ecosystem in balance, right? Nobody would miss one less mallard duck or swan.

A swampy breeze swept across Jacks's nose, and he picked up the gamey scent of the ducks below, their quarry. A primal thrill rose up from his core. He envisioned his jaws clamping down on prey, its fruitless struggle to escape, its fluttering life snuffed out. Jacks wondered if Benoit would lead him on a stealthy descent to the banks of the meer or if they would charge down on the birds all at once.

Then Benoit stopped short of the escarpment and took a different approach through the woods.

Jacks had no idea why. He followed a few paces behind.

They came up to a dusky clearing, and Benoit crouched in the brush of the periphery, still as a statue. On a quick scan, Jacks couldn't make out anything in the open space, but he could smell unwashed clothes and body odor. He peered deeper into the gap in the woods, and at the opposite end, he spotted two men, their faces blackened with grime, camped out with a ramshackle assortment of shopping bags. They were taking slugs from a whiskey bottle.

Jacks watched, dumbstruck, as Benoit crept forward, low to the ground, toward the homeless men.

No.

Benoit glanced back with a forbidding scowl. One of the men stood and walked a few swaying steps into the woods. Jacks heard him unzip his fly. Benoit braced his hind legs, staring at the man. Then, he charged at him.

Jacks leapt after Benoit and caught his back with his forepaws. They tumbled together, snarling. The man who was relieving himself hobbled desperately into the cover of the woods. Nearby, his companion slid back on the ground, too shocked or too drunk to get up on his feet.

Benoit shook away from Jacks. *What are you doing?*

I'm not hunting people.

Benoit batted Jacks's muzzle with his claw and Jacks backed away, stinging.

We need to protect our territory.

Benoit turned his attention to the man on the ground, who was watching their interaction, paralyzed.

"You're a big kitty, aren't you?"

He answered back in a low growl, shuddering with violence.

The man rooted through a plastic bag. "You want something to eat? I've got beef jerky here."

Like a menacing shadow, Benoit buried the homeless man, and he was gone except for his delirious shrieks from the attack. Jacks cantered forward to intervene, but it was too late. Benoit grappled his victim belly-down, clamping down on his neck with bone-crushing jaws and shaking him.

Blood spouted, a raw, grisly scent. Carnal urges sliced through Jacks, pulling him to join in the kill, but a cold wave of shame stopped him. Jacks lunged for Benoit to drag him off the man. Benoit released the limp body and fought Jacks off in a spinning wrangle. Jacks rolled out of their tangle and righted himself.

Benoit went back to his prey, pawing the body over a few

times to make sure he was dead. He looked back at Jacks. His muzzle was wet with blood, and his eyes glinted with pride.

Jacks felt himself shrinking. He should have acted sooner and done something to stop Benoit. Now a man was dead, and what could he do? Go to the police?

Benoit stared at him as though to break Jacks's will. Jacks searched Benoit's eyes and saw no remorse, no hesitation over what he had done. It was a murder simply for sport. Jacks sprang off into the woods.

SIX

JACKS STOOD IN the recess of an apartment building entrance, staring at the neon bodega sign across the street. Bella squirmed in his arms. She wasn't happy about being wrenched away from her bed at the factory, but he couldn't leave her there.

Since running away from Benoit, the question of what to do had been thundering in his head. He hadn't come up with any answer for the long term, but he knew with sudden certainty he had to leave Benoit. What he had done was an abomination. There was no need to kill homeless people to "protect their territory." Benoit hadn't even told him that was his intention. Jacks would never have joined him if he knew that killing people was part of his hunting routine, and now a recollection sent chills the size of icebergs through his body. The news stories from Montréal. Early morning joggers mauled to death by a wild animal. Benoit was that wild animal. Jacks was sure of it now. He wanted him to become one too. Jacks needed to get away.

Taking Bella with him was probably selfish and certainly not practical, but they shared a bond, and Jacks had no connection to anyone else in the world. Benoit didn't really care about her. He had no sentimentality toward anyone. Back at the factory, Jacks had shifted back to his human form, grabbed his duffle bag of clothes, and carried the cat away.

They ended up at the only place he could think of going. He grooved soft lines down Bella's back to calm her. He inhaled and exhaled a long breath. Then he crossed the street and entered the bodega.

A hail of bullets, sirens, and screeching cars came from the cashier counter. Farzan must have been watching some action flick on his phone. Jacks walked up to the counter, trying to look casual.

Farzan's eyes were heavy with fatigue. It was five thirty in the morning, the tail end of his overnight shift. He glanced at Jacks, and his face lit up with surprise and a big smile.

"Twice in one night. What did I do to deserve such luck?" He gestured to his phone screen. "You like old movies? This is a classic. Michael Keaton and Jack Nicholson in the original *Batman* from 1989."

Jacks didn't answer. Farzan took a closer account of Jacks and winced. There was a swollen scratch below his eye from his tussle with Benoit. There was a big duffle bag weighing down his shoulder. Then, of course, there was the tiger-striped cat he was holding. Jacks shifted his weight, uneasily. Yeah, he was a hot mess.

"What happened?"

"I'm sorry. I didn't have any place to go."

Jacks could feel Farzan's heavy gaze on him. When he spoke, it came out stunted. "I got into a fight. With my boyfriend."

Farzan walked around the counter, locked the door, and flipped over the "Closed" sign. Bella fought to get out of Jacks's arms. He let her jump down to the floor and watched her scurry down a grocery aisle.

Farzan came up in front of Jacks. "He hurt you?"

Jacks didn't know how to answer.

"If he's abusing you, you should report it. We'll call the police. They have a domestic violence unit. They're trained in handling all kinds of relationships."

"It's not like that." How could Jacks explain? "I started the fight. And the problem is we were living together."

Farzan studied him. "And what's he doing now? Did he kick you out, or did you run away from him?"

Jacks wasn't prepared for Farzan to be so perceptive. He just needed someone to give him a break and help him regroup for a little while.

"It was both our faults." He gestured to his face. "I know it probably looks gruesome, but it's not that bad. It was a long time coming. We were toxic together."

"Toxic as in physically abusive?"

"No. We never got into a physical fight before."

Farzan frowned. "I'm not sure I believe you."

"Then don't believe me. I'll get out of your way." Jacks wandered down the aisle to retrieve Bella. She had taken off to some hiding place. He felt lousy about pulling her from one place to the next, but what could he do?

"Where will you go?"

"I don't know. Do they allow cats at homeless shelters?"

"No. But they take them at the A.S.P.C.A."

Bella was crouched down low behind a row of cereal boxes. Jacks approached her slyly and scooped her up in his arms.

"This one's not going to a jail for cats." He started back to the front of the bodega. Farzan stood solidly in front of the door.

"Why did you come here?"

"I thought maybe I could hang out for a little while. Just until morning. When I can call some people."

"Who are you going to call?"

"I've got some friends upstate. But I don't want to wake them up in the middle of the night with my stupid drama."

"If they're your friends, they shouldn't care."

"It's just been a while since they heard from me, y'know? I was thinking it would be better to wait until eight or nine so it's not like such a big deal."

"Well, it's not going to work."

Jacks glanced at Farzan, startled.

"My father takes over the shop at seven thirty. He's not anywhere near as charitable as me."

Jacks thought about all night diners. But he couldn't bring Bella there, and he had no money. The train station was a long walk downtown. His whole body was tired. Should he just try to get some rest in a subway station until the morning?

Farzan sighed. "I've got an apartment in the basement of my parents' house. You can get cleaned up and call your friends in the morning."

"Really?"

"Just keep your cat out of my comic books."

Jacks looked at him with a lopsided grin. Farzan shrugged, earnestly indignant. "I've got a collection of over one thousand titles. Some of them are rare editions and worth some money."

SHOWERED, WITH A bath towel wrapped around his waist, Jacks sat on Farzan's faded microfiber sofa, staring at the cordless phone in his hand. Farzan was washing up in the adjoining bathroom. Morning light from the basement windows cast the cluttered apartment in swaths of gold. Bella had gone off exploring the new landscape of second-hand furniture, bookshelves, and polyester carpeting.

Jacks couldn't decide whether or not to call Jonathan. It was hella awkward. The last time they spoke, over two months ago, Jacks had told him he met some guy in Montréal and was staying in Canada for a while. He'd punked out on his share of the rent and probably left Jonathan thinking he was a world-class asshole. And now he was going to call him out of the blue to ask if he could wire some money so he could get out of town?

But what else was he supposed to do? Trying to have that conversation with his mom would be even worse, and he had exhausted his options for people to call for help. He'd pay Jonathan back as soon as he had a job. He only needed like a hundred bucks to buy a bus ticket and get some food. Maybe Jonathan would be chill about it. Or maybe he wouldn't. Should he be worried about his parents filing a missing persons report?

Time seemed to stand still while he wrestled with these things, and he was startled when the bathroom door creaked open and Farzan came out. Jacks quickly set the phone on the coffee table in front of him as though he just finished a call.

Farzan's eyes widened at the sight of Jacks sitting on the couch in just a towel, and then he crossed his arms in front of his bare, skinny torso and looked away.

"Did you call your friends?"

"Yeah. No answer."

"They will have this phone number now. That's good. They'll call you back." He stepped briskly to the bedroom and shut the door behind him with a firm clack.

Jacks smiled to himself for a moment. Farzan was such an adorable little kid sometimes. And he was a goddamn prince, letting Jacks shower at his place. Jacks felt terrible about lying to him, *again*. He was sick of all of his lying and avoidance, and angry at himself for his whole fucked-up situation. He had a duffle bag full of clothes, but they were all unwashed. Changing into another damp, grimy outfit would be disgusting.

Farzan came back into the room wearing an untucked button-down shirt and a pair of jeans. He had some sort of first aid kit in his hands, and he sat down next to Jacks and zeroed in on the scratch across his face.

"This looks more like the work of your cat than your boyfriend." Farzan continued looking him over and found the brown, puffy spot on one side of his ribcage. "You have a mild contusion." He raised his hands and looked to Jacks for his consent. Jacks eased back on the couch to let him better examine the wound. Farzan pressed his fingers lightly around it. Jacks grimaced. "It hurts?"

"It's a little sore."

"I don't think anything is broken. You would be in a lot more pain." Farzan opened his kit, snapped on latex gloves, and retrieved an alcohol swab for the scratch. "This is to clean out the scratch and prevent infection. There is more bacteria and fungus under most fingernails than on a toilet seat."

He started working on Jacks's face. The alcohol swab stung like acid, but Jacks gritted through it. He wanted to be a good patient for Farzan.

"Can I ask you a question?" Jacks said.

"I've got three years to go with my degree, but I'm fully insured for malpractice through the university."

Jacks chuckled. "No, not that. I wanted to know, why are you being so nice to me?"

"Overcompensation."

Jacks shrunk up his brow.

"It's the exertion of effort to compensate for a perceived physical or psychological defect. In my case, the perceived defect is being gay in a Persian family. I have to be perfect in every other way. I'm the first one to go to an American college. I'll be the first to get a medical degree, not that I had a lot of competition. I'm the youngest sibling of four. My sister repatriated to Iran to marry a fundamentalist and barely talks to us. Of my brothers, one dropped out of high school in eleventh grade and has a felony record for bitcoin fraud. The other is unemployed and has three kids by three different women. They've given our parents enough high blood pressure without me contributing to it."

"I think you're a rock star. But you shouldn't have to feel like you have to be perfect. I can't thank you enough. You didn't have to help me out like this."

"It's hasanat. That's like mitzvah for Muslims."

Farzan touched some antibiotic cream onto the scratch. He set down his supplies, looked over his work favorably, and pulled off his gloves. "That doesn't really answer your question, though. About why I'm being nice to you."

Jacks glanced at him.

"When you came into my father's shop, you treated me like a human being. Not some terrorist or crooked Arab trying to cheat you out of money. Anyway, I had a good feeling about you since the night we met. If you weren't already taken, I would have full-on seduced you."

He stood and started toward the bedroom to return the kit but stopped short, with his back still turned to Jacks. "Don't worry. I can control myself. I had plenty of practice with that, going to an all-boys high school."

Jacks watched Farzan disappear back in his room and listened to him rustling around. He wasn't sure what to make of

Farzan's pronouncement. He was probably just being funny, trying to lighten the mood. When he reemerged, he was wearing a light zip jacket and had a messenger bag for his laptop strapped over his shoulder.

"I get back from classes at six. There's food in the fridge and tuna in the cupboard for your cat. Answer the door at your own risk. If my mother finds you, she'll have you moving furniture around the house and running errands for her. Oh, and there's a washer and a dryer through the utility room off the kitchen. If you need to do laundry."

"You don't mind if I hang?"

"You have to wait for your friend to call back, don't you? Besides, you should take it easy to let that bruise heal. Just keep an eye on your cat. That's all I ask."

Jacks retrieved his duffle bag from the floor and rooted through it. He brought out his iPod and handed it to Farzan. "The Death Cab for Cutie track," he explained.

Farzan looked at the device for a moment, and then he pocketed it. "Thanks."

When Farzan left, Jacks picked up the phone again. He called 311 and got transferred to an anonymous tips hotline.

The woman who answered took down his report about witnessing a homeless man being attacked by a panther in Central Park last night. Crazy as it sounded, she handled it matter-of-factly, whether she was used to outlandish reports or desensitized to her job. She told Jacks the police would check out the area, so he figured at least they would find the man's body. Then, maybe, they would put more officers in the park, which would deter Benoit from hurting other people there.

After the call, Jacks fidgeted. What if they caught Benoit or killed him while trying to apprehend him? Jacks needed to stop him from hurting innocent people, but the thought of him being locked up forever in some kind of containment, treated like a freak of nature, felt like a betrayal of his own kind.

He rounded up Bella from a sunbathing spot beneath a window and lay on the couch with the cat on his chest. He rubbed her back the way she liked it. Still, Bella glared at him in annoyance.

"I know," Jacks said. "But what else was I supposed to do?"

SEVEN

WHEN JACKS WOKE, a residue of dreams hummed happily in his head. He was free of Benoit, as though their relationship had never happened, and back to being in college with dozens of prospects in his future. Then, he took account of his surroundings with some dissonance and, gradually, a pinch of panic. Farzan's basement apartment was cloaked in darkness. The casement windows were pitch black. A single patch of light came from some appliance in the adjoining kitchen. He had fallen asleep on the couch and slept away the entire day. How did that happen? He had meant to start working on getting his life in order so he didn't have to impose on Farzan. The last thing he remembered was putting his washed clothes in the dryer and lying back on the couch.

Farzan must have covered him with a woolen quilt. Jacks pulled down the cover from his bare shoulders and went to explore the kitchen. He found a Tupperware bowl on the Formica table. Beneath the bowl was a handwritten note on college stationery. Jacks slid out the note to read it.

Didn't want to wake you. This is chicken kabobs and rice. I *know you prefer hot dogs, but I only restock them on Tuesdays. (Ha, ha). You can heat up your dinner in the microwave: one minute and thirty seconds, <u>stir</u>, then one more minute. There's juice and milk in the fridge. Your scratch should be patted clean with alcohol, and reapply the antibiotic cream one more time. (Supplies are laid out in the bathroom).*

I'm at the store overnight. See you in the morning. Farzan

P.S. I hope you heard from your friends.

Jacks noticed in the corner of the kitchen a litter pan and plastic kitty bowls with food and water for Bella. Farzan was a goddamn angel. Jacks swore to himself he was going to repay him as soon as he got a job. He owed the guy something really big, like a glass display case for his comic books, or a sports car.

Above the countertop and cabinets, Bella had found a perch on the basement sill.

"Hey baby. How're you settling in?"

Bella ignored him.

"You still pissed at me for dragging you all over town?"

Her tail swung, and she chirped against the glass. She was focused intently on something outside. As Jacks remembered, the window faced the backyard. They had come in that way in the morning. There was a stairwell to the apartment door, and it opened into the kitchen.

The door rattled. Jacks spun around in that direction. Someone was jerking the locked door knob and pushing against the frame. The curtain panels over the window pane quivered in distress. Jacks crept up on the door at an angle, trying to see the visitor in the sliver gap between the curtains.

"Jacks, I know you're in there."

It was Benoit. He could wake up the entire house. Farzan's parents could call the cops. Jacks sensed danger in a confrontation, but his greater worry was bringing the tornado of his life into Farzan's home. He had to calm Benoit down.

There was a button lock on the doorknob. He released it and opened the door.

Benoit's face was downcast and grim, and he hunched his shoulders like a bull ready to horn its way in. He pushed past Jacks and paced the kitchen aggressively. Bella jumped down from the window to greet him, and Jacks watched the exchange, worried about Benoit's temperament. Benoit broke his stride, and the cat rubbed the sides of her muzzle against his black combat boots. Mercifully, she appeared to have a mollifying effect on him.

"Why did you leave?"

"Why did I leave?" Jacks repeated in disbelief.

Benoit looked at the litter pan and the bowls on the floor. "This is how you want Bella to live?"

"How did you find me?"

"I thought you might go upstate or to your parents in Pennsylvania. But your scent lingered in the city. I followed it on foot and tracked you here."

His face was ashy, and his hair was windswept. He looked every bit like someone who had walked all the way from uptown Manhattan to southeastern Queens.

"Why, Ben?"

"You belong with me."

A familiar pull reached inside Jacks. Benoit's words, his simple certainty, could swallow him up, and make him believe they were bonded in a primal way. Jacks drew a breath and remembered Benoit's jaguar muzzle covered in a homeless man's blood.

"We don't belong together. You showed me that last night." Jacks stepped back, trembling with a mixture of fear and indignation. "You murdered that man."

"Murder? What a quaint and very human notion."

"You killed a man who just needed someplace to sleep for the night."

Benoit's voice bore thunderously into Jacks's head. *He was in my hunting territory. Scaring off the kills with his noise and scent.*

Jacks winced like he'd been clopped on the ears. Benoit took up a lighter tone. "You'll learn. You think you're still one of them." He crowded up on Jacks, raked his fingers through his thick hair, and grabbed a tuft at the nape of his neck. Jacks tried to resist him, but Benoit raked his stubbly chin across his cheeks, and his teeth closed over his ear. "Don't run away from me again."

Jacks broke away from him. "I *am* one of them."

Benoit glanced at him impatiently. "You're something greater now. I thought you understood that."

"I understand we can inhabit both worlds, but that doesn't mean I'm okay with killing."

"Really, Jackson?" Benoit eyed him deeply, reaching a place Jacks had been trying not to think about since last night at the Harlem Meer. Jacks *had* wanted to kill just because he could, a clawing urge to root out weaker creatures and destroy them, exalting in his power to snuff out life. But that could be controlled, couldn't it? Jacks still held on to a conviction that hurting other people was wrong.

"We're not mates, Ben. Something died in me when I saw you kill that man. We're not the same."

"I *made* you."

"I was somebody before. Yes, you opened up a potential I didn't know I had, but I still know wrong from right."

"What's right and wrong is different for us," Benoit roared. "You need to follow my lead."

Jacks was sick of Benoit's ego. "I don't want to live like this.

I'm not hiding in abandoned buildings and standing aside while you kill people who get into your 'territory.'"

"I'm growing tired of these conversations."

"Good. Then you agree. We're not a good fit."

For the first time, Benoit looked a bit defeated. "Everything I've done has been to keep you safe. If you want, we can check into a hotel." He looked away and grimaced. "More sacrifices so that *you'll* be comfortable."

"That's not even the point."

"What is the point?"

Jacks sighed. As disgusted as he was by what Benoit had done, he couldn't help feeling some sympathy. "Ben, I appreciate everything. And maybe I'm nuts thinking that I can do this on my own. But I can't be with you." He looked into Benoit's eyes. "It's not who I am."

"You need to stop denying your nature. I went through that myself when I first changed. You have a mate. Someone to teach you."

"Then maybe I'm not ready for this. I'll come to terms with my nature on my own. But Ben, you've got to let me go."

Benoit swung around the kitchen, took account of Farzan's written note, and swatted the Tupperware bowl with such force that it rebounded from the counter and flew clear across to the other side of the kitchen floor.

"This is why. He turned you against me."

"That has nothing to do with it."

"Did you go crying to him after our fight? Did he say you'd be better off with him? Of course, he told you what you wanted to hear. He wants you for himself."

"I needed a place to stay. He doesn't know anything about us."

"Where is he?" Benoit swerved through the apartment. He found the bedroom door and threw it open.

Jacks didn't know what to do. Trying to stop him might create a bigger racket. Benoit was so goddamn stubborn. "He's not here," Jacks called after him.

Benoit tramped back to the kitchen. "He thinks he can get between us. He sees your will is weak. He's a distraction. He needs to be gotten rid of." His glance landed on the TV console, which showed the time. Horribly, Jacks watched him putting things together in his head. He knew Farzan worked overnight at the bodega.

Jacks stepped in front of the door. "No."

Benoit came at Jacks, and it was barely a fight. Benoit threw him aside with surprising force. He opened the door, reared into black, muscled hide, and sprang away into the night.

Jacks raced over to the phone to dial 911 but hesitated to make the call. Benoit could cover ground quickly. What if the cops didn't respond in time?

He'd set in motion an unfathomable disaster. Benoit would try to rip Farzan apart. In his blind, jealous rage, Benoit was equally in danger if Farzan had time to hit a panic button in the store or if there were onlookers to call the authorities. Benoit would be gunned down by the police. Most horribly, both of them could be killed.

Jacks didn't have Farzan's cell phone number or the number for the store. But he spotted, hanging on a nail by the door, a key ring from a Pontiac dealership. Farzan had taken his own car to work, but the key was for his father's that he had to move around because they shared the driveway? It was overstepping boundaries, but how else could Jacks make it to the bodega before Benoit?

He threw on some clothes, grabbed the key, and went outside to find the car.

A black sedan was parked in the driveway, and the headlights flashed and the doors clicked open when Jacks pressed the unlock button on the fob. He climbed inside and started the engine.

There was a GPS monitor on the dashboard. Jacks punched in the address for the bodega on the touch screen. A light came on from a second floor window in the house, and someone threw open the curtains to look down. Jacks backed out of the driveway and gunned it down the street with the tires squealing.

JACKS PEELED THROUGH outer borough streets and bolted onto a parkway. He had to get to Farzan before Benoit did. No highway patrolmen or toddling construction vehicles were going to slow him down. The GPS directed him across a bridge and then onto a cross street through city blocks that started to look familiar. Benoit couldn't beat him on foot, could he? Jacks sailed through traffic lights at deserted intersections. Thank God, few drivers or pedestrians were out that late on a weeknight.

The neon bodega sign stood out ahead of him. He cruised toward it and screeched into a parking spot on the corner by a fire hydrant.

Jacks flew out of the car but stopped short of the store. Sounds filled his ears: the distant, whirring parkway, drunken banter from shadowy places, a bus grinding and shrieking on the main avenue some blocks away. The store in front of him was quiet. He drew air through his nostrils, breathing in the sour smell of garbage cans, subway exhaust rising up from the sidewalk gratings, and a trail of greasy food from a Chinese restaurant vent some blocks away. But no Benoit. The moment of delay gave his heart a chance to stop beating like a jackhammer. He wiped his sweat-slick brow on his sleeve and walked into the bodega.

Synth-punk music permeated the store from laptop speakers. The place looked empty. Jacks drew up in front of Farzan at the counter. Farzan looked happily bewildered, and he paused his playlist and stepped away from his laptop.

"What are you doing here?"

"There's no time to explain. You've got to close the store."

Farzan smiled absurdly. Jacks gripped the counter. "I'm totally serious. Your life's in danger. Get your stuff and lock the place up so we can get out of here."

Farzan glanced over his shoulder. They were not alone. Some Spanish dude with squinty eyes was stumbling toward the counter with a big bottle of malted liquor swinging in his hand. He hefted his purchase up to the register. The bottle wobbled on the counter and came to a stop.

Farzan rang up the guy. How was he going to convince Farzan to leave the store? He looked around. At the end of the wall of refrigerators, he saw a door that probably led to a back stockroom and then, maybe out to the street.

A light displacement traveled from above. He caught a trace of Benoit's musky scent. Jacks hurried around the counter and through the swinging gate to Farzan. "We've got to go."

"Jacks, you're not allowed back here. Take it easy. I've got a customer."

Jacks stared at Farzan pleadingly.

A slow, crackling footfall traveled from the drop ceiling. They both looked up to it. Dust flurried down from the rectangular tiles. The fluorescent light panels flickered and sparked, and then the store went dark but for battery-operated lights in the lottery display case and the Bud Light wall clock.

Ceiling tiles broke apart and crumbled to the floor. Like a monster conjured from another dimension, Benoit—300 pounds of black jaguar—plunged down from the ceiling into the store's center aisle.

With sudden sobriety, the Spanish guy grabbed his malt liquor and ran out of the bodega. It was too dark for anyone except Jacks to make out the intruder, but Benoit's presence spread across the store like a terrifying chill. Farzan backed up behind the counter, trapping himself. There was only one way out, through the gate, and Benoit was eyeing that exit.

Jacks grabbed Farzan from both sides and guided him toward the gate. There wasn't time to make it around the counter and out of the store, but he had a straight run down the refrigerator aisle to the back room.

He told Farzan quietly and steadily: "Fast as you can. To the back of the store."

Benoit crept toward them with his jaw slack and the fur on his back puffed out. Farzan's body shook in Jacks's hands.

"What is that? A bear?"

"I'll explain later. You've got to go."

"What about you?"

"I'll distract it," Jacks told him firmly. Then he lied. "I've done it before. While hunting upstate."

Farzan's whole body was quivering. "What if I don't make it?" he said, looking over his shoulder. Jacks followed his gaze and spotted a handgun on the shelf below the cash register. It was too much of a gamble. He didn't trust Farzan to fire a warning shot, and he didn't trust Benoit to be deterred.

Jacks pressed Farzan forward. "There's no time for that. Run for that door and don't look back. Lock the door behind you. Get to your car and drive. Go. I promise you, I'll be fine."

From three yards away, Benoit's green-eyed glare locked in on Farzan, quivering in murderous anticipation.

"Go," Jacks shouted with a shove.

Farzan raced for the back room. Benoit sprang after him, cornering the aisle with a skin-curling scrape of his claws on the linoleum floor. Jacks took a running leap, bore down on the magical spot in his diaphragm, and burst into fur and pouncing limbs in midair. He caught Benoit by his hind legs, and they went tumbling down the aisle together in a massive wipeout that sent cans of coffee and soda bottles flying from shelves.

Jacks heard a door open and slam shut.

When they came to a stop, Benoit pulled himself free and slashed a claw across Jacks's flank.

You can't protect him. He's mine.

Jacks lunged for Benoit's neck, caught a fold of his black hide in his jaws, and worked him onto his back. *You think killing him is going to make me stay with you? It's over, Ben. Face it.*

Benoit launched out his hind legs, jettisoning Jacks into a metal shelf of paper goods that toppled over into the next aisle. Jacks righted himself to get back to the fight. He needed to delay Benoit as long as he could so Farzan had a chance to get to his car.

Benoit hunched and snarled. *I can destroy you as easily as I can destroy that boy.*

Jacks pounced to bury him with his weight. He clamped his jaws on a loose pocket of hide, and they spun over each other and slammed into the back wall of the bodega. Benoit swung for Jacks's eye, but Jacks ducked and swung back, clawing Benoit's ear. He sprung away before Benoit could reply. The maneuver worked. Benoit bounded after him, away from the back end of the store.

Some yards short of the front door, Benoit caught Jacks's shoulder with a claw and set upon him. He gnashed Jacks's hide and gouged the side of his leg with his hind claws. Jacks fought and twisted his body to get free. Benoit clamped down on his neck and wouldn't let him go. Jacks's lungs burned, trying to suck in air, and his body felt ripped apart. His consciousness was fading. Then Benoit released him.

Jacks crawled out from under Benoit's body. One of his hind legs collapsed under him as he tried to stand on it. He wondered if a finishing attack was coming next.

Desperately, he took account of things. Lights were on, maybe from a back-up generator. Benoit had freed him because his attention had turned to the back of the store. Farzan stood beneath a neon exit sign with a baseball bat raised over his shoulder. Benoit swung his tail back and forth, gauging timing and approach.

Farzan called out in a gasp, "Jacks?"

Benoit stalked toward him in the cover of the middle aisle. He slouched to the ground, readying his muscular torso to spring. Farzan's bat wouldn't do him any good. He would never have a chance to use it. Benoit would ambush him and clamp down on an artery in seconds.

Jacks summoned a burst of strength to kick off from his good leg and leap onto the counter. He jumped down to the cashier side and, pushing out from his diaphragm, his fur retracted, his bones and his muscles realigned, and he was back to his human self. He grabbed the handgun from the shelf, released the trigger guard, and pointed the gun with both hands.

Benoit galloped toward Farzan, accelerating. With preter-natural sight and precision, Jacks zeroed in on the target and squeezed the trigger of his gun. He didn't even feel the rebound of the ear-splitting blast. Benoit bowed, and his legs gave out beneath him, still sliding forward from his momentum. His lumbering body came to rest at Farzan's feet.

Jacks dropped the gun. He pushed through the counter's swinging gate, and limped to Benoit. He had saved Farzan's life, but his stomach plummeted, seeing the black jaguar dead. A whimper rose up from his throat.

Farzan's chest heaved rapidly with shallow breaths. "How did you think you could fight it by yourself?"

Benoit? Jacks telepathized.

There was no answer.

Jacks fell down to his knees beside Benoit's lifeless jaguar body. Blood pooled beneath his head. Jacks covered his face in his hands. "I didn't mean to. What else could I do?"

"Are you crazy? That thing was going to kill you." Farzan stepped around him. "Jacks, you're really injured. That leg looks bad. You're probably in shock."

Jacks knew this couldn't have ended any other way, but the violence splayed out in front of him was shameful and chilling. He shut his eyes to it, momentarily wishing everything away. Could he twist and shrink his memories to make himself believe it never happened? He thought about running off, disappearing forever.

Vaguely, he was aware of Farzan talking desperately on his cell phone, and then there was a jump, a shudder against a wall, and a terrified shriek.

Jacks looked up. Benoit had transformed to his human self. He lay at rest, like a naked corpse on the battlefield. Strangely, the sight conjured a sense of calm. Benoit had returned to his original nature. The madness that had gripped him had run its course. Just like the she-jaguar who converted him.

Sirens approached the store. Farzan must have called the police. Soon, officers and ambulance workers would flood into the place. Benoit would be taken away in a covered gurney to a morgue, undocumented, no one to claim his body or to acknowledge his death. Jacks clasped Benoit's shoulder and kissed his forehead.

I'm sorry, Ben.

EIGHT

THE SPECTACLE OF the aftermath was largely lost to Jacks. His adrenalin waned, and he succumbed to the force of his injuries. He barely remembered getting hooked up to an IV and oxygen mask by EMTs and rushed to the trauma unit at Lennox Hill Hospital downtown.

Two days later, his awareness returned in increasingly longer spans. He'd been moved from the critical care unit to a regular bed in the hospital. He was bandaged in many places, lighter dressing around his chest and sides, tighter and thicker around his left leg from high on his thigh to below his knee. Jacks recalled the fight and the injuries that had left him with a lame leg, but he also could feel his body was repairing itself. The hospital staff told him they were encouraged by how quickly his wounds were healing.

Farzan visited every day. Once, he brought his father, his mother, and his brother, Sammy. It was the first time Jacks had met a Persian family. He expected them to be angry about him stealing their car. But Mr. and Mrs. Mohammed were warm and full of gratitude. They brought him fruit, flowers, and shiny, jellied candies and wept with thanks that he fought off a wild cat to protect their son. Farzan must have given them a selective story, including something ennobling about his homeless situation. Jacks didn't ask Farzan about it. When they were alone, they both stuck to easy topics, like Jacks's recovery and the playlist Farzan had made for him if he felt like listening to it. Farzan had uploaded it to his iPod, which he had brought along.

Then, on the third night of his hospitalization, two police detectives came to visit him.

Jacks tried to remember what he had told the cops and the EMTs at the bodega. He was pretty sure he hadn't said anything, and then a fragment from that night returned to him. While he'd been waiting in an ER stall, a nurse asked him some intake questions. Freaked out, he gave her a fake last name and said he had no relatives to notify. He also gave the abandoned furniture factory as his address. They must have taken him in as a charity case. He certainly didn't have health insurance. Jacks hadn't even had any ID. He left his driver's license and his college ID back at Farzan's apartment.

One of the cops, Detective Robbins, was a pretty, thirty-something, Black woman, who was friendlier than her partner. Detective Faraday was a balding, white guy built like an overgrown bulldog. He had a grim, suspicious face. After they introduced themselves, they stood at the foot of his hospital bed. Robbins did most of the talking.

"The responding officers said you were in bad shape. How are you feeling?"

Jacks scooted upright at the head of his bed. "I'm getting better."

"They haven't found the animal that attacked you. What do you remember from that night?"

"Not much. I was visiting my friend."

Robbins looked down at her notepad. "The cashier, Farzan Mohammed, says you saved his life. According to his statement, a black panther got into the store from the roof. You scared it away, and then a man entered the scene and tried to attack Mohammed. You got a gun behind the cash register. Did you know the man you shot?"

Jacks shook his head.

"He hasn't been identified, and the strangest thing is, no one in the neighborhood noticed a naked man walking the streets that night. Do you have any idea how he got there?"

"No."

"Maybe he took off his clothes while he was in the store." Robbins let the sentence hang, almost like a question. Jacks blinked.

"The officer's report says you were kneeling over his body."

"I never shot anyone before. I was pretty shaken."

Robbins smiled like she understood how he felt. Though she tried to look like one of the guys with her uniform and tight ponytail, she had a warm, motherly face. Then Jacks noticed Detective Faraday's gaze locked in on him.

"I'm really sorry. I wish I could be more help."

"You got one of the bad guys. You already helped plenty," Robbins said. "Maybe in a couple of days, things will come back to you clearer." She smiled at him again. Jacks returned a nervous grin. He didn't want to open his mouth, afraid of what would come out. Even the most incidental reply could lead to who knew what kind of questions.

"There's one other thing. We went by the place of residence you gave to the hospital. It's an abandoned building. Can you tell us about that?"

His face burned. "It was just a place I'd been staying. Until I get a job."

"Mr. Mohammed tells us he's offered to take you in while you get back on your feet."

"Yeah. His whole family has been amazing."

The detective glanced at her notepad and turned to something else. "The hospital has you down as twenty-two years old."

"Yep. I'll be twenty-three in September."

Robbins closed her notepad and crossed her arms over her chest. "Where did you grow up, Jackson?"

"Upstate New York."

She waited for more. Jacks improvised a bit. "I had a job up there for a while. I came down to New York a couple of months ago."

"What about your parents?"

"I don't have any. My mom and dad died. Before I can remember."

Detective Faraday broke in. "You telling us you got *no* family? No brothers, sisters, aunts, or uncles? Nobody who's gonna be worried about you?"

"Nope."

Jacks steeled himself. Days ago, when he was languishing with his injuries, he'd considered for a moment calling his mother. But he'd since decided he was never returning to his parents. If they couldn't accept his gayness, they certainly wouldn't accept his cougar nature. They'd want him locked up in an institution.

Faraday looked Jacks over smugly. He was probably twice Jacks's age and thought he was a dumb kid run off from his family because he couldn't handle being a responsible adult.

"Jackson *Cherokee*," Faraday read off his pad. "That's an unusual name. You Native? Or you just come up with that 'cause you're a Jeep fan?"

"No. It's my family name." It was the name Jacks had given

the hospital. Hearing it said by someone else made him feel good. He was starting a new life as the descendant of a proud people who knew about dual souls.

Feeling a little more confident, Jacks asked Faraday, "Has this been in the news? I don't really want to talk to reporters."

Faraday grinned for a half second. "Believe me, neither do we. It was on the local stations the other night, and the *Post* ran a story. Nothing big. You been contacted by reporters?"

"No."

"So, don't give a statement if a reporter asks. Would've happened already if they were interested. Sad to say, but stuff like this happens uptown, and it's not exactly headline news."

Faraday scratched his ear, and his face brightened, suddenly convivial. "Probably our John Doe raised the panther as a cub in his apartment. He couldn't handle it when the thing grew up bigger than him. Those animals belong in the wild, or at least a zoo. Damn shame when one of them has to get put down because of some guy's stupidity." He turned to his partner. "You've seen that show on cable? About the whack jobs who think they can get away with keeping a hyena in their apartment? *Animal Obsessions* or something like that?"

Robbins shook her head. Faraday looked at Jacks, and Jacks shook his head as well.

"You got lucky, Jackson," Faraday said. "Getting attacked by a big cat and living to tell about it? Believe me, you got lucky."

The two detectives left their business cards on the bedside table, where Jacks's dinner tray was sitting. The Salisbury steak was gone, but the mashed potatoes and peas were untouched. Faraday looked at it a second longer than he needed to. Jacks tightened up. It couldn't mean anything to the detective, could it?

"If you remember anything more, give us a call," Robbins said.

"Sometimes it takes a little while for things to pop back into place after suffering a trauma," Faraday said. "Hey—how'd you learn to fire off a pistol like that? You pinged the guy right in the brain stem, killing him instantly, from fifteen, maybe twenty yards away, according to your pal Farzan. They got shooting ranges at orphanages?"

Robbins passed her partner a glance. Faraday kept looking at Jacks expectantly. He didn't answer. His father had taken him to shooting ranges when he was younger, but he had never been good with guns. It was his feline sight and balance that enabled him to make his mark cleanly at the base of Benoit's skull.

"No family," Faraday repeated. "That's a damn shame. You figure you're gonna be staying put in New York for a while?"

"I've got some things to figure out, but yeah. I like it here."

"Always something to do in the big city, isn't there? Well, you take care, Jackson. Get yourself back on your feet."

Jacks didn't feel encouraged. It sounded like what Faraday really meant was: we'll be watching you.

FARZAN AND SAMMY brought Jacks back to their house a day later. Getting out of the car, Jacks favored his right leg due to the gash. It had been his worst wound and was still sore at the stitches, while his other lacerations had sealed up without a trace. A minor medical miracle, his doctor had said. Though the hospital hadn't made much of it. Jacks figured they were happy to discharge him early. He had only stayed at the hospital for four and a half days.

Inside Farzan's apartment, the first thing Jacks did was look around for Bella. He made a full sweep of the space, calling out her name, and then he noticed Farzan watching him, looking stricken.

"She was gone the morning I left you at the hospital. We put flyers around the neighborhood, and I've been leaving food for her outside. I'm sorry, Jacks. I didn't want to tell you while you were recovering."

Jacks staggered past him, out the door, and into the backyard. He scanned the shrub-lined fence, the maple trees, and the space around two sides of the garage. The late afternoon sky was heavy and gray, casting everything in washed out light, bleak as could be. Through outdoor barbecues, flowering trees, and car exhaust, he couldn't get a read on Bella's scent.

He slunk back into the apartment.

"I saw her while you were sleeping that night," Farzan said. "She came down from the kitchen windowsill and had some food. That was maybe ten o'clock. Could she have gotten out while you were leaving the apartment?"

Jacks ached. He didn't want to believe he'd been so careless, but that time span was a blur. It was possible. How else would she have gotten out of the apartment?

He glanced around and sat down on a wooden chair at the kitchen table. Plopping down on the couch felt too imposing, even though Farzan and his entire family had said he was welcome to stay until he sorted things out. Farzan went to the refrigerator and brought out a pitcher of water.

"Want some?"

"No, thanks." Jacks slumped in his seat while Farzan poured himself a glass and took a place across from him at the kitchen table.

His worries about Bella fell away as he realized, starkly, the confidentiality of the moment. He and Farzan had talked at the hospital, but nurses, patients, or some member of Farzan's family had always been close by. Farzan had kept some things he had seen at the bodega from his parents, and certainly from the police. It occurred to him, there were also surveillance cameras in the store, which no one had mentioned. Had Farzan tampered with them? In any case, Jacks wasn't ready to talk about any of it.

"Nice weather we're having, isn't it?" Farzan said.

Jacks glanced at him. Farzan met his gaze for a moment, and then looked away. "We should talk about what happened that night, don't you think? If you're up to it now."

Jacks squirmed under the table. "What do you want to know?'

"That man was your boyfriend."

Jacks nodded slowly.

"He was also the cat."

Jacks looked down at his hands in his lap. How could he explain things?

Farzan stood and walked into the living space. He returned with Jacks's wallet. Opened up. His driver's license, debit card, and Calverton ID showed in the card slots. "Jackson Dowd," Farzan said. "I figured there was a reason you didn't give your real name to the hospital. So, I went along with it." He retook his seat with his hands folded on the table. "You risked your life saving mine. I decided I owed you something, keeping your business to yourself, I guess. But if you're going to be staying here, I have a right to know what's going on."

Sweat beaded his forehead. He shifted in his seat, and then he looked up at Farzan. "This is going to sound insane." Jacks drew a deep breath. "Benoit, my boyfriend, was a werecat." He looked away and didn't wait for a response. "I know it's totally unbelievable, but you saw it yourself."

"There's a Persian superstition that the cat is a *jinn*, a kind of demon that can change shapes. I always thought that was old folklore held on to by gullible people. Now I don't know what to believe."

"It's not like that. He wasn't a demon. It's a kind of awakening of the feline soul that goes back thousands of years."

"Why did he want to kill me?"

"He thought you were a threat. He thought getting rid of you would bring us back together. I tried talking to him earlier that night, but I couldn't reason with him." Jacks scuffed his sneakers on the floor. "I think, at some point, you can lose the part of you that's human. I feel terrible, Farzan. I didn't know he'd react like that when I left him, but I shouldn't have come back here and put you in danger."

They stared away from each other for a while. All things considered, it was going as well as Jacks could have expected. Farzan wasn't in hysterics, or acting like he was crazy. Jacks needed someone to understand and not judge him.

Farzan asked him, flatly: "Are you one too?"

Jacks met his gaze. "Yeah."

Farzan stood up. He stepped around the kitchen, going nowhere in particular. He brushed his hand through his thick black hair again and again.

"I'd never hurt you," Jacks said. "After all you've done for me, you think I could consider for a second doing anything bad to you? That's why I had to stop Benoit."

Farzan halted with his back turned to Jacks. "I've read a lot of comic books, but I never thought..."

"It's not like in the comics." Jacks could see Farzan's hand trembling. "Benoit brought this potential out of me. It's an ancient tradition. From a time when people worshiped feline gods."

"He *turned* you? Like a vampire?"

"No. I don't prey on people."

"What if you lose control? What if something inside you

takes over and you end up hurting someone? I've got my parents living upstairs."

Jacks got up from his seat. "It won't happen. I promise you. Farzan, I'm the same person I was before you knew about this."

Farzan looked him over. He was wary and torn. Shame gutted Jacks. "I've only been like this for three months. I'm trying to understand it, too. And I don't have any place to go. Things were bad with my parents to start, and there's no way they can handle this. I'll go to a shelter, if that's what you want. But you've got to believe me, Farzan. I wouldn't hurt you, or anyone else."

The world pulsed in and out of his vision. What was he going to do? He was homeless, with a couple of dollars in his pocket, unable to provide any kind of ID to start rebuilding his life. He had no one in the world to turn to for help. His family and Jonathan and Gabe probably thought he was dead, and it was better that way. No one would ever understand what he had become. They would be disgusted and embarrassed to be around him.

Warm arms surrounded Jacks. He tried to keep back his tears, but his sadness was too much. He buried his face in Farzan's shoulder, and it poured out of him in choking sobs.

Farzan held him by the arms. "I'm not kicking you out."

Truthfully, Jacks didn't think much about how he had come to that decision. He was overwhelmed by gratitude. First thing in the morning, he would job hunt. He'd take whatever he could get: washing dishes or working at some fast food place. He'd work two or three jobs so he could help out with household expenses and damages to the bodega from the fight, while saving up for a deposit on his own apartment. He swore to Farzan he'd make up for everything and get his own place as quick as he could.

NINE

Six weeks later

NO ONE HAD come into the bodega for a full hour. It was 4:20 in the morning, too early for the sanitation workers to come in for their coffees and newspapers, too late for the people getting off from night jobs to stop by for beer and cigarettes. Jacks had the traffic patterns down pat after two weeks of working at the store. He had inherited the overnight shift from Farzan. Farzan called the hour from 3:30 to 4:30 the "Dead Zone."

Sitting behind the cash register, Jacks sank beneath a somniferous weight. He had been working since seven in the morning at a grocery store where he got paid under the table stocking shelves. Then, he'd headed to a marketing research center to pick up the five to nine shift. They paid cash on a temp basis to annoy people with telephone surveys. When that job finished, he'd had an hour to wash up, eat dinner, and sit down for a few minutes before he had to take a bus and two subway trains to make it to the bodega by eleven. The routine would start again after Farzan's father took over the store at seven thirty.

Jacks had never worked so hard, but he couldn't complain. Earlier in the summer, Farzan started an overnight rotation at an emergency room, and Jacks insisted he would cover the bodega for him, and do it for free. It compensated a little for not paying rent, not to mention the fact that Benoit had tried to kill Farzan. Meanwhile, Farzan refused to accept money for utility bills or groceries so Jacks could save up for the two months rent he would need to get his own place. New York was mad expensive. Jacks was only halfway there. One thing he knew for sure: as soon as he signed his own lease, he was taking Farzan out to a fancy dinner and a live rock club he mentioned he wanted to check out.

If he could keep up his insane work schedule.

All kinds of dubious caffeine supplements and herbal boosters were on display around the counter, but Jacks had never liked taking drugs. What if his body had a bad reaction and his heart went haywire? Or what if it had the opposite effect, like when kids with attention deficit disorder took stimulants to calm down? That would look real good—passed out at the register when Farzan's father walked into the store.

He stood to shake off his fatigue and glanced around the place, double-checking that he'd done all his tasks. The aisles were swept and mopped. The refrigerator cases were Windexed, and the shelves had all been wiped down. The store had never looked so good. Mr. Mohammed had said it himself. Jacks had to keep in motion to stay alert, and the rigorous routine gave his mind some focus so it wouldn't wander off to other things.

Like the urge flickering inside him to transform, to roam free, to find higher ground.

The stacks of morning newspapers could always be tidied a

bit, but his fit of exhaustion was intense that night. His legs wouldn't move, and his shoulders melted into a slump. He stared, unfocused, at the coffee machines, wondering if he could take just five or ten minutes to rest before brewing fresh pots for the early morning customers. He dropped back into his chair. His eyelids drooped, and his vision diffused. He thought of Bella.

He had looked for her all over Farzan's neighborhood since she had disappeared from the apartment. He had even checked out the abandoned furniture factory. Then a vision kept playing over in his head. Jacks couldn't tell if it was a dream washing back into his consciousness or some kind of psychic connection, however that was possible.

It was nighttime, and he was walking along a wide street with a median of parked cars. He could feel the pavement against the pads of his feet, and his body was lithe, trotting on all fours, so light he was practically gliding. It seemed to Jacks that he had transformed into a cat, but it felt different than when he called up his mountain lion self. A line of hedges in concrete planters towered above him. His movement was strange: a sidling motion rather than the skulk or gallop he was used to. He was a cat, but he was a small cat. When he looked down, his forelegs had black and gray tiger-striped markings. Jacks had somehow gotten into Bella's head, or at least he was experiencing a fantasy of that, showing him what happened to her.

Bella only allowed Jacks to see things she was seeing: the open sidewalk ahead, a glance to the side when a car door slammed shut in the distance. She stopped short of a lighted space.

It was the entrance to the lobby of a condominium build-ing. Bella waited, listening for sounds of passersby, and then she fast-tracked by the lobby with a quick look through the glass doors. A sign was imprinted on the carpet of the lobby: The Minnesota or The Missouri? Jacks remembered the thick, Art Deco-style lettering, but the image passed by too fast to be sure of the name.

At the end of the building, Bella turned down a short street with another median of parked cars. Jacks felt a breeze and heard the faint roar of the ocean. Bella was determined to get somewhere, padding quickly along the sidewalk. A boardwalk and two ramps leading up to it were in the shadows at the end of the street, closed off by a chain-link fence and a locked gate.

Bella slinked between the gate posts and entered a darkened, sandy tunnel below the boardwalk. A short way in, she turned her glance to one side.

Yellow-green eyes sparked from the depths of the cold, sandy enclosure. A man emerged from the shadows. He was tall and broad-shouldered with powerful arms. The hood of his short-sleeve sweatshirt was pulled up.

The stranger crouched and reached out his hand for Bella. She trotted toward him. The man's iridescent eyes flared, and Jacks caught two peculiar details. He had a red tuft of beard on his chin and a fiery orange-red tattoo that looked like a gothic letter G on the back of his hand. Then everything washed away.

Jacks didn't like him. If the vision was real, like the feline telepathy through which he had communicated with Benoit, he wondered why Bella had traveled to that spot. Farzan had told him about the beaches in Brooklyn and Queens, and they were miles away from their basement apartment in Richmond Hill.

The door to the bodega swung open, and a swaggering commotion burst into the place. Jacks sat up and turned to the front of the store. A crew of Latino guys in their teens and early twenties had rolled in. They had gold bandanas on their heads, and they wore black jackets and oversized gold T-shirts.

The guy leading the group had a cleft lip, and his face was almost completely covered in tattoos. Four black teardrops below one of his eyes stood out amid a menacing design of tribal signs and lettering. Jacks had seen gangbangers in the bodega before, and they had never made trouble. But there were eight of them, and they looked keyed up.

Some of the guys started grabbing things from the snack racks in the center of the store, stuffing them in their jackets and their baggy jeans pockets. Three others headed for the refrigerator cases and clanged out twelve-packs of beer. Jacks stood up from his seat. He needed to keep track of the activity. His temperature spiked. Were the guys really raiding the store? He didn't want to believe it.

One guy batted his hand down a paper goods shelf, sending bags of paper towels cascading down to the floor. His companions laughed, and then the whole group joined in, swatting cans from shelves, kicking over display cases, and breaking jars in the middle of the aisles.

Jacks shouted at them. "What do you think you're doing?"

One of the guys started hurling two-liter sodas through the store. More groceries got wrenched from shelves, and plastic bottles burst like bombs against the walls. The whole place was getting trashed. His thoughts whirled. There was a panic button for calling the cops, but how long would it take for them to respond? There was also Mr. Mohammed's handgun beneath the counter, but what if waving it at the thugs sent things farther left? They probably had guns themselves.

The ringleader with the tattooed face swaggered up to Jacks, and the guys eased off their demolition.

"Where's the jihad motherfucker I seen here before?" His bloodshot eyes bored into him. The guy was high on something, shifting in his place, sweat glazing his shaved head.

He had to be referring to Farzan, and his word choice pissed Jacks off. "*I'm* working here tonight."

"Guess it's that faggot's lucky night." Goofy snickers broke out from his pals, and they drew up by their ringleader, a pack of young toughs itching to boss someone around. Their ringleader gripped the counter and leaned into Jacks. The spit from his shout showered Jacks's face.

"You tell that Arab piece of shit we don't want his filthy store in our turf."

An accumulation of things—the ethnic and homophobic slurs, the destruction of the store he was entrusted to protect, the injustice of a near twenty-four hour workday coming to this —pulled Jacks together and then beyond himself.

"You shut your fucking mouth and get out of here."

The ringleader twisted up his face. "What did you say?"

Jacks repeated, in an otherworldly voice—cold, unflinching, almost a growl. "I said: Get out of the store, and I might let you live."

The guy backed away from the counter, momentarily thrown off balance. His pals glanced from him to Jacks, looking for some direction. The guy reached to his waist and pulled out a semi-automatic pistol from beneath his T-shirt. He pointed it at Jacks' chest.

"I wasn't gonna pop you, but you piss me off." He held the gun solidly with a finger wrapped around the trigger.

The other guys goaded him on in Spanish. "Hágalo!"

"Mate el maricon."

"Muere, puta."

Jacks ducked beneath the counter. He heard a blast and a violent thud from a bullet puncturing the drywall behind him. Unleashed from an angry, wound-up place in his gut, a transformation sped through Jacks. It was like a thermonuclear reaction with every cell of his body blasting white hot, and then his flesh and bones snapped into shape with an audible pop.

He sprang over the counter, a snarling, mountain lion. His forepaws connected with the ringleader's shoulders, and the momentum sent the guy toppling backward into a display case, trapping him beneath Jacks's 200-pounds of muscled hide.

The gun fell out of the guy's hand. His friends jumped out of the way, swearing in Spanish, and scattering. Before any of them got any wise ideas, Jacks batted the gun with his big forepaw so that it slid out of reach.

The guys closest to the door bolted out to the street. Three others lurched to the other side of the store to protect themselves. Jacks bared his teeth and growled. He wasn't planning on hurting anyone. He just needed to scare them out of the store.

One of the guys fumbled for a gun wedged in his jeans. That second threat of violence set off a deeper instinct inside Jacks. Blind with rage, Jacks sprang at him with his claws outstretched, tackling him and gouging one side of his face with his powerful mitt. The guy fell backward into a metal shelf and went down in a delirious tumble. His two buddies made a break for the door.

The ringleader slid by the seat of his pants toward the door, muttering some sort of protective incantation. Jacks glared at him as he made his way out of the bodega. That left the dude he had taken down by the shelf. His gun had fallen out of his hands, and he lay on the floor in a contorted position. He wasn't moving. He must have hit his head against the shelf.

Jacks nudged his muzzle against the gangbanger's chest. A faint heartbeat tickled his whiskers, and Jacks could smell life stirring inside him. He had to get the guy medical attention. But betrayed by a swarming thrill, his mouth watered for the taste of blood. A vision of clamping down on the young man's exposed jugular vein, claiming the kill, hung delectably before Jacks. He pushed it away and skulked back to the counter. He leapt into the cashier compartment, compacted into his human body, and pushed the button for the police.

A rueful ache worked through his body. He had a hell of a lot to explain. He could tell the cops the store had been raided, but the gangbangers weren't likely to keep their mouths shut about what they had seen. Not to mention that one of them was splayed out on the floor with score lines across his face.

TEN

"I CAN'T BELIEVE you would do this," Farzan said.

He sat across from Jacks at the kitchen table. Dark hollows of shadow had spread across the basement apartment. It was late afternoon, and the high, slider windows provided stingy light. Neither party ventured to do anything about it. Jacks felt like the room was electrified plenty without any additional wattage.

He had spoken to police officers and explained things to EMTs and Farzan's dad. He told them half of the story and added that he scared the gangbangers away with the handgun from the store. He'd erased the surveillance camera tapes, but he told them he rebooted the system at the beginning of the night, and it must have shut down by accident. But Jacks had given Farzan the truth. He'd promised himself he wouldn't lie to him after what happened with Benoit.

"The guys were tearing up the store," Jacks said.

"You could have gotten killed."

"They could have shot me behind the counter."

Farzan stood up from the table. He started in one direction

then another in the little kitchen, working one hand through his thick, black hair, which had grown out from a faux-hawk to something resembling a pompadour.

"There are protocols to follow."

"There was a pistol pointed at me. What was I supposed to do?"

Farzan turned his back to Jacks and was silent for a moment. "You said you could control it."

Jacks's voice rose up in a crescendo. "I *can* control it. But if a group of kids comes bursting into your father's store, wrecking the place and waving guns, I'm gonna react."

Farzan turned around, and then he glanced at the ceiling. His mother, his father and Sammy lived upstairs. He spoke to Jacks in a quiet, measured tone. "You can't work at the store anymore."

Jacks got up from his seat. "Why?"

"You think the cops are going to catch these guys? They'll be back to save face." He leaned against the kitchen countertop and grimaced. "Even if the cops actually find them, there'll be dozens of delinquents from the neighborhood happy to pick up where their friends left off. These kids are like roaches. You stomp them out, and there's a brand new batch ready to terrorize the store."

Jacks's eyes widened. Farzan sounded like Mr. Mohammed, and Jacks wondered how much Farzan agreed with his dad when he went off on racially charged rants about the "local hoodlums" plaguing his business. They hung out in front of the store and scared away customers, Mr. Mohammed said. But they were mostly just kids who didn't have anywhere else to go.

"Not every kid in that neighborhood is bad."

"I'm sure they appreciate your enlightened point of view. You know how many times our storefront has been marked up with graffiti? Or how many times they come in on a grab-and-run? And when we chase them out, they call us Arab scum."

"I'm not making excuses for any of that. I'm just saying..." Jacks trailed off for a moment. "It's a poor community. There's lots of problems and not a whole lot of opportunity."

"That's so bullshit. You want to talk about opportunity? My father brought my mother and older sister and brothers to this country after his textile factory in Iran was firebombed by Islamic revolutionaries. They had no place to go but my uncle's in New York. After I was born, eleven of us were living in a three-room flat.

"We were not the privileged, university-educated Persians of Beverly Hills, and my lovely uncle didn't believe in hand-outs. He insisted that we pull ourselves up by our bootstraps. He never helped my father with connections despite the fact he had a successful business importing fabrics and knew lots of people in the textile industry. My father worked two jobs to buy that bodega so he could get us out on our own. So we would have a future. And we still work our asses off night and day. We always treat our customers with respect, and this is what we get in return?"

Indignation colored Farzan's face. He wouldn't look at Jacks. It triggered an awkward realization. The gangbangers had given Jacks a chance to let them leave peacefully. He was an outsider to their world, just some middle-class white guy who didn't figure into the racial politics that fomented their rage. That outsider status had provided Jacks with a degree of protection. If it had been Farzan or Mr. Mohammed working at the store last night, things might not have played out that way.

He drew up in front of Farzan. "I'm sorry. I get it. It's not fair."

"Don't worry about it. It's not your fault. You were protecting the store. I shouldn't have taken it out on you."

Farzan had never been one to hold back what he was think-ing, but his skirted glances told a different story. At least he had calmed down some. Jacks tried to reason with him. "I know the cops haven't been the best in the past, but they said they'll be watching the store. Your father needs me on the overnight shift. Who else is going to do it? You've got your internship."

"Who's going to explain it to him when no one shops at the store anymore?"

Jacks looked at him funny.

"We might as well be running an African safari. We've had two incidents with big cats in less than two months."

Jacks shrank inside. He hadn't meant to draw attention to himself. He'd covered his tracks the best he could, and the cops on the scene had seemed satisfied by his explanation that the kid he'd knocked out had scraped his face against a shelf. But Jacks understood what Farzan meant. People talked. Word spread.

"You're not going back to the store," Farzan said with finality.

"What am I supposed to do? I want to contribute around here."

"You're doing plenty. You've got your other jobs during the day."

Jacks *had* work off the books at a grocery store. It was his best-paying gig: one hundred bucks a day, but he had to call his boss that morning because he was held up by the police and needed to straighten up the bodega. The grocery store manager told him not to bother coming in later, and the message was pretty clear. If he didn't show up that morning, there was no point coming back. It wasn't easy finding jobs that paid under the table.

"Who's going to work the store at night?" Jacks said. "You're not dropping out of medical school because of this."

"We'll tell my father you can't be working around the clock anymore. Sammy is unemployed. *Again.* He can cover the store for a while."

Jacks didn't like the idea. He was tired of feeling worthless.

Meanwhile, Farzan's expression brightened in amusement for some reason.

"What?"

"You don't have to worry about disappointing my father. You've become his latest hero. First you saved my life, now you saved his store."

"Well, at least someone likes having me around."

Farzan eased up closer and placed his hand on Jacks's shoulder. "If I'm being honest, what you did was badass. I'm sorry for flying off the handle. It's actually infuriatingly admirable how compassionate you are about the kids in that neighborhood." They looked at each other and then both glanced shyly away. That had been happening a lot when they were alone together in the apartment. It was just tight quarters, Jacks figured. But this time, neither one of them budged, and, in a heartbeat, Farzan leaned in and kissed Jacks. It was soft and tentative at first. Then both of them pressed further, and they were kissing open-mouthed.

Farzan backed away. His face was bright red. "I'm sorry. I shouldn't have done that."

Jacks held Farzan's neck and kissed him again. Maybe the rush from confronting the young thugs earlier in the day was still motoring through him, but it felt right, and every charged moment of living together in the small apartment had accumulated to a tipping point. In a blink, he was lifting Farzan onto the counter with the thought of stripping off his pants.

Farzan reached under Jacks's shirt. His hands were teasingly cold against Jacks's shoulder blades, and then he undid Jacks' belt and tugged off his jeans.

Farzan untucked his Oxford shirt and hastily unbuttoned it. "You can tell me if we're moving too fast."

Jacks opened Farzan's shirt and tasted one of his dark brown nipples. A trace of men's body spray sparked against his tongue. He lapped a trail up Farzan's chest and up the side of his neck. His feline sensitivity kicked in, and scents swarmed into his brain, visualized like a burst of bright colors. The cadence of Farzan's breathing filled his ears, wanting, swelling. He brushed his nose against Farzan's soft lips, and spread his hands toward the warmth between Farzan's thighs.

Farzan bowed his head and spoke quietly. "I guess it's not moving too fast for you. I didn't know." He raked his hand through Jacks's hair and kissed his face. "It's what I wanted. What I always wanted. Since the day you came into the store."

The thrill that coursed through Jacks came crashing down, and he stopped what he was doing. He was attracted to Farzan, but his head had been too crowded to consider that they could be boyfriends. If that's what Farzan was saying.

"Okay. Change of plans. I guess it's not what you always wanted." Farzan scooted back on the counter.

"It's not that." He clasped Farzan's arm, but he couldn't find words.

"I shouldn't have said anything." Farzan pulled his arm away and started buttoning his shirt.

"It's not your fault."

"Of course it's my fault," Farzan said sharply. "I was an idiot. Again." He finished his last button and stepped around Jacks.

"Farzan, listen. Can we talk about this?"

Farzan halted.

"I didn't mind. Obviously. I just..." Jacks swiped his face. "I'm not there yet. The way you said. God! You're looking at me like I'm such an asshole."

"That's not my asshole face. It's my please-spare-me-the-it's-not-you-it's-me face. I get it, Jacks. It's not the first time for me. We'll pretend it never happened." He walked to his bedroom and shut the door behind him.

THEY DIDN'T SPEAK for the rest of the day. Jacks lay on the sofa, flipping through TV channels with no particular interest, and Farzan stayed in his bedroom, studying for school or whatever. Later that night, Farzan washed up in the bathroom while Jacks was having a plate of microwaved chicken nuggets in the kitchen. Dressed in his hospital scrubs, with a duffle bag thrown over his shoulder, Farzan trudged past Jacks on the way out the door. He mumbled a goodbye and didn't even glance at Jacks.

Jacks went over to the kitchen cabinet by the refrigerator. He had seen a bottle of whiskey in there, practically untouched, probably some random holiday gift Farzan had received. Farzan wasn't much of a drinker. Jacks opened the cabinet and brought out the bottle. He screwed off the cap, and poured himself a couple fingers of the glistening, amber liquor. It scorched going down, all the way to his stomach, and it made his body delightfully heavy and warm.

He poured a second drink and swallowed it down. He needed to shut his mind off. Too many things were stressing him out, like how he was going to find another off-the-books job? Did Farzan want him out after what happened? He could have gone along with it. He liked Farzan. It wouldn't have been so hard to say he'd wanted to be with him from the start, too. A lot easier than living on the streets and trying to survive.

Jacks tipped the bottle to refill his glass. It just wasn't the time for him to get involved with Farzan that deep. He remembered that moment, sniffing over the gangbanger he had taken down, when his feline urges nearly overwhelmed his better sense, driving him to dominate, to destroy. Jacks had told Farzan he could control his wild cat soul, but the truth was, he didn't really know.

"All cats kill," Benoit had told Jacks. "It's time for you to learn."

The apartment rocked a bit. The alcohol was doing its thing. His body felt like one big sandbag. He'd only slept something like five hours in the past two days. Jacks put the whiskey bottle away, washed his glass, and swayed into the living room. He passed out on the pull-out sofa bed nearly as soon as he laid down.

ELEVEN

HE WOKE UP the next morning at eleven. It was a Thursday, and Farzan always came back to the apartment after his internship to take a nap before his afternoon classes, but there was no sign of him having come or gone.

Jacks found his cell phone on the kitchen counter and called the marketing research center. He wasn't scheduled to work that day, but with some luck he could pick up a shift. The supervisor told him the study he'd been working on was finished. She might be hiring for a new project in a couple of weeks.

Jacks fell back on the pull-out sofa bed. For the first time in weeks, he had absolutely nothing to do. The empty apartment made Jacks jittery. The idle hours loomed in front of him with dread. It was too much time to be alone, facing the fact that he had no idea what he was doing with his life. Nobody would ever accept who he was, not even Farzan, really.

He sat up on the creaky bed. That train of thought was going to take him to a dismal place. Instead of feeling sorry for himself, he needed to keep moving forward and get the money for his own place. Now that Farzan was pissed at him, the timetable for moving out may have just accelerated.

He looked to Farzan's bedroom door. He had told Jacks he was free to use his desktop computer, though Jacks felt weird about barging into Farzan's room, especially after that morning. But to seriously job search, a computer was a hell of a lot better than trying to use his cheap Android phone. Jacks got up, clad in the boxers he had slept in, and wandered into the bedroom.

Sitting down at Farzan's computer desk, he faced a cluttered Windows desktop on the monitor. With his heightened feline senses, Farzan's scent was like a cloud surrounding him. It wasn't unpleasant; it was appealing, actually, but it emphasized the fact he was invading Farzan's space. Well, what could Jacks do? He needed to use the computer, and meanwhile, Farzan's odors had his body humming in a strange sort of arousal. Jacks couldn't shake it off. An instinct compelled him to snoop.

He clicked open a photo gallery, and a grin spread across his face. Farzan had pictures from his college graduation, family gatherings, and a handsome headshot he must use for a dating app. He looked happy. He had such a close-knit family. Farzan complained about his mother's nagging and his older brothers' laziness, but it was obvious how much they all cared about each other.

In the glint of the monitor, Jacks caught his own silhouette. It hit him that he was an outsider, looking in on someone else's life.

Jacks had told himself no self-pitying. But the feelings gripped him hard. Farzan's photos were documentation of a normal life, something Jacks hadn't had even before he became this...thing. But he'd had friends and plans. When he'd run off with Benoit, he'd been six weeks away from graduating with a bachelor's degree. He and his roommates talked about moving to New York City together, waiting tables or whatever they needed to do for work until they could get real jobs.

Now, it was like Jacks was dead to everyone.

He couldn't even pick up the phone to call his friends from college. There were too many things Jacks couldn't explain. It hurt like razor blades to his heart. Jacks needed badly to share with someone what had happened to him. There were terrible parts, and there were amazing parts. He could hear and smell and see things he never could before. His vision at night was as sharp as it was during the day. He could telepathize conversations. His body could rejuvenate itself from wounds. Benoit, who was more than two hundred years old, had told Jacks he would age one year for every twenty.

But how could anyone take that in without freaking out? Any rational person would want him to get medical or psychiatric help. He'd be quarantined and studied and treated like some kind of mutant. Tears burned in his throat. Could a person live for three hundred, four hundred years without anyone knowing who he truly was? Never having a friend?

Glancing at the monitor, he noticed a photo folder labeled: "me & jacks." He clicked it open. It was a dozen or so shots that must've synched from Farzan's iPhone. The discovery filled him with a magical warmth.

There were pictures of him recovering in the hospital. Another of Jacks with Farzan's family, which he stared at for a while. Farzan's father, who they called baba, his mother, who they called maman, and his older brothers, Sammy and Rahim. It was a Sunday dinner, and everyone had been teasing Farzan's mom that she had made too much food, though they were all smiles sitting around the table with heaping plates of chicken stew, lamb, rice, and lentils.

The only shot of Jacks and Farzan was a goofy pic Farzan had taken on a Saturday afternoon they both had free. Jacks told Farzan he wanted to go to Times Square so they took the subway to midtown Manhattan. He had never seen streets so crowded, nor all the enormous video screens and brightly lit up signs. They strolled around, stopping here and there to watch street performers. Then they happened upon the theater that was showing *The Lion King.*

Farzan had insisted on the spot: that lion head icon from the musical hanging above them. He could be so light-hearted about Jacks's nature at moments, but most of the time Farzan treated the subject as off-limits, as though if they both ignored it, it would just go away. In the photo, Jacks had his hand on Farzan's shoulder, and he blinked at the wrong time. Farzan's brown eyes were wide and sparkling. Jacks could see how much in love he was. Farzan had taken Jacks in when no one else in the world would help him. He was his certified guardian angel.

But did Farzan love him, or just the parts that he chose to see?

Jacks closed up the photo gallery. What he really needed to do was to learn who he was. He needed to know if he was dangerous to other people or if it didn't have to be like that. If his feline nature could be managed in some way, he could explain that to Farzan, and they could have an honest conversation about what he was and what the implications were. Maybe Farzan could handle it, and he'd understand why Jacks was hesitant when they got physical. If he couldn't, well, at least Jacks could leave knowing someone in the world didn't hate him.

Jacks thought back to his recurring dream about Bella. That could be a good place to start. He wasn't going to learn how to get a handle on his feline telepathy from humans. The idea would have seemed bonkers to him four months ago, but he wondered if he could get information from other cats. He and Bella had shared a bond. For all he knew, that dream had been

Bella telepathizing to him with some message. Or maybe she was giving him clues of where to find her. Jacks focused on that vision where she had traveled to meet that vagrant man with the red goatee.

Jacks called back the unfamiliar, night-shrouded board-walk. What stood out more was the tattoo on the man's hand. It was a fiery, orange-red Gothic letter G. Jacks pulled up images from a search engine, scrolling through several pages until he recognized the symbol.

The image he found looked like it was hand-sketched. It linked to some guy's website: "Conspiracy-Watch with K.C. Anderbeau." Amateurish, the site was filled with weird artwork and photos along with rambling posts about UFOs, government cover-ups, and secret societies. Jacks's eyes rolled back in his head a bit, but he read through the guy's blog post about that flaming red G tattoo.

They call themselves The Glaring. They came from a medical experiment the Nazis were working on in the 1940s, which the U.S. military found when they stormed Berlin. They thought the public couldn't handle it, so they turned everything over to the O.S.S. (which later became the C.I.A.). The feds thought they could contain it, but now there's hundreds, maybe thousands of these hybrid beings living among us. Since posting this sketch, my site has gotten over a million hits and a steady stream of death threats. They look like people but they're not. They've got fangs like vampires and they don't just suck blood. They eat people! Anyone with REAL information about this group should email me ASAP!!

Jacks remembered Benoit telling him there was information about soul shifters out there, but there was also a lot of bullshit. This certainly seemed like bullshit, but Jacks typed "The Glaring" into a search engine anyway, just to see what came up.

He found nothing interesting at first. Pages and pages of

hyperbolic political articles, mostly about the *glaring* facts, the *glaring* inequality, and on and on. Jacks sighed. Then he was overcome by a cheeky whim. He typed into the search field: "How does a werecat join the Glaring?"

Most of the returns were nonsensical, but at the bottom of the first page, Jacks delayed on a URL for a site called "Glaring Revolution." No description, and the link took him to a page that was completely black except for an icon in the upper right corner where you could choose the language. Spanish, English, Portuguese, French—the drop-down menu looked like it covered every language on the planet. Jacks chose English, and in a blink, fiery orange-red gothic words faded in.

Restricted Area: Show your Claws or Vanish from our Sight.

Jacks laughed out loud. The page was probably built by some Thundercats geek. A cursor blinked for him to enter a password. Jacks typed in "Cheetera" just for fun. She was the buxom feline heroine from the cartoon series. He hit "enter" on the keypad.

The monitor blacked out. Jacks clicked his mouse. Nothing happened. He tried hitting keys. The monitor screen was still dead. It wasn't a power outage. Farzan's overhead light was still on. What the fuck? The computer had powered down, all by itself?

A violent rap at the door shook through the apartment.

The hair on his forearms stood up. He stared at the computer monitor. It had to just be a coincidence. Jacks shook off the eerie feeling and wandered out to the living space. Curtains were drawn over the door's window. He rummaged through his pile of washed clothes to throw on a pair of joggers and a T-shirt.

Was it Farzan's mother? He stopped in the bathroom to quickly brush his teeth. The door rattled with another impatient knock. Jacks wiped his mouth and hurried to the door to answer it.

Two police detectives stood at the entrance: a pretty, thirty-something Black woman, and an older white guy with a snide smile. The sight turned Jacks to stone. They were the same detectives who had questioned him at the hospital after the incident with Benoit. He glanced at their badges to recall their names. Detective Robbins and Detective Faraday.

"Hi ya, Jacks," Faraday said. "Imagine us meeting again so soon."

"We have some questions about the incident at Mr. Mohammed's store yesterday morning," Robbins said. "Can we come in and talk?"

Jacks stepped aside to let them in. The doorway led into the kitchen, which was really the only place for guests. The open sofa bed took up most of the living room. Jacks gestured to the two chairs at the kitchen table. Faraday waved off the offer of a seat, and Jacks sat down with Robbins. Faraday was looking around the apartment.

"You sleep down here with Mr. Mohammed's son? Farzan?" he said.

"Yeah." Jacks felt suddenly defensive, though he didn't know why. "There's a pull-out couch."

"I see that," Faraday said. "With all the room they got upstairs, why you two hole up down here, practically living on top of each other?"

"Farzan's brother moved back home."

Faraday looked up at the ceiling. "How many bedrooms they got up there? Three? Four? From the outside, it looks like a big house."

Robbins shot a wearisome glance at her partner. "We didn't come here to run a home inspection."

Faraday shrugged blamelessly. "I'm just curious is all."

"Jacks, we're here to follow up with your statement to Officer Melendez yesterday," Robbins said. She brought out some papers and a black notepad from her briefcase. Faraday leaned against the countertop behind her, glancing around the space, as if something incriminating was looming around.

"The young man who was taken away from the bodega that morning, his name is Alfred Quiñones," Robbins said. "Did you know him?"

"No."

"Did you ever see him in the store before?"

"I never saw any of them before that night."

Robbins nodded. Her warm aura put Jacks at ease. She sorted through her papers. "Based on your description, we brought some photographs we thought you might be able to ID." She slid a glossy mug shot across the table. The guy's cleft lip and tattooed face were unmistakable to Jacks.

"Yeah, that was one of the guys. The leader of the gang, I think. The one who took a shot at me."

Robbins brightened with a satisfied grin. "Javier Hernandez. He goes by Cholo on the streets. He's got quite a rap sheet. Just released from prison on an armed robbery conviction."

"Did you find him?"

"Not yet. And Mr. Quiñones isn't exactly cooperating with the investigation. It would help us if you could be as precise as possible about what happened in the store."

His hands were cold and sweating beneath the table. "What do you want to know?"

"You said that this guy fired a shot at you. What happened then?"

Faraday leaned into the conversation.

"I ducked under the cashier counter." Jacks raked his hand through his hair. "I don't know...I guess the guys didn't expect him to do it so some of them got spooked and ran."

"What about Quiñones?"

Jacks pulled out exactly what he had told the cops the other morning. "I saw him reaching for his gun. I went to tackle him and knocked him into a shelf."

Robbins nodded slowly.

"Not too tough, these gangbangers," Faraday said. "You telling us one of 'em shoots, they all turn into fraidy cats, and you got time to run around the counter and body slam Quiñones? No offense, Jackson, but you ain't the most intimidating guy to look at. Especially to a group of thugs, some of who done time."

"That's what happened."

"That's what happened," Faraday repeated, dubiously. He strolled over to the table. "Not the way Quiñones tells it. We all got a big kick outta this at the station. Y'see, the kid's convinced he got attacked by a mountain lion. Right there in the store." Faraday slapped his hand down on the table. "Bam—a mountain lion appears from outta nowhere. Just like what happened about a month ago when you and Farzan got attacked by a black panther. What do you make of that?"

Jacks shrugged his shoulders.

"Normally, I'd say it's the dumbest excuse I ever heard from a perp. But we got it on public record from just a few weeks prior, a wild cat loose in the neighborhood. First, it attacked some homeless guy in Central Park, then it waltzed into Mr. Mohammed's store. When the D.A. gets wind of it, he's not gonna be so keen on pursuing charges against these gangbangers." Faraday shrugged his bulldog shoulders. "What do we got? No video. Coincidentally enough, Mr. Mohammed's security camera had a malfunction or something, just like the night of the homicide. It's your word against theirs about what happened in the store. Might've just as easily been an animal that wrecked the place, and Mr. Mohammed's looking to pin it on some kids from the projects. Quiñones's got a gouge down his face that sure as hell don't look like it came from a tumble to the floor. So tell us, Jackson. What really happened?"

"I told you. The guys were raiding the place."

Faraday hunched over the table, and he barked at Jacks with full force. "Who're you protecting Jacks? Mr. Mohammed? Farzan? Somebody in the neighborhood who's got a big cat they can't control?"

His insides compacted, readying to unleash a transformation to fur and claw. He could picture lunging out of his seat to strike Faraday by the neck, fangs puncturing a blood vessel, twisting the cop's neck with his jaws to finish him off so he'd never try to intimidate him again. A glimpse of Robbins in his peripheral vision brought him back. He had to keep it together. He imagined his feet growing roots into the floor, and he replied to Faraday. "I don't know what you're talking about."

Faraday rolled his eyes and retook his glowering position leaning against the counter. The pressure in the room seemed to ease up, but in the silence, some awful implications occurred to Jacks. Farzan's father might have no recourse bringing charges against the thugs. He might get turned down by his insurance company and have to pay for the damage to his store. Farzan's prediction echoed back. People in the neighborhood would hate his family even more. They'd lose customers. The gangbangers would come back for revenge.

"None of these guys make the most reliable witnesses," Robbins said. "But if there's anything more you can tell us, it would help us make the case to the D.A."

Jacks stared down at the table. There had to be some way out of the mess he had created for Farzan's family, but what could he say?

"I told you everything that happened."

THE TWO COPS left, and his mind raced again. They thought Mr. Mohammed had told him to concoct the report. Since he had deleted the security cam footage from that night, he didn't have anything to prove the gangbangers wrecked the store. At least that kid Quiñones hadn't seen him transform into the mountain lion that attacked him. But Faraday was running with the only plausible theory. Someone associated with the store, probably Mr. Mohammed, kept big cats. Besides Quiñones, a half dozen thugs had seen a mountain lion jump out behind the cash register. They'd be questioned by police.

Jacks wondered if he should turn himself in, explaining everything, to clear Farzan's family. He hadn't been involved in the incident at all. That would be the right thing to do.

But what would happen then? He'd probably be locked up on the spot. They'd think he was a dangerous freak of nature. Questions about the second incident would lead to the first. Jacks might be charged with Benoit's murder.

It felt like he'd be turning himself over for execution.

He hadn't done anything wrong. Jacks had been protecting the store, protecting himself. His righteousness grew, lifting him above the shitty circumstances and laying open an inner acknowledgement. It had felt good to transform that night. His dual soul was natural to him. He liked his feline body, his ability to burst forth with crushing power. Why should he feel ashamed of that? Maybe his mistake had been trying to deny the feline part of him. Farzan didn't want to face it, but Jacks had to. He alone was responsible for leading his life as a man with the cougar spirit inside him.

Jacks would set out on his own. He had saved up about a thou from his jobs, and he would use it to get out of town and lay low someplace else. He would leave a signed confession. He could even video himself on his phone and send it to the police. Then, Mr. Mohammed couldn't get blamed for what happened to the store. Farzan could tell his father as little or as much as he wanted to. Wherever Jacks ended up, he knew how to hide if the police were looking for him.

He wanted to explain things to Farzan before he left. But Farzan didn't come back from class at six o'clock like he usually did. Jacks waited another hour, and then he called Farzan's cell phone. It went to voicemail.

"Hey, it's me. I really need to talk to you. In person. Okay?"

Jacks packed his things into his duffle bag and watched the clock. He prayed Farzan would come home before his overnight shift at the hospital.

WHEN NIGHT FELL, his restlessness grew like he was being physically attacked from the inside out. His skin ached and burned. He scratched until his forearms were scored and puffy red, and then he took a hot shower.

Jacks dressed and sat down on the sofa, facing the TV. His skin had numbed, but a creepy crawly feeling assaulted his legs. He stood and paced around. His legs wanted to wander. His feline self wanted to get out. But Jacks couldn't do that. Farzan could come home at any moment.

He went to the kitchen and downed a shot of whiskey. It scorched his throat a little, but it didn't make his face warm or relax his body. He tossed back a second shot and then a third. He was still completely sober. His body was too pumped up. If anything, the alcohol made him feel more irritated, more caged in.

Jacks paced back and forth, burning up with aggression when he reached a dead end. The basement apartment had never felt so confining. He swerved around, losing track of his steps, bumping into the couch, knocking aside the living room end tables. Something was reaching into his core, arousing violent impulses. Was it the alcohol? It almost felt like an allergic reaction.

Then he noticed it. A whiff of a corrosive stench getting stronger, nearer, making the hair stand up on his scalp.

Jacks looked to the open window above the kitchen. The offensive ammonia scent was coming from out there. It was something or someone he had to destroy.

Jacks tried to rein in that impulse. He was so tensed up, thirsting for a fight, he might hurt someone innocent along the way, never mind leaving Farzan with more police drama to worry about. Jacks needed to find the source of that smell and keep a level head until he did. He'd never encountered such a strange and dangerous smell before, and he wondered for a moment whether it was real or something otherworldly. The scent was so strong and noxious, it should have drawn screams of terror, police sirens, hazmat workers to clean it up. He spotted a bag of garbage that needed to go out to the bins around the side of the house. Jacks grabbed it. He was going to confirm there really was an awful smell out there.

The odor was even stronger outside. The inside of his mouth curdled, and his shoulders clenched. It wasn't exactly nauseating. It was taunting, like some jokester banging on the windows of the house, or banging on his temples. Jacks stuffed the garbage away and clanged down the lid of the can with extra force. Then, he picked up a more familiar scent and swung toward the street.

In a pool of light from a street lamp, he spotted a tiny figure on the sidewalk. Bella.

Jacks staggered toward her. His heart swelled, and his wound up energy dissolved at once. The tiger-striped tabby crouched low to the ground and didn't move.

"Hey baby. Where have you been?"

From three steps away, Bella puffed up her fur and hissed

at him. Jacks halted. She had never been skittish with him before. Bella's eyes were flared and glinting red. Jacks concentrated on one thought and telepathized to her.

What's wrong, baby?

The dreadful stench washed over him like a radioactive wave. Jacks stared beyond Bella to a shadowy spot beneath a tree. A figure moved toward him, unveiled in the glow of a streetlamp. Jacks saw a hooded short-sleeve sweatshirt and a shadowed face elongated by a red tuft of beard on the chin. The man from the boardwalk.

Jacks judged his approach. They stepped wide circles around each other like repelling magnetic poles, staring each other down. The stranger was the source of that offensive smell, some pheromone asserting dominance. Jacks was sure then that his vision from the boardwalk had been real, a psychic forewarning.

"Who are you?" Jacks said.

"Heya, Jacks," the sketchy guy said, self-satisfied.

"Yeah, I'm Jacks. And this is my cat."

Bella crouched between Jacks and the stranger, swinging her tail back and forth. Jacks needed to get her inside and away from the man. He tried compelling her with a willful glare. Bella hunched up and growled at him.

"She ain't your cat no more."

"What did you do to her?"

"I didn't have to do a thing. She came to me, and she led me to you."

His yellow-green eyes twinkled. He had the same haughty attitude as Benoit, a big cat bullying his lessers, but he was different. Jacks felt no undercurrent of seduction. They were two toms who wanted, needed to tear each other apart. The spot in his gut throbbed, wanting to be released.

A beat-up sedan cruised down the street, bringing Jacks

back to his surroundings. He couldn't transform and attack this stranger right across from Farzan's parent's house.

The stranger also loosened his posture, seeming to share Jacks's concerns about having things out on the street. "What say we talk inside?"

Jacks approached Bella again, stooping slowly, non-threatening and gentle. She shrank back and hissed. Jacks reached his hand toward her, and she gave him a smarting strike with her claw.

The stranger made a chuffing noise. Bella turned and scuttled toward him. He bent down and lifted her in his arms.

Jacks looked at Bella, cradled by the stranger. He felt like he had been abandoned by his best friend. He studied his adversary. The guy looked young, and he was thin and pallid, like he'd been surviving on the streets for a while. That didn't make him any less dangerous, but Jacks needed answers. Even though he'd turned Bella against him, the stranger was the only werecat Jacks had ever met besides Benoit. Jacks led him and Bella into Farzan's apartment.

"YOU'RE NOT WHAT I expected," the man said.

"How do you mean?"

They stood in the living space, and the man was shifting around, looking at the corners of the tiny, low-ceilinged apartment. He was agitated, probably by Jacks's scent, especially now that he had entered what amounted to his den.

"I expected more from the werecat who was brazen enough to turn against his own kind."

Jacks looked him over guardedly. Unsheathed from his hood, thick ginger-colored hair crowned the stranger's head in helter-skelter peaks, and he had coarse sideburns in addition to the pointy beard on his chin. He stood a couple of inches taller than Jacks and was lean and solidly built, like a boxer. Jacks figured he could handle the guy if things came to that, though he wouldn't get out of it without some bruises. His attention turned to Bella who was weaving affectionately through the stranger's legs. Jacks looked up at him.

"Who are you?"

He smirked, obviously enjoying having the upper hand. "Nobody important to you."

Jacks stepped in front of him so he was inches from the stranger's chest. "How'd you get my cat?"

The man smiled broader, revealing a crooked incisor. "She came to me. She told me about you and Benoit. How you betrayed him."

Jacks stood back and looked down at Bella. He didn't want to believe it, wasn't sure how to believe it, but the possibility couldn't be denied. Why else would she show up with a stranger, growling and hissing like he was a murderer? Jacks must have underestimated how deep her bond with Benoit was. She had run away seeking vengeance for his death. But what had his vision of her been about? He and Bella had somehow stayed psychically connected, perhaps unbeknownst to Bella?

It was suddenly staggering to Jacks—the world of small cats. He envisioned a citywide network of strays, witnessing events from shadowy stoops and alleyways, passing along the information to their werecat brethren. How many cats had been watching him since he killed Benoit? Jacks turned his attention to the gothic tattoo on his hand. The information he had found on the internet had been dubious, but it was all Jacks had.

"Tell me about that tattoo. What's the Glaring?"

"Let's just say they're a group that doesn't take well to human apologists. You're lucky I'm the first to get tipped off by your cat."

"How does that make me lucky?"

"Because you have something I want."

The stranger wandered through the apartment, filing through bookshelves, tossing things to the floor, and yanking open drawers. Jacks gained up on him and grabbed his arm.

"What do you think you're doing?"

The stranger tugged his arm away. "You have something of Benoit's. It belongs to his kind, not a traitor."

Jacks had collected Benoit's antique leather travel bag from the abandoned furniture factory after his death. He had looked over the stuff in a mire of grief: Benoit's clothing, his forged travel documents going back hundreds of years, some cash, and a collection of odd-shaped keys. Jacks had given the clothing to charity, given the cash to a cat rescue organization and kept the few odds and ends in the travel bag figuring he would decide what to do with them later. It hardly seemed like anything of value was left, but he didn't want to say one thing or the other.

The guy dismantled the kitchen, well off the trail of the goods, which told Jacks he had never met Benoit. If he had, he would have picked up his scent from the bag Jacks had stashed behind the sofa. But Bella was on the job too, up on her hind legs like a meerkat and angling her head around the apartment. Jacks had to stall them while he worked out what to do.

He stepped heavy-footed toward Bella, blocking her way, and she scampered into the bathroom. Jacks quietly shut the door behind her.

"Did you know Benoit?" he asked the stranger.

The man threw open the mop closet in the kitchen. "Don't matter."

Jacks strode into the kitchen. "It matters to me. You have no right to his belongings. You're just some scavenger who wants to pick over his stuff."

"That's shocking sentimentality, Jacks. You murdered

Benoit, your mate, and now *you're* fit to decide who deserves his things?"

"It wasn't a murder. He was out of control. I was defending someone he was going to kill."

The stranger's eyes flared. "Werecats kill. What a pathetic creature you are, rallying to save a human from your own flesh and blood. Do you even know how to be a werecat?" He turned back to rifling through the kitchen. "I can't imagine what Benoit saw in you, though they say some geezers get soft and simple-minded in their old age."

Jacks wasn't about to bring the guy over to his side of the argument. He imagined roots growing from his feet into the floor like when he had been talking to Detective Faraday. He needed to understand things.

"There's a story on the internet that says the Glaring is the result of a secret medical experiment."

The stranger snorted. "Humans have active imaginations. Kind of like you, thinking you could get away with offing your mate."

"What is the Glaring? Some werecat police force?"

"You're such a kitten. You'll find out soon enough about the Glaring, and I promise you, it won't be pretty."

Jacks heard Bella's unhappy mewl from the bathroom and talked over it. "What are they? A secret society?"

The guy bumped by Jacks while crossing the kitchen to try a drawer beneath the sink. "You ask too many questions."

Jacks stepped behind the stranger as he batted out cleaning products from beneath the sink. His proximity rattled the guy, encouraging Jacks to delay him even more. "What are you looking for?"

The guy stood up and looked around at the kitchen cabinets.

"How do you even know I have it?" Jacks said.

"Suppose I don't know for sure. But I'm starting to think it'd be a whole lot easier looking for it without you around." He swung back to Jacks, curling his lip. There was a blink of transformation—a flash of a saliva-dripping feline jaw and fangs. He was on the edge of rearing into a wild beast. Jacks held strong. His adrenalin was mounting. He could explode into his cougar self in the space of a breath. Then the stranger glanced over to the living space. He was adding something up.

"Where's the tabby?" He swept past Jacks, heading for the bathroom door.

It occurred to Jacks whatever Benoit had left behind must be more important to this guy than killing him for betraying his kind. He could've tried to kill Jacks out on the street and rifled through his apartment later. Jacks's human sense was telling him the guy was just a weaselly thief. Jacks needed to raise the stakes to get rid of him. While his back was turned, Jacks reared into cougar muscle and tawny hide. He sprung from the kitchen to the living space and launched himself at the stranger, flattening him on his stomach and crippling him under his weight.

He pressed his muzzle into the guy's neck, growling. *What are you looking for?*

Quick as a lightning pulse, the stranger transformed beneath him—a golden jaguar with black rosettes, fully grown, snarling, and bucking to get free. His feline manifestation was about the same size as Jacks, but as a jaguar, he could get an advantage with his thicker limbs and crushing jaws.

Jacks hesitated too long to finish him off with a bite to his jugular. His opponent heaved Jacks over and got on his fours. He swiped his clawing foreleg wildly for Jacks' muzzle.

Jacks batted off the attack, retrenching steadily until he was backed up against the couch. A strike from the werejaguar scored one side of his foreleg. He tried another tack.

What'll the Glaring do when they find out you stole Benoit's things?

The werejaguar snarled. *Who says you'll live to tell them?*

Jacks stared into the jaguar's bloodthirsty eyes. *What'll you do about Bella?* The guy had used Bella to find Jacks, probably promising her revenge. Now he needed to keep track of her because she'd have to be disposed of once he got what he wanted. Jacks scrambled out the open door. He prayed the werejaguar would chase him, and a few leaps into the backyard, he heard an avalanche of movement behind him.

He stampeded through the backyards on the block, jumping fences, swerving around patio furniture and children's playground sets. He knew a place they could have things out without involving witnesses: a sunken train track overgrown with weeds and brush. Jacks had noticed it while walking to the bus stop. The railway looked like it hadn't been used for half a century.

The jaguar kept up with him, bursting through the yards like a tornado. Jacks switched into a higher gear. He had to stay ahead until they got to the spot. Middle Eastern music and lively voices traveled from up ahead. Mostly Arab and Indian families lived in Farzan's neighborhood, and someone must be having a backyard party a few lots up. Jacks couldn't bring the jaguar through there. He scrambled down a driveway and into the street.

Out in the open, he tried to take account of his surroundings. He had to move quickly, but he didn't want to arouse a scene. He just needed to get to the end of the block and make a right on the avenue that bridged over the train tracks.

Parked cars lined every open space along the block—people who had come out for the backyard party. Jacks spotted two women in chador walking up the driveway to the house. He dodged across the street and onto a lawn a safe distance away.

Where was the jaguar? Jacks glanced over his shoulder to check on his chaser's progress.

A burst of movement hurtled toward him. Before Jacks could react, the jaguar lunged. He caught Jacks's hindquarters, but Jacks shook him off and barreled away.

From a safe distance, he drew up behind a hedge to check out what he had left behind. The jaguar was wiped out on the lawn. He had lost his balance while trying to tackle Jacks. The ladies across the street had stopped to stare, chattering in their foreign language.

Jacks had to keep the jaguar going. He limped out from the hedge, overplaying his wounded haunches. The jaguar locked in on him, and he got up to pursue.

Jacks galloped down the street, and near the end of the block, he shot behind a house where he could get access to the train tracks from the cover of trees. He saw a high wooden fence ahead. He sprang for the top and used his forepaws to pull himself up and over. He dove for the other side of the fence just as the jaguar vaulted to the perch.

Jacks braced for his fall, but his landing was clumsy, and his hind legs nearly flew over his back. The jaguar plunged on top of him, and they tumbled together down the brushy bank of the train tracks.

They lunged for each other with their muzzles. One bite from the jaguar would be enough to cripple him or burst a vital artery. Jacks slashed at the jaguar's nose and eyes. At the bottom of the slope, he rolled out of their tumble. A fog of fur swarmed around him.

One of the jaguar's eyes was closed shut and bleeding, but he was locked in viciously. *We both know you ain't getting away from me. Tell me where you put Benoit's stash.*

Jacks held his ground, and in a blink, the jaguar leapt for Jacks's haunch. Jacks spun around and swatted his opponent's snarling muzzle. One claw connected with his wounded eye. The jaguar recoiled with a bestial shriek that shattered the summer night.

Jacks pounced on him from the side and clamped down on his neck. A pent up brutality powered through his core. He sunk his fangs deep into the jaguar's hide with an audible puncture of his flesh. The jaguar flailed. Jacks straddled the beast with his forelimbs and bore down with his weight. With his fangs snaring the jaguar's neck, his victim's movements drove his deadly bite deeper.

Warm blood saturated Jacks's jowls and seeped into his mouth with a satisfying metallic taste. The jaguar's body quieted. Jacks's heart pounded in his chest, but gradually, through the suffocating pin of his body over his prey, he could feel the jaguar's fluttering pulse, struggling for survival. In a strange way, it was like cradling a baby to sleep. He held on tight to the jaguar until his pulse trailed away to nothing.

He released the limp body, which fell curled in defeat on the gravel of the train tracks. A swell of pride rose up in Jacks. It was his first kill. Beyond himself for a moment, he wished someone was around to see it. He felt invincible, as though he had grown into a giant, capable of crushing any enemy that crossed his path.

Under the stark wash of the moon, the jaguar's spotted fur shriveled into pale skin, the feline torso shrank and realigned, and the stocky head, arms and legs retook their frailer human form. The red-haired stranger lay pale and naked. His neck was gored. His midsection was all ribs and a sunken stomach. He couldn't have been much older than Jacks.

Jacks drew back. His thirst for dominance fell away. This was what he had done. He had taken someone's life. If he hadn't, the werejaguar would have taken his, but the bloodied lifeless body was a horrid sight. Why did it have to come to this when they were the same kind, just trying to survive?

Now an invisible stopwatch was ticking. He had to hide the deed, to make it look like something else, or to quickly disappear from the scene. The lighted bridge above the ravine looked deserted. The only sounds were a truck rumbling down the street from some distance away and, faintly, the music and commotion from the party.

Then he looked over a bank of the ravine. He saw one, then two, then many pointy-eared silhouettes in the shadowy brush. Like miniature wraiths in the night, they seemed to hover above the death scene. Here and there, pairs of elliptical eyes glinted in the moonlight, narrowed in judgment. Jacks wondered how long they had been there, drawn out from their hiding places to witness the attack. He circled around himself. How many were there—dozens or hundreds?

A chorus of greedy whispers filled his head.

It's Jacks.

What did he do?

He killed Bernard.

Let's tell.

TWELVE

IN HIS HUMAN form, Jacks hobbled back to Farzan's house, favoring his gouged leg. It was the same one Benoit had shredded in their fight earlier that summer, and Jacks made a wry mental note that he needed to protect himself better the next time he got into a wild cat brawl. Farzan's blue Ford sedan was in the driveway. Jacks steered around it into the backyard.

The door to the basement apartment was wide open just as he had left it. Jacks made his way down. His cargo shorts and T-shirt were in tatters, but the wound to his leg had stopped bleeding. The hike from the train tracks had been hellish.

Farzan's voice called out before Jacks even saw him. "Jesus, Jacks. What happened?"

He was wearing his hospital scrubs and straightening out the furniture. The place looked like it had been ransacked by burglars—books pulled off of shelves, drawers thrown open, the living room rug bunched up in odd places like the humps of an underwater sea creature. The laminate floor tiles had deep scars from the flight of two big cats.

As he took a full account of Jacks, Farzan's exasperated face turned stricken. "Oh my God." He rushed over to support Jacks and walk him over to the couch.

Seated, Jacks caught his breath and luxuriated for a moment as the strain of his limbs dissipated. Blood soaked through the cuffs of his cargo shorts and coated his leg down to his sneakers. In the light of the apartment, he could see that was the least of his walking horror show. He had wiped his bloody mouth on the sleeve of his vintage Nirvana T-shirt. More of Bernard's blood was blotted in dull crimson patches across the front.

Farzan's hands shook as he stood in front of Jacks, gauging what to do. "I'll get bandages. Take off your shorts."

Jacks unbuttoned his shorts and delicately slid them down his briefs and all the way to his calves. The simple action felt like his leg was getting shredded all over again, and he swooned a little and sat back down on the couch. An angry purple gash stretched from the outside of his thigh to his knee. Around it, the skin had bloomed yellowish pink. Jacks told Farzan, "Can you shut the door?"

All the way back from the train tracks, he had been trailed by the little phantoms, scuttling under cars and skulking along front yard hedges. They had been watching him as though stalking weakened prey. They were too small to pose a danger, but Jacks was spooked. The strays were watching his every move.

Farzan shut the apartment door and went to his bedroom. He came back with his medical kit. Kneeling in front of Jacks, he cleaned his leg with alcohol wipes that made Jacks's eyes tear up.

Farzan shook his head. "You have to go to the E.R."

Jacks glanced at the wall clock. It was 10:45. Farzan had fifteen minutes to make it to his internship on time.

"*You* have to go to the E.R."

"I'll call out."

"You don't have to do that." He knew if Farzan missed a night of his internship, he would have to make up the time. Farzan was already working and studying every day, around the clock, so how was he going to fit in more hours at the E.R.?

"You're in no shape to go to the hospital on your own. You need stitches, antibiotics, a tetanus shot—"

"I'm not going to the hospital."

"Jacks, please, don't be stubborn."

Jacks raised his voice. "I've got no insurance. I already owe fifteen thousand dollars from the last time."

"My father said he'd pay for that."

"It's not that bad. Can't you just put a bandage on it?"

"There could be infection. It won't heal properly without stitches."

Jacks gazed at Farzan steadily. "It's going to be fine."

Farzan blinked, and then Jacks' meaning spread across his face in an uneasy shadow. When he had gone into the hospital after his fight with Benoit, he'd had lacerations to two-thirds of his body. They put him in critical care for a day, shifted him to a regular room the next, and discharged him two days later with barely a mark on him.

Farzan immersed himself in bandaging Jacks's leg. When he was done, he stood and threw up his hands. "This is insane." He staggered around the room. "You called me with this urgent message. I rushed back from my uncle's house in New Jersey. And I come home to find this *scene* from a slasher movie." He shifted back to Jacks, shaking. "I don't know how I'm supposed to react to this."

"I'm sorry about the damage to your apartment. I'll pay for it. I saved up some money."

Farzan stepped closer and spoke in not much more than a whisper. "I'm not talking about the apartment."

"Then what? You're talking about me?" Farzan waved for him to lower his voice, but Christ, if his fight with Bernard hadn't woken his parents, they had to be out of town. "Twenty-four hours ago, you were acting like you wanted me to be your boyfriend." Jacks stretched out his arms. "This is me, Farzan. Me and my crazy life. I didn't ask for this to happen, but I was defending myself. I was protecting your apartment from someone who was ripping it apart."

Farzan wiped his face with his hand. "I don't think it's healthy. For you, for me, for anyone. Every time you go through that change, something terrible happens."

Jacks leaned forward from his seat. "Let me explain."

"I don't know that I want to hear it."

Silence engulfed the room. Jacks studied Farzan, who looked away timidly. He wrung his hands until his knuckles were white, and a teardrop fell.

Jacks pushed himself up so he was standing on his good leg. "You thought you knew me. But you only saw the parts you liked."

Farzan shuffled over. "You shouldn't stand. You need to keep the leg elevated."

"I'm serious, Farzan. If we're going to be friends, or more than that, both of us need to face what I am." Farzan waved and pleaded with his eyes for Jacks to sit down. "When you kissed me, it was like you really understood, and didn't care. Like it was possible for someone to feel that way about me." He sat down to appease Farzan. "And I got scared. For you. Or me. Both of us. I don't know. But I'm ready to talk about this. I just need you to listen."

Farzan took a seat a little way down the sofa, legs crossed. "Put your leg up," he said. Jacks did so and tried to figure out where to start.

A ragged mewl blared from the bathroom. Both men turned to the closed door.

"Oh, Bella came back," Jacks said. "Do you mind letting her out? She should hear this too."

JACKS RECOUNTED THE visit from the police detectives, Bella's return, Bernard, what he had learned about the Glaring, and the fight down at the train tracks. Farzan seemed to be doing his best not to flip out.

Meanwhile, Bella sat brooding on the kitchen window ledge with her legs tucked under her. She had skittered away when Farzan let her out of the bathroom. Discovering no way out of the apartment, she had appropriated her favorite perch.

"When you feel like you're about to transform, what's it like?" Farzan said.

"I don't know. It feels natural to me now, I guess. It's just something that's always inside me. Like a suit of armor I can pull out." He scratched his ear. "But it's more than that. It's releasing a part of me that can be fearless, that can do things my human self could never do."

"Do you want to be like that all the time?"

"No. There's things I can do in my human body that I can't do as a cougar. They call it two-spirit, like dual souls. Benoit gave me the power to change physically, but the potential was always there. I think I've felt it all my life, but I didn't know what it meant. I barely knew anything about Native people and animal spirits, even though it's that blood in me that made this possible. My ancestors, the Cherokee, had a spiritual bond to the cougar, and it wasn't so strange to them that people can possess a dual nature." Jacks shared what he had learned. "Their shamans dressed in mountain lion hides. Their hunters studied cats so they could learn from them. When they had to face their enemies, they had ceremonial dances to channel the cougar warrior spirit."

Farzan sank into his seat, weighted down by incomprehension. Jacks remembered that Farzan had never seen him as a cougar. He had only seen Benoit's transformation, and that had been horrible and violent.

"I don't turn into a monster," Jacks said. "I don't lose my mind and start wanting to kill everyone."

Farzan stood up from the sofa, glancing at his medical textbooks on the bookshelf. "There's got to be some explanation. We'll find a specialist. Someone who can treat you—"

"I don't want to be treated."

"It's not normal."

"It's normal for *me*."

That silenced Farzan, though he looked pale and worried. When he spoke, his voice was small. "Okay. It's normal for you."

"I really need you to respect that." Jacks gazed at Farzan, and Farzan nodded, timidly.

"I'm trying to understand. It's not the easiest thing, y'know?"

Jacks stretched out his arms. "Ask me anything."

"Who are these people who are after you—the Glaring?"

"Bernard said they're after me. He was just a thief who wanted something of Benoit's, so I don't know, but I think it's true." Jacks thought better of expanding on that by telling Farzan about the large clowder of cats who were spreading the news across the city and probably beyond by now.

"That means it's not safe for you here?"

Jacks nodded.

"It's not safe for any of us, is it?"

"They want me." Jacks sighed. "So, I need to move out,

which I have no fucking idea how I'm going to do. But for you and your family, I have to leave."

Farzan looked at Jacks in alarm. "Where will you go?"

"I'll figure it out."

"You have a thousand dollars. That won't last you long. You're in no shape to be traveling anyway. You need to rest."

"*Now* you want me to stay?"

"I never said I wanted you to leave." Farzan retook his place on the couch besides Jacks. "If you're in danger, you don't have to go through it alone. You're better off with people. My maman always says that."

Jacks clasped his hand. "Thanks. I guess I was hoping you'd say that."

Farzan hid his face shyly. Jacks could tell he was still confused by everything he had heard, but he didn't pull his hand away. In fact, he gripped and massaged Jacks's hand while they shared a quiet moment. Maybe Farzan didn't care what he was. They'd been drawn to each other since he came to the bodega in the middle of the night, buying out the cold cuts and canned meat.

He was bursting to tell Farzan everything. He'd killed a goddamn jaguar! Jacks tamped down on the rush of pride it aroused. That would be too much to share with Farzan. Jacks looked at Bella, who was staring down from the window ledge. *She* would understand. The little tabby knew what it was like to make a kill, to dominate the things in her world—a mouse, a bird, a caterpillar. He and Bella locked eyes, and Jacks telepathized to her. She jumped down from her perch, trotted over, and rubbed her muzzle against his ankle, purring, submissively.

Farzan shifted uneasily in his seat. "What'll you do about Bernard?"

"I don't know. Call it in anonymously?"

Just then, police sirens travelled from the street. Jacks tensed up. The cops were getting closer, and an ear-splitting cavalcade of fire engines and ambulances followed them.

Farzan went outside to check it out, leaving Jacks to wonder how fast he could hop-step to gather his things and get out of the neighborhood. Bella scampered back up to the kitchen ledge and squatted. She stared out the window with her tail lashing behind her.

In short time, Farzan returned. His face was twisted with worry.

"Someone beat you to the police. They're down by the train tracks. Did anyone see you?"

"I don't think so. Just the cats."

Farzan stormed toward Bella. "This is *your* fault." The cat recoiled and hissed.

"Take it easy," Jacks said.

"She led Bernard to you. She's a little demon."

"He betrayed her too." *Didn't he, Bella?* Bella's ears pinched back, and then she turned to the window.

Farzan went back to the living space, hovering and shaking his head. "This is bad, Jacks. Even if no one saw you walking down the block covered in blood, those detectives will want to talk to you again."

Jacks propped himself up on the sofa cushions. "I know. I've got to get out of town."

"How? Where will you go?"

Jacks braced his leg while he turned and stretched his body so he could reach over the back of the sofa. He grasped one strap of Benoit's black leather valise and pulled it up over the sofa and onto his lap. In the front zipper pocket, everything of Benoit's that Jacks had held on to was wrapped in a vintage, silk handkerchief. Jacks unzipped the compartment and brought the stash out. From the corner of his vision, he noticed Bella watching like she had zoned in on a nesting bird.

"I've got to figure out what Bernard was looking for. To find some answers."

"Answers to what?"

"I don't know exactly. People who knew Benoit. Someone who can tell me about the Glaring and how to get them off my back."

Farzan sat down beside him. "How do you think people from Benoit's past are going to help you? If they cared about him, they're not going to be too friendly when they find out you killed him."

"I don't think Benoit left behind many people who cared about him. He was a loner. He never stayed in one place for long. Anyway, I'd rather find one of these werecats before another one of them finds me."

The silk handkerchief was rich blue with a pattern of gray and silver wildflowers, and it looked expensive. Benoit had lived in distressed jeans, untucked button-down shirts, and combat boots, but maybe, at some time, he had worn it in a dinner jacket. He'd also been around for over two centuries.

Jacks unpeeled the folds of the handkerchief. The contents were like long-forgotten items in a kitchen utility drawer. Faded and expired travel documents. Broken pieces of antique watches. A half dozen keys of many shapes and sizes.

Jacks flipped through the passports and the tourist visas. Benoit had really seen the world. There were so many customs stamps, so many countries: France, Indonesia, Mexico, India, Vietnam. But what could the documents be worth to anyone?

"A key can be valuable," Farzan said.

"They could be keys to anything, anywhere in the world."

Farzan pointed to a long, flat silver key with a clover head. "That looks like it's for a safety deposit box."

Jacks's eyebrows shot up.

"Baba has one. He doesn't keep any important documents or expensive jewelry in the house. Not after they took everything away from him in Iran."

It sounded like a good lead. Jacks remembered Benoit telling him he was living off an inheritance, and he moved his assets every ten years. Most likely, he would have kept an account in a country with favorable banking policies.

Farzan was one step ahead of him. "Look at his most recent passport."

Jacks found Benoit's passport from Canada. There were stamps from Morocco, Mexico and, dated just one year ago, Barbados.

Watching from over Jacks's shoulder, Farzan pointed at the stamp from Barbados, knowingly. "Caribbean banks. They're notorious for hiding money."

Jacks turned over the plated key in his hand. There were no markings on it. It was light and simple. An eerie chill passed over him.

"What if he had a lot of money?"

"Then you can buy me an apartment and a new car."

"No. I'll give it away. Either to someone who knew him or to charity." Bella had crept up, trying to hide in the shadow of the coffee table, stalking the shiny key.

All three of them turned to the window, listening to another round of sirens. They faded away in the night, leaving the crime scene. Bernard was being carried away to the morgue.

Would there be a house-by-house investigation for witnesses? Jacks hardly knew how these things worked, but a tight pit formed in his stomach. He couldn't wait and see if things blew over after Bernard's murder. He had to leave town soon.

Jacks leaned over and kissed Farzan on the cheek. Farzan smiled, but his body was stiff and quivering.

"What was that for?"

"For putting up with me."

Farzan raised his arm and pulled Jacks closer, interlacing their hands across Jacks's stomach. Burrowing together with Farzan felt warm and safe, but as the situation sank in, a lump pitched in his throat.

"I have to leave."

"I'll go with you."

"I wish you could. I'm not going to lie. I'm a little scared of what I'll find. But you've got medical school. Besides, it'll look suspicious if you run off too."

He explained his plan to leave a confessional video about his part in the incident with the gangbangers. Now, he would add to it what happened with Bernard so the police could put that matter to rest as well. If Farzan disappeared, they would think he was in on it.

Farzan argued against the plan. "It's not fair. You acted in self-defense both times. If you run, they'll consider you a fugitive. The FBI will get involved. You won't be able to enter the country again."

"I'm already a fugitive. You really think there's any way to defend me when people find out what I am?"

Farzan started to speak but stopped when Jacks squeezed his warm, graceful hand. He had to understand the legal system wasn't equipped to handle his situation, no matter how innocent he was. "It's the best thing for me and the best thing for your family. If I stick around here, we're all in danger. From the police and other werecats."

Jacks felt a displacement on the couch. Bella had jumped up on the cushioned seat. She purred and watched them.

"What do we do with *her*?" Farzan said.

"She'll be fine. She promised to protect you."

Farzan snorted. "How's the little snitch going to protect me?"

"She'll keep a lookout. And if any of them do show up, she'll be able to communicate with them so they know they're looking for me in the wrong place."

Bella climbed over his lap and stepped onto Farzan. She rubbed her muzzle against his arm, purring. Farzan looked like he had been cornered by a venomous snake.

"She almost got you killed. How can you trust her?"

Jacks gazed at Bella steadily. "It's hard to explain. She's linked to soul shifters. All of them are. House cats, strays. But her master's dead. She'll be loyal to me now."

Farzan frowned. "I don't trust her, changing allegiances so easily."

Jacks rubbed Bella behind her ears. As much as it would have made sense, he couldn't place the slightest edge of anger toward Bella inside of him. She had bonded to Benoit then bonded to Bernard for her own reasons. Now she had pledged herself to him. It was just the way with cats.

THIRTEEN

JACKS WASHED UP in the bathroom with a hand towel and a sink of soapy water to clean the night's grime from his face, his armpits, and his other accessible parts, while balancing himself on his good leg and trying not to get his dressing wet. The pain from Bernard's gouge was subsiding. His skin was knitting itself back together. He wouldn't be surprised to wake up in the morning, unwrap the bandage, and find his leg completely healed.

He changed into a pair of boxer shorts and peg-legged into Farzan's room. Farzan sat at his computer. Jacks stepped behind him and checked out the monitor. He'd pulled up a list of flights to Barbados for the next day. Another browser tab had search results for Barbadian banks.

"You should take the bed tonight. It'll be more comfortable," Farzan said.

Jacks sat down on the edge of the mattress. "Lie down with me. That can wait until the morning."

Farzan's shoulders tensed. "I'll print this out. You can

decide tomorrow. But there's a direct flight from JFK at eleven for three hundred bucks."

The printer rattled and whirred. Farzan closed out his browser, then went over to shut his door, no doubt mindful of Bella harassing him. He stopped in front of Jacks.

"How's your leg?"

Jacks rustled onto his back with his leg stretched out. "It's just a little stiff." He patted the mattress next to him. "Come over here."

"What does lying down with you entail?"

Jacks snorted out a laugh. "I'm not going to give you a tongue bath. Unless you really want it." Farzan didn't look any less terrified. "I just thought it would be nice to share the bed tonight. We don't have to do anything. We really don't. Unless, it turns out we're in the mood."

Farzan peeked at Jacks and sat down on the bed, next to him, a little tentatively. "If this is going to be a sympathy-fuck or a nice-knowing-you-fuck, I'm okay with that. But I want to make some things clear..."

Jacks took Farzan's hand, kneading it in his, pulling it to his lips so he could kiss his fingers. "You don't have to talk."

"I'm a gay Persian with attention deficit disorder. If I can't talk, I'm liable to stay up all night staple-gunning animal prints to the wall and creating mood boards on Pinterest."

Jacks pressed his tongue against the tip of Farzan's index finger, feeling the tiny grooves of his fingerprint. Then he swallowed the finger down to the bottom knuckle, siphoning, biting it lightly with his teeth, burying it in the warm, wet space beneath his tongue.

Farzan's voice deepened. "I just need to know...if we do this...where we stand."

Jacks unbuttoned Farzan's shirt and clasped the sides of his ribcage, pulling him closer. He kissed and nuzzled against Farzan's shoulders, which were smooth and warm.

"I mean, it's not that I'm opposed..."

Jacks sucked his neck and pried open his belt to dig his hand between Farzan's legs.

"Jacks..."

His voice was distant. He smelled so good, and he was hardening from Jacks's touch.

Farzan's voice came more forcefully. "Jacks."

Jacks blanked. He had lost track of the conversation.

"I asked you a question. If we do this, where do we stand?"

"I want to be your boyfriend." The simple honesty surprised Jacks himself.

Farzan stroked Jacks's hair. "That's a good answer. But the timing? Not so good."

"I don't know what else to say."

Farzan nudged out a comfortable position and dug his fingers through the back of Jacks's hair then stroked his arm. "You can send me postcards from Barbados. That's romantic, I think. You can write about how much you've been lusting for my body."

Jacks pressed his hips against Farzan's and brushed his thumb against the hairs at the nape of his back. "That sounds very *Prison Wives*."

Farzan plunged his tongue inside Jacks' mouth. They kissed like that for a while.

Farzan broke their embrace. "When will I see you again?"

"I wish I knew. It'll never be soon enough. I'll get settled somewhere. You can come visit. I really want this to work out."

"Don't say anything unless you mean it."

"Of course I mean it. I never met anyone like you." Jacks pulled Farzan closer for another open-mouthed kiss.

They made love in the most intimate way, side-by-side so

Jacks didn't have to trouble his bandaged leg too much. Afterward, Jacks held Farzan tight and interlaced their hands on Farzan's chest. "Was it everything you wanted?"

"Yes and no," Farzan said.

He glanced at him with a crooked grin.

"It would be better if you weren't leaving in the morning."

Jacks traced circles over Farzan's hand with his finger. "I know. I've got to figure some things out. But I swear, I'm coming back to you."

Farzan broke away and propped himself on his elbow. "If that's your promise, it doesn't matter what happens between now and then. We'll be thousands of miles apart. If someone else comes along for a night or two, I don't care." He looked at Jacks severely. "Just don't tell me about it."

Jacks thought it was a strange thing for Farzan to say after they had made love for the first time. But that was Farzan—always practical, and always thinking ahead. "Same for you, okay?"

"I don't think you need to worry about that. I just don't want you to feel controlled or weighed down by me."

"Babe, I want this as much as you."

"I just want you to be happy."

Jacks stroked Farzan's face. "I'm happy."

Farzan settled back into Jacks. Gradually, Jacks started taking stock of what laid ahead. He would be leaving for Barbados in the morning, and he had never traveled on his own. He had never even been to a foreign country, except for Canada, and he'd be using a good chunk of all the money he had on the flight. The police would be after him. Some secret werecat society might be after him as well. Jacks held Farzan tighter and tried to push the worries out of his head. But he wouldn't be getting much sleep.

EARLY THAT MORNING, he carefully scooted out of bed and made his way to the bathroom. His leg itched terribly from the bandage. When he peeled it off, the skin was pink and still a little sore, but the six-inch gash had completely sewn itself up. Jacks splashed some warm water on his face. He quietly stepped back to Farzan's bedroom and stole a place under the covers.

In the darkness, Farzan turned to him. "I want to see you."

Jacks wasn't sure what he meant, but he sounded wide awake, like he'd been having trouble sleeping too.

The night lamp clicked on, and Farzan sat up. "I want to see you the way you are. When you go through that...shape-shifting."

Jacks had a bad feeling about it, though he didn't know why exactly. He'd had a mental pep talk about not being ashamed of himself. But what if Farzan was frightened or disgusted?

"I should know you. The *whole* you, like you told me," Farzan said. "Don't you think?"

Now he was using Jacks's own words against him. He drew a deep breath and wrestled with his reservations. They were about to be separated for a long time. If he left without letting Farzan see that part of himself, it would be continuing the game they had been playing, skipping around the realities of his dual soul.

"Okay." He sat up on the bed, which was a full-size mattress and tight for the two of them. "You should move back a little."

Farzan shifted over to the edge. Jacks closed his eyes and focused on the magical spot below his diaphragm. He could do the transformation gradually, where it felt like he was turning himself from the inside out, but that might be too gross for Farzan to take in. It helped if he had some adrenalin spiking to make the explosive change, but there was nothing urgent about the current situation. He imagined gripping his magical spot, crushing it in his fist, balling up that energy so tightly that it burned white hot. His body shuddered, his bones snapped violently, and he could feel his horizontal realignment. Jacks opened his eyes.

Sitting on his haunches, he took up two-thirds of the width of the bed. Farzan scooted back and tumbled onto the floor. When he recovered, his face was bright with shock and wonder. It was something Jacks had never seen before, as though Farzan hadn't believed it was possible until that moment.

Farzan stepped around the bed, checking out Jacks's feline self from different angles, like a scientist conducting an examination. It was weird being studied like that. Jacks understood Farzan needed to get used to seeing him that way, but after a while, he heaved a big, fang-bearing yawn. He wished he could say something the way he did with Bella.

"It's amazing." Farzan inched up closer and held his hand out, waiting for permission to touch Jacks's fur. Jacks leaned toward him, and Farzan stroked one side of his shiny, golden neck.

"It's beautiful." Farzan corrected himself: "You're beautiful."

Jacks nudged his head against Farzan's hand, and Farzan rubbed his furry crown and touched his ears. A purr motored through Jacks's body.

He shrunk back to his human self. Farzan sat down next to him on the bed and held one side of his face in his hand.

"How many guys can say they have a boyfriend who can do *that*?"

Jacks smirked.

"Would you be upset if I told you I like you better this way?"

"Be careful what you say. If I get hungry in the middle of the night, I might just eat you for dinner."

Farzan pulled Jacks close with one leg draped over Jacks's hip. "I think I like you both ways."

Jacks ran his hand down the smooth side of Farzan's back and up again. "Really?"

"Really."

They made love again, and afterward, Farzan finally fell asleep in his arms. Jacks was tired, too, but not sleepy. He shut his eyes. He had a boyfriend. That felt really good. Whatever challenges lay ahead of him seemed just a little less terrifying. He had Farzan. And Bella. He wasn't alone in the world.

FOURTEEN

THREE DAYS LATER, Jacks was walking up the paved path to the Beechfield Bank of Barbados. Gabled, with a wraparound porch, the bank looked more like a Victorian home styled for entertaining than a place of commerce. He'd already checked out three banks since he'd arrived in Barbados two days ago, and his cyber-sleuth partner Farzan had uncovered there were only six banks on the entire island. His odds were getting better. Plus, last night when they had talked on the phone, Farzan said he'd researched Beechfield and found that many foreigners set up offshore holdings there.

A detail caught Jacks's attention, and he halted on the sunbaked, dusty walk. The awning above the porch was emblazoned with a gold insignia of a dragon, like a medieval coat of arms. He wondered if Benoit might have found a certain irony in the barbaric imagery. As he stared, dread bit at Jacks. Inside the handsome building could be the answer to a mystery Bernard had tried to kill Jacks to solve.

The tropical heat was brutal, especially as Jacks wore slacks, a button-down, and a blazer he had picked up at a retail shop in JFK. He wiped the sweat from his face with a napkin, took a deep breath, and stepped up to the bank's porch and through the double doors.

Blissful air conditioning greeted him. The place was quiet and tidy, with freshly vacuumed carpeting, cherrywood desks, and a shiny counter for the bank tellers. Security cameras were visible in the corners of the ceiling. A uniformed guard chatted up a young Black lady at one of the front desks. Jacks strode past them. The messenger bag strapped to his shoulder felt radioactive, its contents ready to burn through the nylon fabric and expose his sham.

Farther down the bank's little bay of desks, Jacks spotted an older Caribbean man whose nameplate said he was Mr. Applewhite. Jacks summoned a big, friendly smile.

"Good morning. I have some business that I think requires the manager." Jacks took off his messenger bag, opened the flap, and brought out a manila folder. "One of your customers recently died, and I've been appointed to handle his estate."

Jacks showed the bank officer his passport, Benoit's death certificate, and a notarized letter. The death certificate was real. Everything else was fake. Farzan had said his older brother Sammy was good for nothing, but he didn't give Sammy credit in the area of forging documents.

The bank officer looked everything over as though he had been presented with a thirty-page search warrant written in Latin. Jacks leaned his weight to one side while a rivulet of sweat streaked down his brow.

"I'll call the manager for you." Mr. Applewhite took a second look at the passport. "Mr. Heathcliff?"

Jacks nodded and tried to keep a poker face. It was a cheesy alias, but Farzan thought it would be easy to remember and funny as hell. The bank officer gathered the documents, and Jacks watched him climb the stairs, walk along the second floor balustrade, and disappear into a private office.

The security guard took a break from flirting with the young, pretty girl and tipped his hand from his forehead. Jacks gave the guy a little wave. He felt so awkward, standing in the middle of the bank. Should he sit down at one of the chairs in front of Mr. Applewhite's desk? It felt presumptuous. He shouldn't act *too* casual, should he? He decided to wander over to the bank's display case of brochures.

The brochures advertised mortgage rates, credit cards, and auto loans. He pretended to browse them and picked up a glossy trifold. He looked up at the second floor. Was it a bad sign things were taking a while? Jacks had no idea. The manager was probably just tied up.

He spotted Mr. Applewhite coming down the stairs, followed by an older Black woman in a bright mustard skirt suit and a patterned headscarf. Her expression was hard to read. Jacks hiked up a grin as she approached. She held out her hand in greeting.

"Mrs. James," she said.

"Donovan Heathcliff." Jacks shook her hand.

"Let's go up to my office."

Mr. Applewhite drifted back to his desk with a strange, parting glance. Maybe he was just curious because he hadn't been part of such dealings before, or maybe Jacks was paranoid. He followed the bank manager up the stairs.

Mrs. James's office was a carpeted, wood-paneled room big enough for a gathering of twenty people. Jacks sat across from her at a tidy executive desk while she tapped up something on her keyboard. Her monitor faced away from him.

"Typically, we're notified by the lawyers when one of our international customers passes away," she said. "You traveled all this way to take care of this business yourself?"

"Yes, from Manitoba." The bank manager's mouth made a little O. Jacks relaxed a bit. He and Farzan had hatched a back-story for their exchange. He'd been biking with Benoit in Canada. There had been a gruesome tractor trailer accident. No next of kin. But that was if he needed to elaborate, and he wasn't sure he did quite yet. Instead, he improvised. "Mr. Hemmingstone, my lawyer, told me he would call ahead."

Mrs. James frowned. "Lawyers," she groaned. "What is it they say? What's a hundred lawyers at the bottom of the ocean?"

"A good start."

She let out a shrieking laugh that sliced through Jacks and made him chuckle nervously. He rummaged in his pants pocket and pulled out a long, flat, silver-plated key. "There's also this." Jacks placed the key on the bank manager's desk.

Mrs. James looked down at the key and nodded. "Yes. Mr. Guichard had several accounts with us *and* a safety deposit box. I only met him once. About a year ago. Such a nice, young man. Much too young to have left our God's green earth."

Jacks gazed at her sincerely. In truth, Benoit hadn't been nice, and he had been over two hundred years old. Not that Mrs. James could have guessed his real age. She swiveled in her chair, searching for something in the credenza behind her. The moment of sentimentality was squelched.

When Mrs. James swiveled back, she had papers. She pushed them across the desk. "Some forms for you to fill out while I make a copy of your passport."

The lines and boxes on the forms swam in his vision.

"We'll also need a reference letter from your bank." Mrs. James placed a business card on top of the documents. "There's an email address and a fax number on there."

"Oh, I'm not transferring his accounts."

Mrs. James's eyebrows rose.

"I've come to cash them out."

The bank manager regarded him as though she was expecting the punchline to a joke. Hearing none, she folded her arms and looked at Jacks. "Did Mr. Guichard's lawyer inform you of the nature of his client's holdings with our institution?"

His mouth opened and quickly closed.

"Our Diamond customers find it beneficial to transfer their assets. Or they may choose to set up a new account with us. We have a brochure that explains an array of options." She brought it out from her desk drawer. "Most of Mr. Guichard's assets are tied up in investments and securities. If you liquidate them entirely, you'll lose thirty to forty percent of their value based on local and international tax codes. Here, you'll see the annual caps on withdrawals to avoid tax penalties. By setting up another Diamond account, you can choose your own portfolio based on a variety of growth strategies."

That sounded complicated and time-consuming. "I'm only here for a couple of days."

"I'm afraid it will take longer than that. We are obligated to freeze an account for thirty days after notification of a death. It's a legal requirement in the event anyone should come forward to contest the claim to Mr. Guichard's estate."

Anxiety snaked through his body. Farzan's research hadn't turned up that complication. Jacks didn't think anyone else knew about Benoit's offshore accounts, but thirty days felt like an eternity to wait. What he really wanted was the contents of the safety deposit box. That's what Bernard had been looking for. There could be another way to get to the box, but it was risky. He needed to talk to Farzan.

Mrs. James watched him with motherly sympathy. "Your lawyer should have explained all of this to you. I'll print out the account statements, and you can take some time to decide how you would like to proceed." She tapped some keys, and the laser printer behind her churned out pages. Then, she looked over her desk blotter calendar, took up a fancy gold pen, and circled August 28. "If we issue a death notice today, the accounts will be released to you on August 28th. We can open an account here under your name, or if you choose to transfer to another institution, we'll need some forms filled out, and it can all be handled electronically. And of course, we need a way of contacting you during the period of public notice. Where are you staying, Mr. Heathcliff?"

Jacks hesitated. "The Primrose Guest House."

A shadow passed over Mrs. James's face. His insides sank. He hadn't expected to share that information. The Primrose Guest House had the cheapest rooms on the island at $95 a night with a shared bath. It was a forty-five minute bus trip out of town. Hardly the type of accommodations one would expect for someone claiming what was sounding like a sizeable inheritance.

"It's just for a night or two," he said. "I'll forward you a number where you can reach me outside of the country."

Mrs. James handed him the printout and the key, and she went to copy his passport in an adjoining room.

Jacks bounced his knee. There were so many lies to keep track of, and now this waiting period, during which the police were investigating Bernard's death back in New York City. How long would it be safe for him to stay in one place?

FIFTEEN

"THIRTY DAYS?" FARZAN said. "What if they run your passport? The ID number was fine for getting you through TSA, but if the bank digs a little deeper, they're going to see it's for Sammy's ex-girlfriend's grandfather who died last year."

Jacks tipped his cell phone away from his ear, feeling attacked by the anxiety coming from the other end of the line. He sat down on the creaky twin bed in his room at the Primrose Guest House, and he scratched the back of his neck. "I know. That's why I'm thinking about going with Plan B."

"Plan B?"

"Ye-ah. Like, getting into the safety deposit room on my own."

Farzan's voice raised an octave. "No way, Jacks. You're not charging in there as a mountain lion."

"I could try getting in after the bank closes."

"You think you're Catherine Zeta-Jones? There'll be surveillance cameras and locks to break through and alarms."

"I'm just trying to figure out my options."

"What options? This was a bad idea that's gotten even

worse. Get yourself on a flight while that passport Sammy made for you still works."

Jacks flopped back on the bed and sighed. Where was he supposed to go? He couldn't go back to living with Farzan when there were werecats like Bernard looking for him.

"Have the cops been by?" Jacks said.

"No."

"Anyone else?"

"No."

"How's Bella?"

"She's fine. You want me to put her on the phone?"

Jacks grinned. He wouldn't have minded trying to telepathize to her to see if she had picked up any information from the strays, but she was a sore spot for Farzan. Jacks could feel her presence close to Farzan through the phone, a purring energy.

"I just want you to be safe," Farzan said.

"I know. But I can't give up on this. I have to wait it out. No one is going to come forward. The bank manager believes me. She gave me all these forms for transferring Benoit's money. I didn't even tell you..." Jacks stood up from his bed and walked over to the dresser countertop where there was a pile of folded papers. He sorted through them for the bank statement. "Benoit had 15.6 million dollars in stocks and bonds."

There was a sharp silence on the other end of the line. Jacks imagined a jaw hitting the floor back in Queens. He cracked up with laughter. "Still think I should abandon ship?"

"I think I'm coming down there to run away with you to Brazil."

"Samoa or Vanuatu, remember? No extradition."

"This is fucking crazy, Jacks."

Jacks laid back down on his bed. He drummed two fingers against his lips. "Like I told you, I'm not stealing the money. I'll try to find one of Benoit's relatives. He didn't tell me much about his family, but he said his mother was from Columbia. If I can't track down anyone who was related to him, I'll give it to charity."

"My noble boyfriend. But you don't have to give it all away. After all the trouble Benoit put you through, you're entitled to keep something."

"I'll keep a few bucks to buy you a souvenir."

"What, like a seashell fridge magnet?"

"What do you want? A straw hat? Flip-flops?"

Farzan took a moment to respond. "I want *you*. Back here. Safe and sound."

"I want that too. If it was possible, I'd be on the next flight."

They spoke easily after that, just about everyday things: Farzan's internship, his family, the little bit of the island Jacks had seen so far. Jacks wished Farzan had been able to come with him. It would be like a real vacation for the two of them, hanging out on the beach and having rum cocktails for lunch. He had seen signs for jet skiing, parasailing, scuba diving — all things he had never done. Jacks had never gone away with a boyfriend before. Hell, he'd never travelled farther than New Jersey by himself.

"Tell me this is all going to work out," Farzan said. "That I'm going to see you again. That we'll look back on this and laugh."

"It's going to work out." He needed Farzan to believe it, even if he wasn't a hundred percent sure himself.

AFTER THE CALL, Farzan got up from the sofa to stash his prepaid cell phone, which was a little untraceable contingency for keeping in touch with Jacks. He stopped short on his path to the bedroom when he noticed Bella staring at him from her spot on the kitchen windowsill.

"What?" he said. "I haven't decided how I feel about *you* either. It's your fault he had to leave the country."

Bella turned her attention to the window, decidedly disinterested in the conversation. Farzan went into his bedroom to hide the phone under the mattress.

When Farzan thought about what she had put Jacks through, his temples burned and throbbed like he was sprouting horns. Maybe he should trust Jacks's judgment, his feline telepathy, but Farzan couldn't change how he felt about the turncoat cat.

By the digital alarm clock on his nightstand, he had an hour and a half to nap before heading off to the hospital for his overnight shift at the E.R. Farzan shut his bedroom door. He took off his T-shirt and jeans and placed them in his hamper. He hit the overhead light switch, plunging the room into darkness, and laid down above the covers in his boxer briefs.

His body was a mess of nervous energy. Jacks wouldn't do something foolish like trying to break into the bank, would he? He could be shot or locked up in jail or sent back to the U.S. to face double murder charges. Farzan flopped onto his side, adjusted his pillow, and flopped over again. What did they think they were doing? Neither one of them knew how to pull off an international heist. Farzan had never even skipped a class and come up with some dishonest excuse to tell the professor. He waited for the "Walk" sign before crossing the street. Meanwhile, Jacks needed to be guided through how to book a flight online. They were a terrible con-man team, but it was insane for Jacks to try this thing alone. He should have insisted on going with him. They were thousands of miles away from each other, with only a pair of flimsy cell phones to stay connected once or twice a day.

Farzan hated being so helpless. His head swirled with anxious thoughts, and if he couldn't turn them off, he would never get to sleep. He had an eight-hour shift to get through at the hospital.

He just wanted things to be perfect with Jacks. He couldn't try to control him. That's where he had gone wrong in his past relationships. Farzan's first boyfriend in college had called him "smothering." The next and last, an older, closeted Persian man from an online dating site, had told Farzan that if he had wanted a nagging wife, he would have stuck with sleeping with women.

Farzan needed to chill out. Technically, he and Jacks had only been boyfriends for a few days, and it was complicated. That's why he'd said Jacks was free to fool around while he was abroad with no questions asked and no information volunteered. Farzan hoped Jacks didn't, but he wanted to be modern, mature, and realistic about their relationship. Or was he self-sabotaging it by saying that?

The door clacked like someone was pushing on it to get in.

Farzan stared at the door, mystified at first. Then scratching and high-pitched mewling infiltrated the room. Why the hell was the damn cat bothering him?

Farzan climbed out of bed and stomped toward the door to scare Bella away. A violent rattle tore through the darkness and stopped him in his tracks.

He froze. It was the outside door to the apartment. The door knob shook forcefully, and then there was an explosive shudder, like someone was trying to break open the door with a body slam.

Farzan's heart leapt out of his chest. What did he have in his bedroom to ward off an attacker? His laptop? A wire hanger bent into a hook? He went to his closet and grabbed the only weapon he could think of: one of his steel-tipped Doc Martens.

A lock cracked, and he heard the outside door fly open.

On the tips of his toes, Farzan stepped to his bedroom door. His hands were trembling. He twisted the doorknob gently and cracked the door open, hiding behind it, so he could peek into the living room.

In the faint aura of a single standing lamp, he saw a young Asian man with windswept hair and a black T-shirt clinging to his muscular torso. The stranger looked around, orienting himself to the basement apartment before he spotted the bedroom. Farzan shrank behind the door, gripping his boot, controlling his frightened breaths. He could call the police, but getting authorities involved could lead to questions about Jacks.

He peeked out to the living space again. It looked like the intruder had magically disappeared at first, then he caught, low to the ground, a man-sized cat with downy, speckled fur. It was skulking toward the bedroom.

Farzan watched, paralyzed by the wild beast. The Asian man must have picked up his scent and transformed into a snow leopard. By the ferocity of the cat's yellow-green eyes, Farzan felt certain he intended to make a kill whether or not he found Jacks. He had nothing to fend it off but the boot in his hand. He had no place to run. The bedroom was a dead end.

Bella scuttled into the space between the wereleopard and the bedroom. Farzan stared in disbelief. Was she crazy? The big cat could gore her with a bat of his claw. Bella puffed her fur out, and she hissed murderously at the wereleopard.

The wereleopard stilled his progress and shrank up his head. Then he came back at Bella with a fang-bearing growl that shook through Farzan's body and turned his joints to jelly. Bella held her ground and glared at her opponent. Farzan was terrified Bella was about to be crushed in the big cat's jaws. It could practically eat her whole.

Then, a miracle happened. The wereleopard eased off from

his snarling posture, and he circled Bella, just sniffing her out. Bella pivoted around, keeping her eyes locked on the beast. The wereleopard snorted and moaned a feline complaint. Bella answered with a shrill mewl. It was some kind of cat communication. Jacks had said Bella would protect him from werecats, though Farzan hadn't fully believed it at the time.

The wereleopard's limbs lengthened into human arms and legs, and his fur drew into his skin with the speed of freakish, reverse time-lapse photography. His muzzle and his ears realigned, and in a blink, he was back to his human form: a young man, lean and muscle-toned, crouching on the floor. He stood and gave Bella another look-over. She sat back on her hind legs with an unbreakable stare. The stranger smiled with an undercurrent of mischief on his face. He turned and walked out the door.

Farzan looked at Bella with wonder. She licked her paw and scrubbed one side of her muzzle. What could she have told the wereleopard to make him leave so easily?

The answer hit him all at once. The wereleopard wanted Jacks. The only thing that would have deterred him was knowing he was looking in the wrong place.

He staggered out of the room toward Bella. "What did you tell him?"

The cat's eyes narrowed and flared, as though it was in very bad taste to accuse her. Farzan rushed back into the bedroom to get the cell phone beneath the mattress.

SIXTEEN

THERE WASN'T MUCH in the vicinity of the Primrose Guest House. For more than an hour, Jacks had walked along the shoulder of a country highway, headed to a resort town recommended by the night attendant. It was a desolate and occasionally dangerous trek. Along the way, the headlights of cars and trucks had emerged from dark hollows in the road up ahead or behind him, and the drivers sped past Jacks without any thought of clipping whatever was on the narrow shoulder.

Jacks had needed to get out of his closet of a room at the guest house. At nighttime, his feline sensitivity peaked, and the world bloomed with curious scents and sounds. The four walls surrounding him felt like a cage.

Tropical warmth still clung to the island at night. He had ventured out in an open Oxford shirt, cargo shorts, and flip-flops. He figured when he found the town, he'd people-watch and maybe treat himself to a can of soda. It's not like he could afford to spend any more than that. With the money he had left after buying his plane ticket, he could swing renting his room for two more nights, and now, that money had to somehow stretch a month. Meanwhile, when he checked the pockets of his shorts, he realized he'd left his cell phone charging back in his room. What a bone-headed thing to do! He should have his phone on him at all times in case Farzan needed to reach him.

Jacks considered heading back to the guest house. Then he noticed a valley of dotted lights just down the road. Farzan was at the ER overnight. He'd be safe there, wouldn't he? With the hospital security and all the people around, it was probably one of the safest places for him to be. It looked like the town was no more than a mile away. He'd just take a quick look around, and he could transform into his mountain lion self to gallop home through the countryside. He'd only be away for a couple of hours.

The highway rounded banks of gated vacation communities and joined a seaside mainway with high-rise beachfront apartment buildings and luxury resorts. Jacks crossed the four lane boulevard to gaze out at the ocean where there was an open view between the buildings.

The sound of breaking waves and the breath of the sea inspired awe. Jacks had only seen the ocean once before, in Atlantic City, New Jersey, and the nighttime Caribbean vista was far more beautiful. It reminded him he was on a tiny dot of an island in the middle of a vast ocean. As he looked around, he realized this was a whole other kind of beach community. The rolling lawns in front of condominiums were landscaped as impeccably as golf courses. People kept the noise down. When they needed to get around, they drove luxury SUVs and sports cars.

The highway edged along the coast toward an inlet marina encircled by two-story villa-style condominiums. That looked all kinds of interesting to Jacks, so he headed over for a closer look. The private enclave was like a palace with little beaches, gazebos, and a yard of berthed yachts. The lights of the villas glinted in the calm, dark inlet water.

He came up to the main entrance with a security booth and a toll barrier across the drive. A fancy sign read: Port St. Charles Marina, Boat Owners and Residents Only. That was a minor deterrent. He wanted to check out those yachts. With his night vision, he zoned in on the marina warden from a good thirty yards away. The young guy was caught up watching something on a TV screen in his boxy, lighted workstation.

Jacks stalked up on the entrance and crept quietly around the lawn side of the security booth. He hoisted himself up the seven-foot concrete wall bordering the property and scanned for passersby. There wasn't a soul out on the drive or the nearby parking lot. He jumped down in a nearly soundless landing on a grassy lawn.

Inside the compound, he could just act like he belonged there, though he preferred to skulk around, not running into people. A walkway rounded the property's lobby building and led to the interior of the marina. Jacks crept into the shadowy cover of palm trees, waited out some sounds from the lobby, and fast-tracked down the walk and around the building.

The marina lit up like Christmas in front of him. Going to a private university in upstate New York, he had met students from wealthy families. They had come from boarding schools and talked about their parents' vacation homes in Florida and Colorado. But this place looked like it was for a totally different class of people. The grounds were pristine. The homes were two-story, multi-terraced properties, and everybody seemed to have a yacht docked at the marina.

Live jazz music came from a private club near the lobby of the community, where most people must've been gathered. Jacks spotted a few outliers here and there—staff in button-down shirts and shorts and neatly-dressed couples strolling around the promenade. He anticipated their routes and altered his course to the shady margins of the walk in order to give them a wide pass. When the way was clear, Jacks stepped along the promenade to check out the boats.

Some had triple decks and fancy cabins for entertaining dozens of people. They had funny names: "Aquaholic," "Seas the Day," and "Screw Loose." The boats got bigger as Jacks approached a channel that opened up to the sea.

He saw a long pier down that way that launched out to the water for even bigger yachts. It looked to be deserted. Jacks headed toward it, excited to check out those mammoth boats. He came up to a black steel and glass extravaganza, decorated with outdoor lights, a luxury hotel on water. Next to it was an oversized, catamaran-style ship that looked like it could carve through a glacier.

He heard music from the end of the pier. A fast beat. Electronica. Like something from a European nightclub. The sound didn't interest Jacks so much. He liked alternative rock and synth-punk mainly. But he was curious to see what kind of people were out partying at the prime berth at the Port St. Charles Marina.

Jacks approached at a cautious clip, ready to dash back the other way or dart down one of the darkened mooring docks if a security guard came around. The music was coming from the last yacht on the pier. It wasn't the biggest boat he had seen, but it was impressive. He went over to take a closer look.

It had to be one hundred, two hundred feet long. The yacht had double-tiered cabins and a glass-enclosed cockpit on the top. The main cabin was vast and sheathed by shiny black reflective windows. People inside could see out, but Jacks couldn't see in. That palatial cabin was where the music was coming from.

The back of the hull bore the name of the vessel: Maarten's Pride.

Jacks's nostrils twitched. A magnetic pull tugged at his gut, eerily familiar and dangerous. But the scent he was picking up didn't spur an urge for violence like when he had crossed paths with the werejaguar Bernard. It had an aggressive male edge, but it was inviting, alluring. Jacks wanted to get into the party going on in the massive cabin, but his human instincts held him back like straps of ice.

A glass door to the cabin slid open, and a figure stepped out. Jacks retreated to the shadowed side of the pier where he could still see what was going on but had room to make a break for it if he had to. The man called back to his friends in a language Jacks didn't recognize. Jacks watched the stranger walk over the gangplank and step onto the mooring dock. Focusing his feline vision, he saw the man was tall and dressed in linen pants and a tailored shirt, unbuttoned down his long torso to his navel. The man stopped and stared through the shadows at the exact place where Jacks stood. Jacks couldn't move. The stranger's eyes flashed like iridescent sapphire gems, and he strolled to the pier, looking merry.

"Hello there."

Jacks held himself warily. He'd found a werecat. He could tell by his scent and the way his eyes captured light in the dark. This one had a few days' growth of beard on his cheeks, his upper lip, and his chin, giving him a casual and untended masculinity. He looked to be in his late twenties. Jacks couldn't see if he had the same flaming orange tattoo as Bernard. His hands were hooked in the pockets of his pants. He probably came out of the yacht because he sensed Jacks.

He made a spur of the moment decision. He wasn't going to run away. He desperately needed to learn more about his kind, and it was one in a million odds that he'd found someone on the tiny island.

The man came up an arm's length from Jacks and rolled back on his sandaled heels. "It's a nice night for a prowl."

He was a few inches taller than Jacks and a pleasant puzzle of features: short, thick African curls of hair, a golden complexion, and a strong Caucasian jaw and nose. The man brought out of his pocket a tiny silver snuff box, tarnished with age and shaped like the coiled horn of a gazelle. He unclipped the top and held it up to one of his nostrils. A whiff of its contents, earthy and potent, wafted to Jacks. The man offered it to him.

"Oh. No thanks."

The man grinned. His eyes had turned to crystal, watery pools. He replaced the trinket in his pocket and held out his hand.

"Maarten."

Now Jacks could see for sure he didn't have a Gothic tattoo on his hand. "Donovan," Jacks introduced himself.

Maarten's grip was warm and lingering. Jacks gently retrieved his hand. "I like your boat."

"You're American." Maarten's mouth curled into a flirtatious smirk. "A New World cat."

Jacks wasn't sure what he meant. New to being a werecat?

"Are you here on holiday?"

Jacks couldn't help smiling, stupidly. "No. Business."

Maarten scowled. "That sounds all sorts of boring. What business could you have on this island paradise?"

"I've got some things to settle for a friend."

Maarten looked Jacks in the eye. "A friend?" His face brightened in amusement, over what Jacks wasn't sure. The guy might've been a little loaded from whatever he kept in that fancy snuff box.

He shifted his weight. "Yeah. I'm just here for a couple of days." The heat from Maarten's body lapped at him.

"Are you here alone, Donovan?"

The guy had mischief on his mind, and however alluring that might be, Jacks suddenly got cold feet. He glanced over his shoulder at the route back to the marina. "I'm sorry. I didn't mean to be gawking at your yacht. I should get going."

"I asked you a question."

He didn't mean to be rude, but Maarten was being rude, wasn't he? "Yeah, I came here alone. But I'm not *alone* alone."

Maarten's eyebrows narrowed teasingly. For some reason, Jacks couldn't bring out that he meant he had a boyfriend.

Then Maarten held his shoulder with his warm hand and leaned in so close that Jacks could see the whites of his canine teeth. "So wonderfully, wonderfully, wonderfully, wonderfully pretty. You know that I'd do anything for you. We should have each other for dinner. We should have each other with cream."

Jacks was baffled for a moment. Maarten broke out in a laugh. Jacks blushed and smiled, recalling the strange verse from *The Love Cats* by the Cure.

"You don't have to be afraid, Donovan. I only bite with consent."

Jacks yawned nervously. "I'm not afraid. Just beat from traveling. Nice to meet you."

"What a pity." Maarten gestured to his yacht. "I was going to invite you inside. Give you the grand tour."

Really?

"Ah well. Some other time then? We'll be here all week."

We?

Maarten's blue eyes simmered. "Can I count on you? I'd like to see your wonderfully pretty face again."

Jacks summoned some swagger. "Maybe."

"That's not good enough. You'd keep me waiting on a maybe?"

Jacks smiled at his persistence. "Nice to meet you. We'll probably see each other around town."

As he walked back to the marina, Jacks felt Maarten's heated gaze, like a spotlight on his back, all the way down the pier.

WHEN JACKS GOT back to his room, he went straight for his cell phone on the top of his dresser. The screen startled him. Four missed calls and a text message: "R u up?" He tried calling Farzan back, but it went to voicemail. It was almost three in the morning. He was probably just busy at the hospital, right?

Jacks laid down on his twin bed, setting the phone on the mattress at close reach. One of his knees bounced. Something terrible could have happened. Or Farzan might have just wanted to say goodnight again before he left out for the E.R. If Jacks called Farzan's parents' house or Sammy's cell phone to ask questions, he might be getting them alarmed in the middle of the night for no reason.

It was better to wait things out. Farzan would call back when he got a break around three thirty. Jacks wasn't sleepy anyway. The encounter with Maarten had his head crowded.

Was the guy dangerous? If Maarten meant to harm him, he played it with subtlety. He acted more like he wanted to get down Jacks's pants than wanting to kill him to protect his territory or avenge Benoit's death as Bernard said that Glaring group would do. Maarten seemed to know nothing about Jacks, though that could be a different kind of trap. He might have been trying to get Jacks into his boat so he and his friends could shred him to pieces.

A restless, achy energy wormed through him. He stood and paced around his little room. There was a luxury yacht down at the harbor filled with men like him. If they weren't interested in murdering him, well, they were exactly the people he should be talking to. Maybe he should've accepted Maarten's invitation. Heat rose to his face. The guy was hella hot, and his friends were probably hella hot too.

He slowed down to think things through logically and practically. Yes, he needed to learn about the werecat world. Maarten might have information about this werecat faction the Glaring. Checking them out was a huge opportunity that had fallen into his lap. But was it just a coincidence they had showed up at the same little island where Benoit had a fortune at an off-shore bank?

At three thirty-two, his cell phone chirped and lit up. Jacks sprung for it on the mattress. "Hi."

Farzan's voice was low and annoyed. "Where have you been?"

He sat down on his bed. "I'm sorry. I went out for a walk and left my cell back in my room."

In a rush, Farzan told him about the visit from the Asian wereleopard.

Jacks shot up like a spring. "I'll catch the next flight back there."

"I'm fine, Jacks. He's gone. I don't think he's coming back."

"How do you know? There could be others —"

"They're looking for you, not me."

The sharpness of his voice shocked Jacks silent.

"Jacks, Bella communicated with the guy somehow, and he left in a hurry. The reason I've been trying to call you all night, while you were wandering around on your own, is because...I know this sounds insane, but I think, I'm pretty sure she told him where you are."

"She wouldn't do that. She was protecting you."

"I'm not convinced she was protecting me. I've gotten warmer vibes at a bar filled with New York Rangers fans watching Fox News. The guy broke down the door with his body to get into my apartment, and she told him something that convinced him to leave. She must've told him you're in Barbados, don't you think? She already led one werecat to you."

"I dunno." Jacks scratched his head. "She could've told him to look for me somewhere else. Kathmandu, for all we know."

"I don't trust her. You should get out of Barbados."

"Where am I supposed to go?"

"I'll wire you money. You can get a flight to, I don't know, another island at least."

"Babe, I'm not taking your money. I should be wiring money to *you* to fix your door." Before Farzan could break in, Jacks went on. "Listen, this proves that other werecats are after me. They're going to be after me wherever I go. I'll try to make a psychic connection with Bella. She might be able to help me stay a step ahead."

"What if she wants you to step into a trap?" Farzan said. "No. I'm coming down there."

"Hon, please. I appreciate it. I really do. But you don't have to fly down here and screw up your internship. I couldn't live with that. I couldn't live with you getting hurt. This is my mess, and I swear, I can protect myself if it comes to that."

"It's not just your mess. I'm invested in this too, y'know?"

Jacks understood what he meant. Farzan cared about him a lot. It warmed his heart, but at the same time, there was no way in hell he was putting Farzan in danger again. For a delicate moment, it occurred to him that the only way he could ensure Farzan's safety was to break things off, say something awful so Farzan would never want to see him again. But Jacks couldn't bring himself to do that.

"I know you are. But babe, I'm the one who knows about this world. You get that, right? And I'm telling you to trust me. I'm going to be fine. We'll check in as often as we can."

The other end of the line was quiet for a moment. "Just promise me you'll be careful."

"You, too. You should keep your bedroom door open, so Bella can get in there and warn you, just in case."

Farzan huffed.

"Just consider it, okay? We're going to get through this." Jacks looked at the date on his screen. "Hey, it's now just twenty-nine days until I can get into Benoit's security deposit box. We got through one. We'll take it day by day."

Farzan relented. His break was over, and he had to get back to seeing patients. They exchanged I miss yous and goodbyes.

After, Jacks curled into himself on the bed. It was a small comfort that Farzan hadn't been mauled by the wereleopard, but because of him, a werecat broke into Farzan's home and came close to killing him. Was he a coward for not ending their relationship then and there?

Still, he couldn't hurt Farzan like that. He didn't want to push him away. Jacks realized he was being selfish on some level, and it sucked. But he just couldn't end their relationship that night.

His thoughts turned to his encounter with Maarten. He felt a sting of guilt about not having mentioned it to Farzan, but he had to try talking to Maarten and his friends. Farzan wouldn't like it. He would say it was much too dangerous. But Jacks had to go with his instincts. He needed to find out what he was up against.

SEVENTEEN

MAARTEN'S PRIDE WAS at the pier when Jacks snuck into Port St. Charles Marina the next night. But as he crept along the promenade toward the big dock, the scene was quieter. Track lighting outlined the double-decker boat, but no bass-heavy electronica emanated from the cabin with its black reflective windows. Maarten and his guests could have gone to the club. They could have gone into town. They could be asleep for all he knew. He wondered if he had made it there too late.

He had tried to plan his arrival for around the same time as when he'd met Maarten the night before, but picking out what to wear had eaten up time. He had never been around people who owned yachts. Cargo shorts seemed too casual. The suit jacket he had worn to the bank seemed too businessy. In the end, he had decided on his best pair of jeans, his dress shoes, and his Oxford shirt, tucked in. He sprung for a taxi to take him into Speightstown so he wouldn't be dripping with sweat from making the trip on foot. That was an expense he really couldn't afford. He needed this visit to be worth it.

As he walked toward the gangplank to the yacht, he picked up the beckoning scent that had snared a hook into his gut the night before. He deciphered a trace of jasmine, which was intriguing. Staring at the boat's reflective windows, he briefly broke his stride. A dangerous premonition spooked him.

If he went into the boat, he might never come out.

That was just nerves. Jacks unfastened a chain at the gangplank and walked across onto the deck. Now, he could hear faint, downbeat instrumental music from the cabin. He came up to the sliding door from where Maarten had emerged the night before.

Every surface of the cabin was opaque. He leaned his ear against the sliding door. The only thing he could hear was the music. He rapped his knuckles lightly against the glass and waited. He heard no sound of movement from inside and was starting to feel like an idiot. *One last shot.* Jacks knocked a little louder.

A few seconds later, the door slid open just enough to frame the head of a light-skinned woman with messy curls of black hair. She glared at him fiercely. The shape of her nose and her blue crystal eyes said she had to be related to Maarten.

"Hi. I'm Donovan. I met Maarten the other night, and he invited me to drop by."

She looked at him a moment. With an arm fastened firmly across the door, she turned to the interior of the cabin and shouted back in a foreign language. It was German or Dutch, he guessed. A muted voice called back.

The woman gave Jacks a disapproving look, but she pushed the door open a little more and stood back to let him through.

The cabin was bathed in red fluorescence. Hanging from the middle of the ceiling, an enormous crystal chandelier sent gouges of light floating through the room. It was vast and much more sparsely furnished than Jacks expected. The space was open and carpeted, with lounge areas around the periphery. A rectangular balcony on the second floor overlooked everything. A heady masculine scent saturated the indoor space.

He followed the woman into the mire of the cabin. Her curvaceous body, clad in a flowing sundress and hemp sandals, seemed to glide through the room. She led Jacks to the far end where he saw a shadowy gathering of people on an oversized high-backed couch. He nearly stumbled over himself. He was clearly overdressed, crashing a different kind of party than he'd imagined.

A half-dozen men lounged on the imperial couch, their bodies and limbs entwined like an opiate-infused cuddle pile. It was a feast for Jacks's eyes, dark-skinned, light-skinned, Asian and European men, each one with a scruffily handsome face and a lanky, muscle-toned body. They wore unbuttoned shirts, and their pants were slung loose around their hips. Some guys wore only briefs. Hands raked idly through overgrown heads of hair, caressed shoulders, slid over thighs. Mouths and noses nuzzled against bearded cheeks and necks. Their collective purr reverberated through Jacks. Things stirred below his belt.

They glanced briefly at him as he approached. The guys' vibe was cliquish. Above the huddle, he spotted two overfed domestics, one orange, one black, perched on the back of the couch like sentinels. They fastened their suspicious eyes on Jacks.

He was so swept up by the scene, it took a moment to spot Maarten in the midst of it. He was slouched in the center of the couch with two bodies leaning lazily against him on either side. He looked up at Jacks, and his sapphire eyes sparkled.

"The New World cat returns."

The other men studied Jacks, undecided, skeptical.

"He's the American I told you about," Maarten said to them. "Here in Barbados to take care of some business for a friend. I'm glad you kept your promise." He raked his fingers through the golden, tousled quiff of his nearest companion and smiled sublimely. "You picked the perfect time to get acquainted. Join us."

He glanced to his other side, and a dark, muscular man smirked and spread his thick thighs, creating a small triangle of space for Jacks to sit down. He couldn't help feeling flattered to be invited. Truly, his mind was blown. They were all gorgeous, and they were all werecats. He was very nearly swallowed up by his desire to dive into their warm bath of sexual heat. He gulped down the knot in his throat.

"Actually, I was hoping I could talk to you."

Maarten raised his eyebrows in his humorous manner. "Talk?"

Some of his companions chuckled. Others peered at Jacks challengingly. Nonetheless, he soldiered on. "Yeah. Y'know, to finish up our conversation from last night."

Maarten glanced at him briefly, and then he turned with a grin, attending to the plucking of his fair-skinned neighbor's budded nipple. "I'm a bit preoccupied at the moment. I don't recall our conversation being particularly consequential, but you can grab me for a chat later. Meanwhile, you're free to join us. Or perhaps you simply prefer to watch."

Men peeked at Jacks from around the couch with bland appraisals and superior reproaches. Maarten's tone didn't sit well with Jacks, and as for his companions, no matter how hot they were, he didn't like being looked down on.

"I really need to talk to you. It's about my friend."

"Why talk when you can just *be*?"

The sentinel cats raised themselves on their front legs and stared at Jacks.

"You said you'd give me a tour. We can talk along the way. I promise, it won't take long."

Maarten scowled.

"It's really important," Jacks said.

He detected a slight displacement beside him. The woman who had led him inside the cabin had shifted her weight impatiently. He had forgotten about her.

"You've met my sister Annika?" Maarten said.

Jacks turned to her, trying to break the ice. Her wary expression didn't change. Annika spoke to her brother in their native language. It was practically a shout. Maarten answered in a querulous tone, but whatever Annika said had enough reason or threat to it to make him sit up from the couch. His companions watched him. The sentinel strays glared haughtily at Jacks.

"All right, New World cat. I did promise you a tour."

MAARTEN LED JACKS from the main cabin to a passageway that opened to the yacht's stern deck, facing out to sea. The furnishings were grand and stylish, from the half-moon bar, chaise lounges and cushioned sunbathing platform to a sunken dining area with tables and benches. From ashore, the yacht was impressive. Aboard, it was like walking into some billionaire's world as portrayed on a travel documentary. The boat was big enough to entertain thirty, forty, or fifty guests. Jacks wondered if there were more people aboard than the seven or eight he had seen.

The night air met his overheated skin, tempering his flush of nerves and shy arousal. Maarten walked him over to a railing and leaned against it, facing him. His high-shouldered frame was draped in an unbuttoned shirt and drawstring slacks. Beyond him, a red beacon blinked on the water.

A playful look sprung up on Maarten's face. "Here we are. So, why were you so intent on getting me alone?"

Jacks took up a space beside him with his elbows on the railing. He had rehearsed a sketch of the conversation in his head, but now his head was floating from the wild reality that he was aboard the luxury liner, standing with its werecat owner.

"Why did you call me New World cat?"

Maarten studied him, sidelong. "You're a recent convert, aren't you?" He drew up closer and clasped one side of Jacks's face. "Young, innocent, and curious."

Already, he was struggling to focus on the questions he needed to ask. All he could do was lean away from Maarten, slightly, hoping he would elaborate.

"You're a cougar," Maarten said. "A younger branch of the family tree."

"What are you?"

"*Panthera Leo*. Old World felid. My kind tramped the earth one million years ago, while yours were stuck in the DNA of a common ancestor, along with the little domestics."

"So, you're a panther?"

"I'm a lion. The top notch of the tree. Along with the tigers."

Jacks wondered if that explained the men's superior attitude. They were like Europeans looking down their noses at Americans. He was sidetracked for a moment, considering how many varieties of werecats there could be. They were all the result of an ancient mysticism, the invoking of the feline gods to merge man and beast. A common ancestor meant a giant, prehistoric cat.

Maarten looked at Jacks with dismissive amusement. "That's why you called me away from my friends? For a lesson in genealogy?"

"Did you know someone named Benoit Guichard?"

A spark shone in Maarten's eyes, but he quickly disguised

it. He turned back to Jacks with his mouth curled up in a dirty schoolboy grin. "Suppose I did? What will you give me to tell you about it?" He hooked the cuff of Jacks's jeans with his bare foot, working its way up the inside of his calf. "What was he? An old flame? A hot screw?"

Jacks was scalded for a moment, and meanwhile Maarten touched the side of his chest and kneaded the taut muscle. "He liked you, didn't he?" He slid his fingers over Jacks's perked-up nipple. "Did he make you cum with his mouth?" He grabbed Jacks's backside. "Did he fuck you here?"

Jacks redirected Maarten's hand. "I didn't come here to mess around."

Maarten's face lit up fatuously. "Really?"

Jacks laughed nervously. "I've got a boyfriend. Back in New York." He hid his face for a moment. Should he have said that much?

"That's quaint. But there's always room for more, isn't there?" Maarten placed Jacks's hand on the crotch of his slacks. The fine linen barely concealed his heated girth. "I'd like to watch you going down on me. Would you shut your eyes, or would you keep them open?"

Jacks didn't move his hand at first. His body was damp and eager from the feel of Maarten's arousal. The suggestion blew up in his mind, giving Maarten head on his luxury boat, under the stars, against the breeze of the Caribbean. He backed off to clear his head.

"Why be a prude?" Maarten complained. "Do you know what's the best part about being a werecat? You can fuck whoever you want. There are no diseases." He opened his arms to their powerful wingspan. "Our bodies mend themselves."

The implications kindled a suppressed fantasy—sex with no rules or responsibilities, but his conscience held him back once again. He couldn't cheat on Farzan. They'd just started something good. Besides, he needed information, and the idea of exchanging sexual favors for that went against his pride. Jacks breathed out in exasperation. He was in way over his head, thinking he could dig up information like an undercover detective. It was risky, but all he could think to do was level with the guy and see what led from there.

"I lied to you. My real name is Jacks." He peeked at Maarten. He didn't look put off. "Benoit was my mate. He reared me." Jacks cleared his throat. "He died recently. I know he used to come down here. I'm looking for people who knew him."

He glanced askew while he prayed Maarten wouldn't be angry about his deceit. Barely skipping a beat, Maarten drew up to him flirtatiously again.

"I've learned to never take what a werecat says at face value."

"Should I assume the same of you?"

Maarten beamed with his rakish smile. "Naturally. But as you've seen, I advertise my motives quite plainly." He picked at Jacks's hair. "You're welcome to stay the night if you need a place to crash."

"Thanks, but I've got a room."

"You're a challenge, aren't you, Jacks? But you should know, a werecat on his own doesn't last long in the world."

"I'm not alone. I mean, I *am* down here, but I've got people." Jacks was cautious about saying much about Farzan, particularly as he was human. "Listen. Can you just be straight with me? Does the name Benoit Guichard mean anything to you?"

"So persistent! He must've been a spectacular mate. As I've heard, there's nothing hotter than sex with your maker."

Jacks looked at Maarten squarely. He had a hunch that the

guy was playing with him precisely because he had information Jacks wanted.

Maarten yawned. "I knew Benoit. About a year ago, he stayed with us for a while. But it wasn't his scene."

"What is this scene?"

"We enjoy life. We enjoy each other."

"Do you kill?"

"All werecats kill. But there are other pleasures." He brought out a tiny, horn-shaped snuff box from his pocket. He offered it to Jacks, and Jacks shook his head. Maarten flicked open the clasp and took a deep snort through one nostril.

"What is that?"

"Valerian." Maarten held out the silver horn, and his sapphire eyes lit up with that watery glow. "It's the best catnip in the world."

Two impulses, at opposite ends, fought inside Jacks. It was dangerous to try the stuff with Maarten. He had no idea what kind of effect it would have. But even a second-hand sniff made Jacks feel delightfully light-headed. A little more would be even better, like submerging his brain in a heated bath. How could he expect to gain Maarten's trust without accepting his offer? It would help to loosen their conversation so he could find out things he needed to know.

He reached for the horn.

A sharp jolt hit him behind his eyes. He gripped the railing to steady himself. Was he already feeling the drug? How could that be? He closed his eyes, and it felt like the world was expanding into an infinite void of black. He heard Bella mewling to him.

Something was wrong. An image flashed in his vision. He saw a young Asian man skulking around the outer deck of the yacht. Things looked different than the way Jacks had come. It was a covered walkway facing out to the marina from a height. He looked up to the upper deck, searching.

A downy, spotted leopard crouched in the shadows of the balcony above him, staring down. Its eyes were wide, and it was quivering for a strike.

Jacks grasped for a plan of action while the leopard's yellow-green eyes fastened in on him like a death grip. Maarten watched Jacks with a grin, apparently amused by his companion's strange behavior and unaware of the intruder.

In a heartbeat, the leopard plunged from the upper deck. Jacks braced himself and tensed up the spot below his diaphragm.

Before he even had to wrangle with the cat, a white lioness sprang out of the cabin and collided with the leopard. The two beasts landed on the deck in a tornado of fur and gnashing muzzles.

Jacks grabbed Maarten by the arm and pulled him toward the dining area at the end of the deck. When they reached cover behind a bench, Jacks zoned in on the melee. He had never seen a white lion. She was beautiful and terrifying. Every part of her body was muscled for killing efficiency.

The lioness had the advantage of height and weight, and she quickly wrangled her opponent into a submissive position and clamped her jaws on the leopard's neck. An ear-splitting yelp severed the night. The leopard's body went through a squall of shudders, and then it lay dead.

The lioness released her kill. The leopard's dark blood stained her muzzle and the tuft of hair on her chest. She raised herself on her rear limbs to an impossible height. Her fur receded into her skin, and her body shrank and realigned into human form. Annika.

Maarten staggered over to his sister, and they bantered back and forth in their native tongue.

Jacks watched the dead leopard. Gradually, its spotted fur drew back, and its curled body morphed into its human form. It was a young Asian man, just like Bella had telepathized to him, and just as Farzan had described. He had come on an assassination mission.

Jacks gained up on Annika. He couldn't bring out words from his mouth. He was grateful, but he wasn't sure if it was safe to explain why the Asian wereleopard was after him. Would she and the others turn on him as well?

Annika called Maarten's attention to something around the side of the cabin. Jacks went after them. Back on the shadowy pier, there were dozens of little, flashing feline eyes — spying strays up to mischief. They must have come out from their hiding places in the little seaside town after learning what the wereleopard was planning. As Jacks knew their kind, they would spread the information, possibly to that mysterious group, the Glaring.

Annika bumped past Jacks and stormed into the cabin, barking orders. A pair of uniformed deckhands came out to pull in the gangplank and untie the yacht's moorings from the pier. Jacks watched the bustle of activity in a daze. They were going out to sea.

EIGHTEEN

THE EMERGENCY ROOM was like a medic's tent in a heavy artillery zone. Farzan eked out a space in the hallway to hunch over his tablet. He tapped in the disposition of his last patient, a gunshot victim. Mercifully, the bullet had just grazed one side of the young man's face. It had been a mess to suture up, but fairly harmless stuff compared to other patients he had seen that shift.

The night had started with a boy who had been hit by a car while on his bike. Both his legs had been crushed under the tires. Then there was a woman who swallowed a bottle of painkillers and needed a gastric lavage. Farzan's third patient was an elderly burn victim who had been pulled from a grease fire in her apartment. The examination stalls were full, and people were sitting on the floor in the waiting room.

To make matters worse, the hospital's HVAC system had broken down. The maintenance crew had thrown open every window on the floor, but it didn't make much of a difference. The place was thick with stagnant, summer heat. Farzan's hospital scrubs clung to his skin. There was an E.R. superstition about all hell breaking loose on the night of a full moon. But Farzan had checked it out on his meteorology app. The full moon was a week away.

The attending physician shouted from down the hall, "Mohammed, get over here."

Farzan closed up his tablet and walked over. Dr. Rabinovich was the AP all the interns hated. Though he'd been practicing for twenty years, he'd been passed over for all the better appointments in the hospital. He must have seriously pissed off one of the medical directors, and he took out his grudge on anyone he had power over. Besides, he was a lousy doctor who did the bare minimum to cover his butt and didn't really teach anything. He just reserved the right to lay blame when an intern made a mistake.

Farzan followed Rabinovich into a curtained stall with his intern counterpart Yesenia Martinez. An EMT with browned blood covering the front of his shirt took his leave with a downcast gaze. The patient on a gurney looked like he had been packaged for meat delivery. Blood soaked through the EMT's bandaging of his torso. One of the patient's arms hung loose from the shoulder, dislocated at a disturbing angle. The tendon had likely been torn from the bone.

Yesenia and a female nurse worked together to get a catheter down the patient's throat and hook him up to a ventilator. Rabinovich pointed Farzan to a heart monitor. Farzan quickly wheeled it over to attach the transmitter to the wrist of the man's good arm. Miraculously, the patient's breaths fogged up the ventilator mask Yesenia had fit around his nose and mouth.

His heartbeat was rapid and shallow. The patient had lost a prodigious amount of blood, and the IV drip from the ambulance was nearly depleted. Farzan went to grab another electrolyte bag. Rabinovich really needed to order a blood transfusion. If they didn't take care of that immediately and sewed up or cauterized the wounds, the guy was a goner. He was already in a deep stage of hypovolemic shock.

In a blink, the heart monitor flatlined, and the patient stopped breathing. Yesenia leaned in to apply heart compressions. Farzan sprang for the defibrillation equipment in a cabinet of the stall. Manual resuscitation wasn't going to work. They would need to shock the heart to get it going again, and that meant applying an electrical current directly to the patient's chest. Rabinovich took up surgical scissors and cut through the bandages.

When Rabinovich peeled back the sheared clothes, Farzan did a double-take. He had never seen such a mauling. The patient's sternum and a good third of his ribcage were exposed by massive, jagged scores. Farzan hesitated with the defibrillator paddles. Thick blood, nearly black, had oozed out of the chest cavity. Even if he could get the guy's heart beating again, how were they going to sew him up?

Rabinovich shook his head. "We'll call this one D.O.A."

The room fell still for a moment. From beyond the stall, an EMT's radio chirped, and a staticky message ate up the silence. Farzan's head pounded from what he had witnessed. He didn't take notice of the EMT's conversation.

The radio cut out, and the young guy with the bloodstained uniform stepped into the stall. Sweat beaded his face. He looked to Rabinovich.

"There's three others just like this one on their way over."

THE YACHT CLIPPED out to the night-shrouded sea. From the stern deck railing, Jacks watched the little bright dots of Port St. Charles Marina disappear on the horizon. Maarten and Annika had left him alone since they motored out from the pier. They were inside the cabin, discussing something. He had a bad feeling about it.

His cell phone was out of service range, and it only had twenty percent battery left. Not that calling Farzan could help in any practical way. He was thousands of miles away, across a vast ocean. But Jacks wanted to hear Farzan's voice and let him know what was going on. He tried shutting his eyes and imagining his thoughts traveling across sea and land and reaching Bella, but he couldn't find a connection. Had Bella sealed up her mind to him or had something happened?

Maarten and Annika approached from up the deck. He wore a muted expression, and she looked put-upon and aggressive. It was time for Jacks to come clean with them.

"I didn't know that guy," he blurted out, before they even made it down the stern deck stairs. "But I know why he was after me." He told them about killing Benoit to save Farzan, and Bernard tracking him down to steal something of Benoit's. He added what Bernard had told him about the Glaring and that he had killed the thief in their grapple. The truth was all Jacks had. It felt much easier sharing his story with people who were like him. They didn't think it was bizarre, or that he was crazy.

Annika said to her brother, "We drop him at the next port."

"That's fine with me," Jacks said.

"He won't last a day," Maarten told Annika.

"He made his own bed. He can lie in it."

"I can take care of myself. Just turn us around, and I'll go back to Barbados."

"You have no idea what you're up against," Maarten said.

"I handled one of them back in New York. I could've handled the one tonight." Jacks glanced at Annika. Obviously, she'd had a problem with him from the start. "I appreciate what you did, but I didn't need you to get involved."

She eyed him haughtily. "I had no choice. You brought your drama into our home."

"And I'm sorry for that. All I'm saying is, I agree with you. Take me back to Barbados, and I'll deal with things myself."

Maarten got in between them and turned to Jacks. "One on one, you might have a chance. What will you do when you're stalked by a group that hunts in packs?"

Jacks didn't have a response to that. If he was honest with himself, he was pretty sure he would be roadkill. Meanwhile, Annika came at her brother in a foreign rant. Maarten responded to her in an even tone. Though Annika was clearly fiercer, her brother seemed to have the final say, the lion to her lioness.

"Tell me how to get them off my back," Jacks said to Maarten. "I didn't do anything wrong."

"You did *everything* wrong."

"What was I supposed to do? Let Benoit kill an innocent bystander?"

"To the Glaring, no human is innocent. You're trying to apply reason to an organization that's held a grudge for centuries. That's why we don't waste time with them. They're little, scorned children who can't let go of the past."

"What's their grudge?"

"It doesn't matter."

"I want to know."

"Take your pick. Colonialism. Exploitation. Industrialization. Basically everything that's happened in the world over the past five hundred years. If they could stop squabbling among themselves, they might actually stand a chance of exterminating humankind, like they say they'll do."

Jacks remembered Benoit telling him very few of their kind were left. It had saddened him to hear it at the time, and he knew enough about European imperialism to follow what Maarten was saying a bit.

"They want to wipe out humans to avenge the past?"

"Put simply, yes."

"Where do you stand?"

Maarten glanced at his sister. "We stand aside." He turned to Jacks. "Humans do a fine job killing themselves without any of our help. The Glaring is a fractured bunch of bunglers. Look how they waste time tracking *you* down. As though by making you an example, they'll inspire solidarity. Cats are far too independent to be impressed by such ploys."

That reminded Jacks of Bernard, who had come after him to steal Benoit's stash before the Glaring could get to it. Jacks told Maarten and Annika the story, hoping they might have some idea about what Benoit kept in his safety deposit box at the Beechfield Bank.

Maarten took it in with an impatient yawn. "Maybe Bernard wanted Benoit's money. Benoit was only with us for a week. He didn't talk about his personal life."

Annika looked at him with much more curiosity than Jacks had noticed before, but she didn't say anything.

"We'll have a room made up for you on the upper deck," Maarten said.

"I can't stay here. I've got things to do in town."

Maarten looked Jacks over with a fatuous twinkle in his sapphire eyes. "Then I hope you're a good swimmer. We've set a course for the night. In case you choose to stay, I'll send down our cabin boy Willem to help you get settled."

With that, he left Jacks on the deck. It was just him and Annika for a moment. Annika seemed to think better of saying what was on her mind. She followed her brother into the cabin.

FARZAN WAS SO sick of hearing Jacks's automated voice mail message, he felt like flinging his cell phone out the window of his compact Ford. Maybe it was just service issues that morning, but it was more than a little annoying he hadn't received a call or a text from Jacks in more than twenty-four hours.

Daybreak cast an eerie pallor over the city. The other drivers seemed dazed, preoccupied. Farzan watched one, then two, then three police cars gun it down the shoulder of the road with their siren lights blinking. It reminded Farzan of his father driving him to grade school on the morning of 9/11. The satellite news station on his car radio wasn't reporting anything unusual, but he felt, uncannily, it was just a matter of time before the horrifying news broke.

Twenty patients had come into the E.R as victims of big cat attacks. Only one survived after they put in a trach tube and hooked him up to artificial respiration. It took two hours to stitch up his back, arms and face, and he was sent up to intensive care where his status would be touch-and-go depending on how the blood transfusions went.

There'd been quiet sidetalk about possible explanations. One of the EMTs said he heard about a breakout of animals from a zoo. Farzan knew better. There had to be more werecats in town like the wereleopard who had been by his apartment. Bella had gotten rid of one, but a whole crew of them must have come into town. And they weren't just after Jacks. They were attacking people indiscriminately.

Farzan turned onto an exit ramp and rumbled through the tree-lined backstreets to his parents' house. Luckily his mom and dad had gone upstate to a cabin for the week with Sammy and his brother Rahim's three kids. Farzan had forty-eight hours off from the hospital. He was supposed to drive up to the cabin to join his family after he got cleaned up and packed some clothes. Now he wasn't sure if he should forgo those plans and head to the airport to book a flight to Barbados. How was he supposed to make these decisions? Why couldn't Jacks pick up his phone?

As he pulled into the driveway, Farzan caught sight of a smoky gray cat laying in the middle of the drive. He stomped on the brake pedal, and it leapt out of the way, narrowly averting Farzan's screeching tires.

He shut off the ignition, threw open the door, climbed out, and shouted a string of curse words in Farsi at the cat.

"Fucking jinn."

The cat glared back at Farzan from the brush along the house. He grabbed his duffel bag with his change of clothes from the hospital and went around the house into the backyard to the entrance to his basement apartment.

The neighborhood was oddly quiet. People were just waking up, he supposed. But the blank silence was unusual at seven thirty in the morning. Something was missing. As he gazed up at a rustle of wind in the trees of his backyard, he put a mental finger on it. He didn't hear any chirping. No birds were around at all.

Farzan looked around the yard and saw an albino stray hanging around the side of the garage. Its fur was yellowed and patchy, and it narrowed its blue eyes at him.

He turned and fast-tracked toward the apartment. Then he nearly stumbled into another cat on his path. The cat recoiled, puffing out its calico fur and hissing. More cats emerged from the shrubby growth along the backyard fence. Nine or ten of them skulked forward warily, their suspicious eyes fixed on Farzan.

He hurried down the stairs to his apartment. Fumbling for his key ring, it fell out of his shaky hand and onto the concrete doorstep. Farzan snatched them up and worked the key into the door. He pushed it open and shoved it closed behind him.

Bella paced the apartment with her tail swinging.

He shouted at her. "What did you do? Invite all your friends over for a party?"

The cat jumped up on the kitchen counter and onward to the ledge of the casement window. She complained with high-pitched mewls as she stared outside.

Farzan charged into his bedroom with his duffel bag. Wherever he was going, he needed a couple days' worth of clothes, plus his toiletries. He emptied the contents of the duffel bag into the hamper and went to his dresser to grab underwear, socks, and T-shirts—just the stuff he could decide upon quickly. A clowder of alley cats surrounding the house couldn't be a good thing.

A feline shriek knifed through the apartment. It sounded like Bella was being torn limb from limb. Farzan rushed out to the living space.

The cat was in her same place by the window. She looked entirely unharmed. He stared at Bella. What the hell was wrong with her?

A fist shattered through the window panel of the door, and an arm groped through and twisted the knob. Before Farzan could pitch a breath, the door burst open, and a spotted jaguar plunged into the apartment.

He backed up against a bookcase. The werejaguar—150 pounds of muscled fur, claws and fangs—locked in on him. Its long, spotted tail swung like a whip. Thoughts raced through Farzan's head. He had looked up on the internet what to do when confronted by a big cat. Don't play dead or try to run away. Stare back, make noise—anything to try to look too big and dangerous for the thing to attack. He looked into the jaguar's menacing eyes and shouted, half in English, half in Farsi.

"Madar jeneh. Get the fuck out of here. Torke jinn. I'll kill you torke pedersag."

The werejaguar didn't flinch. A low growl rose up from its bearded throat and pitched higher into a humid, fang-bearing snarl. Maybe bluffing worked on wild cats, but it didn't work on werecats. The beast was going to shred him with its claws and clamp down on a major artery. Farzan reached for the biggest object on the bookcase: his anatomy textbook, and he hurled it at the cat's head.

The cat sprung out of the way, and the book just clipped its hind leg. Farzan rifled more ammunition: a dictionary and his hardcover Harry Potter collection. The cat dodged the first two books, and then *The Prisoner of Azkaban* connected with its muzzle, inciting a vicious growl. There wasn't much hardcover ammunition left, and Farzan had no route to escape. If he tried to run off in any direction, he'd be buried by the werejaguar.

Then he heard Bella's feisty caterwaul. The tiger-striped tabby lunged from the kitchen onto the jaguar's head.

The werejaguar spun around to fight her off. The coffee table went skidding aside, and the living room turned into a squall of fur and lashing claws. Bella was a fraction of the big animal's size, but she had it backing away from her. Unfortunately, that positioned the raging jaguar nearer to Farzan.

Farzan grasped a plan. He waited until it was inches from him, and then he pried his hands behind the bookshelf and put all his strength into pulling it away from the wall so that it would fall on top of the jaguar. Two hundred pounds of Ikea compressed wood, stocked with eight crates of comic books and four shelves of sci-fi paperbacks, buried the animal. The werejaguar was stunned motionless. Gradually, its body twitched weakly beneath the mountain of debris, and Bella climbed on top, sniffing for life and settling like the victress atop her opponent. Farzan stepped around the disaster area. The werejaguar wasn't going anywhere for a while.

He jumped at the sound of a voice from the doorway. "What the hell?"

Farzan swung around. It was Sammy. His older brother's pudgy face was ashen in disbelief.

"What are you doing here?" Farzan said.

"I stayed back to drive up with you. I thought you might be tired after working all night."

Farzan swiped the elbow of his sleeve over his sweaty face. If he had come home just a few minutes later, the werejaguar might have busted into the house and attacked Sammy on account of his rare whim of brotherly generosity. Farzan softened a bit, considering that he could use some help.

"We need a sedative. Valium, morphine, something like that."

"Ketamine?"

"Fine. And bring one of Baba's syringes that he uses for insulin."

Sammy started out the door to retrieve the stuff from upstairs. It wasn't any secret he bought prescriptions over the internet to sell them to college students. Not that Farzan approved, but when it came to shady situations, Sammy could be counted on to not ask questions.

He remembered something and called after his brother. "Grab the old carrying case. The one Maman used to take her poodle to the vet." Farzan went back into his apartment and exchanged a glance with Bella, who was still sitting atop the wreckage, smoothing out her battle-ruffled fur with her pink, sandpaper tongue. After he and Sammy drugged the werejaguar and dropped its body somewhere, they needed to get upstate to make sure everyone was safe. It wouldn't be a

bad idea to bring Bella along.

NINETEEN

JACKS AWOKE TO a disorienting scene. Besides the bed being much bigger than the one he remembered at the Primrose Guest House, its furnishings were luxurious. Six downy pillows, soft cotton sheets, and a down comforter. Had he tele-ported overnight to a five-star hotel? The room had gleaming, dark wood paneled walls, ceiling moldings, a big, flat screen TV mounted on the wall across from him, and a glass pitcher with water and a silver ice bucket on the table by his bed. It was air-conditioned to perfection and smelled freshly clean.

Jacks slung his legs over the bedside and smiled through a facepalm as the previous night came back to him. For someone who had skipped the country on a fake passport and had a couple hundred dollars to his name, he supposed he could have woken up in a lot worse places.

When Maarten's cabin boy, Willem, had shown him to the bedroom, the room had been dark, and Jacks had been physically and mentally drained. He'd managed to strip off his sneakers, jeans and shirt before climbing into bed and promptly passing out. Now, he noticed the floor-to-ceiling curtains drawn over what he guessed must be a window that stretched the length of the wall. He stepped over in his socks and briefs to take a look.

Parting the curtains, he saw a blue-gray ocean beneath a flawless blue sky splayed out before him. He opened the sliding door and stepped out on a furnished balcony for two, above the side deck of Maarten's yacht.

The sunlight felt glorious against his skin, and the endless seascape made him feel like an adventurer. Then he noticed a faint trail of music and warbly crescendos of playful chatter from below. People were gathered at the stern deck, which was hidden from his angle.

He went back into the room and found his cell phone on the nightstand. The clock read 11:14 a.m. There was still no service, and the battery was drained down to a red sliver.

He had to get a cell phone charger. Or find another phone that got Wi-Fi. He ached thinking about Farzan worrying. Not that it was his fault he'd ended up in the middle of the ocean with no cell service, but he had to explain that to Farzan and make sure he and Bella were okay.

Jacks considered throwing on his jeans and shirt from last night, but he was anxious to get downstairs and figured, based on what he had seen of Maarten and his guests, no one would be scandalized by him walking around in his black briefs. He actually might fit in better. He quickly checked himself out in the mirror. His body had filled out considerably since his trans-formation, and his underwear was clean. He peeled off his socks, grabbed his phone, and stepped out to an unfamiliar hallway.

The music from the stern deck was faint, but he could follow it. He found his way to the open gallery above the loungy hall of the main deck and took a staircase down. Then he traipsed through the passage to the stern deck Maarten had led him through the night before.

Outside, he halted for a moment, squinting from the shock of sun that glared brutally from every surface of the deck. As his eyes adjusted, he took in the scene in fragments. A pair of guys he recognized from last night were picking food from an enormous buffet. Others were stretched out on the cushioned platform in designer bathing suits, curled up together on the chaise lounges, and chatting over plates of food at a mahogany, half-moon bar. Jacks's arrival prompted a glance or two, but they soon went back to their preoccupations.

He walked over to the nearest guest, who was sucking the meat from a crab claw at the bar. It was the hulking guy who had offered Jacks a seat between his legs on the cuddle couch, and in the daylight, wearing only a fuchsia sarong, his heaving chest looked like it could repel bullets.

"Have you seen Maarten?" Jacks said.

The guy looked up at Jacks, swallowed his crab meat, and wiped his lips with his big hand. "Good morning."

"Good morning. Sorry, I didn't mean to be rude. I'm Jacks. I came aboard last night."

His companion belched. "I remember." He passed an amused look to his friends at the bar.

Jacks's smile deflated. "Um, is Maarten around?"

"Haven't seen him." The guy took up another crab claw from his plate.

Jacks looked out to the deck and waved his cell phone. "Anyone have a charger?"

No one answered. They didn't even look in his direction.

"Anyone have a phone?"

They were pretending he wasn't there. Jacks's face burned. He felt like a total idiot, and coming down in his briefs had been a horrible idea. Everyone was in stylish beachwear, and they were sun-bronzed while his bare body was vampiric pale. Normally, he would have written them off as a bunch of stuck-up assholes. But he had finally found others of his kind, and somehow he still didn't fit in. What did they think was so wrong with him?

Someone came up behind him. He turned and saw Maarten, who was outfitted for sunbathing in snug, thigh-length, striped trunks.

"Good morning, Jacks. How did you sleep?"

Jacks itched his head. "Great. Thanks for putting me up in a room. But I need to make a phone call."

Maarten raised his voice. "Have you met my friends?" He pointed people out, and they waved half-heartedly in turn. "This is Kwame, Nicolas, Somsuea, Thierry, Lars, Jean-Luc, and César." The only name that stuck for Jacks was Kwame, the big guy in a sarong with whom he had tried talking at the bar.

"Are you hungry?" Before Jacks could answer, Maarten called out in Dutch to a man behind the bar. It was the cabin boy, a young guy with close-cropped, platinum-dyed hair, wearing a tidy, white polo shirt, and ironed khaki shorts.

"Willem will make you a plate from the buffet. What do you drink? We have every kind of liquor, coffee, calf's milk —"

"Water is fine. But I really need to make a call." Jacks rattled the phone in his hand. "I'm almost out of battery and not getting service."

Maarten regarded Jacks's phone like it was a tacky novelty. "Such a nuisance, aren't they? None of us keep them. But I'm sure you could borrow one from one of the staff."

Jacks searched around the deck hopefully, but Willem had disappeared, and he didn't see anyone else who looked like staff.

Maarten clasped Jacks's shoulders with both of his strong

hands and massaged his tightly wound muscles. "Relax. After breakfast, you can phone whoever you want. The captain even has a laptop you can use to check your email. When we make port in Trinidad, you can see about getting your cell phone fixed."

Jacks didn't need his cell phone fixed; he just needed a charger. Before he could explain that to Maarten, he doubled back to Maarten's statement.

"Trinidad? How far is that?"

"We'll be there by tomorrow night."

He felt like the floor beneath him was giving way. His luggage was sitting in the guest house back in Barbados. He had no idea what they would do with it if he didn't check out by noon or pay up for another night. While Jacks explained this, Maarten looked entirely unimpressed.

"I've got to go back to Barbados. I don't even have a change of clothes."

"We'll phone the guest house. You can pay up the room for the week and have your luggage retrieved by messenger."

Jacks leaned forward, confidentially. "I don't have that kind of money."

"I do."

Jacks didn't like the idea of Maarten paying. More importantly, he needed to get back to Barbados in case the bank called about transferring Benoit's holdings. But what could he do? He couldn't make some rude scene and insist they turn the boat around.

Maarten wrapped his arm around him and directed him farther out on the deck toward the dining area. "Meanwhile, we have plenty of swimsuits that you can borrow. But first: You eat."

They descended some steps to one of the dining tables, set with a white tablecloth and fancy napkins in metal rings.

Jacks's tension lifted a bit. Maybe Maarten knew what was best. Barbados could be swarming with the Glaring after the strays had witnessed last night's scene. Jacks still had over three weeks until the bank would let him into Benoit's safety deposit box. He just needed to call Farzan, and he could do that after breakfast.

By night, Maarten was suave perfection. That morning, sitting across the table from Jacks, with his arms stretched behind his neck, he seemed more real. His lion's mane of thick brown hair was untended and a bit misshapen. He pried a grain of sleep out of the corner of his eye and flicked it overboard. The sunlight showed the whiskers on his chin and jawline, spare in places. These things fed his fascination. Maarten was an overgrown kid, a pampered prince, and his lack of self-consciousness was disarming.

Apropos of nothing, Maarten leaned back in a chuckle that made his honey-colored ribcage shudder. Jacks wondered if Maarten ever worried about anything.

"I don't think your friends like me too much," Jacks said.

Maarten pshawed.

"Your sister doesn't like me."

"Annika can be a bit protective about who we take into our fold."

"Is that what's happening? You're taking me into your fold?" Jacks looked out to the sea. "Or am I being held for bounty?"

"If you prefer, we could have you bound and gagged."

"I think your friends would prefer it."

Maarten sat up a bit. "I wouldn't mind seeing you bound and gagged. Do you like S&M?"

Jacks scoffed, though he had never really given it much thought.

"Spanking?"

"You don't stop, do you?"

Maarten's sapphire eyes glimmered. "Tell me about the wildest sex you ever had."

Jacks once had a threesome with Jonathan and their philosophy TA. Sex with Benoit had been superlative, but he wasn't sure where talking about such things would lead with Maarten. "Nothing too wild. I guess I'm pretty dull."

Maarten made a long face. "Are you feeling sorry for yourself, Jacks? Among so many gorgeous creatures?"

"Yeah. It's obvious I don't fit in. Or is everyone pissed at me because of what happened last night?"

"You fit in, Jacks." Maarten's eyes passed over his bare shoulders and torso. "You could use some color, and what is it Americans say? To loosen your attitude?" He peered over his shoulder at the guys lounging around the deck, and he slid forward so he could lean across the table. "I'll tell you a secret. I fucked every one of them."

Jacks blinked.

"Sometimes, all on the same night." Maarten's arm disappeared beneath the table, and Jacks felt a hand on his knee. "Do you like being fucked, or do you like to do the fucking?"

Jacks made a face more reproachful than he was feeling. "I'm not in the mood for either, if that's what you're asking. A man just died last night a few steps from where we're sitting."

"Yes, I remember a time when it wasn't pleasant witnessing such a thing. But you'll discover the world goes on. I'd be happy he was killed before he killed me, and this is exactly my point. You need to lighten up. We're only talking about sex. It's fun to talk about, isn't it?"

It seemed to Jacks he had good reason to not feel loose or light, but he couldn't decide on what to say. Meanwhile, Maarten slid his hand up his thigh, squeezing playfully. "So, what is it? Do you dream of being on all fours with a queue of men taking turns filling your rump with their cocks? Or would you like it better with their hairy ankles on your shoulders, pounding their arseholes one after the other?"

Jacks glanced away. Was he being uptight? Maarten had a point about counting his blessings, and they were only talking about sex. "Recently, I've been kind of versatile."

"Recently?"

"I started seeing someone."

"I remember now. You mentioned a boyfriend. A primmy, wasn't it?"

"What's a primmy?"

"It's what we call humans. Short for primates."

Jacks frowned.

"There's no shame in it," Maarten went on. "Primmies can be hot, if you find the right one. We've all taken them to bed from time to time." He fixed on Jacks. "So, it's a new relationship. Have the two of you been fucking each other silly?"

Jacks laughed. He didn't mention he and Farzan had only slept together once. He was glad Maarten wasn't judging him. He wasn't like Benoit. He certainly wasn't like Bernard. They came from totally different worlds, but he was the kind of guy Jacks would've liked to be friends with if they had met just normally, like at a bar.

Willem brought over a tray of food—steak tartare topped with a soft-boiled quail egg, some very rare lamb chops, and a quartet of tuna sashimi. Jacks's mouth watered. His body craved protein, and ever since his transformation, he preferred his meat rare, even better if it was uncooked. He looked around the table. There was no silverware.

Maarten watched Jacks, bemused, and then he scooped up a swath of the minced meat with his finger and plunged it into his mouth. Jacks picked up a piece of fish with his index finger and thumb and ate it in two bites. It was fresh and delicious, the best raw fish he had ever eaten. He picked up another piece and chewed it in one mouthful, and then he fed himself from the platter briskly.

"It's delicious," he said, between chews. Remembering his manners, he gestured to the plate while there was still some food on it. "You want some?"

Maarten waved his hand for him to go ahead.

After Jacks swallowed down the last lamb chop, Maarten leaned across the table again. He wiped the crease of Jacks's mouth and licked drippings of blood from his finger.

Jacks sat back, while his overfilled stomach throbbed. "How long have you guys been..." Jacks glanced around the boat. "Doing this?"

"My first ship was built in 1987. This one is a recent upgrade," Maarten rapped his knuckles on the fiberglass hull. "German engineering. Just five years old."

1987 was two years before Jacks was born. Maarten looked to be only a few years older than himself, but he had learned that werecats aged much more slowly than humans. "So what do you do? Just sail around the world?"

"Just sail around the world," Maarten said with a smile.

"If you don't mind me asking...this ship is insane. How do you afford the lifestyle?"

"Annika and I have some investments in Cape Town."

"Is that where you grew up?"

Maarten lost a bit of his glow, but he recovered with his signature confidence. "That's where we escaped from."

"How do you mean?"

"We haven't been back in over twenty years. Too much politics and fighting and all that nonsense."

Jacks wondered if he was talking about the struggle over Apartheid. Though he was too young to have seen the actual events in the news, he had grown up inspired by the story of

Nelson Mandela and his victory over racial injustice. Based on their light skin and features, Jacks guessed that Maarten and Annika were mixed-race. He asked Maarten: "Was your family Afrikaner?"

"On our mother's side."

"So, what happened? Why did you leave South Africa?"

Maarten looked off in the distance for a moment. He came back to Jacks with a tone of finality. "It's not a very interesting story."

Jacks suspected it was a very interesting story. But he had hit a nerve, and he let it go. Somewhere between a question and a statement, Jacks said: "You know the Glaring."

"We've crossed paths from time to time."

He shifted in his seat. "So, am I a goner? You said they're trying to make an example of me."

"After last night, that's clear. But they know better than to bother me. You're safe here."

"I appreciate that. But I can't be running from them for the rest of my life. Do they have a leader? If I could explain my situation...I don't know...is it possible I could make them understand I'm not a traitor? Killing Benoit was my only option."

Maarten looked at him in amusement. "You're expecting to make an appeal? They don't exactly operate according to a United Nations charter."

A thought came back to Jacks. "I don't get it. Benoit told me there was a time when werecats and humans coexisted peacefully. If the Glaring is so proud of their heritage, that ought to mean something to them, shouldn't it?"

"You're assuming the werecats hunting you are rational, when they're actually idiots. They blame humans for the massacre of the old traditions, but they answer back with the same wanton violence. It's an imitation of the species they loathe. War, terrorism, genocide. There's no hope for humankind nor werecatkind. That's why we've chosen a different path."

That was intriguing to Jacks for a moment. "I've got to find my path, too. Suppose I wanted to try to get through to them."

"You'd be charting a short course for yourself, but you could try. They have a capitán of sorts. He goes by the name Tepe."

He gazed at Maarten eagerly. Maarten heaved a sigh. "You would have to find him, and he's rumored to be secluded in a remote region of the Amazon. There are werejaguars and were-ocelots that would much sooner kill you than let you speak with Tepe. And even if you found him, he would probably kill you himself rather than entertain a conversation. Why risk that when you don't have to?"

It certainly did sound dangerous, pretty much a suicide mission. But what options did Jacks have?

"You've got a life here," he told Maarten. "I'm trying to make one too."

"It's not that difficult, Jacks." Maarten gestured grandly with his hands. "You see how we live. We do what we want, whenever we want. It's a party that never ends. And it's by select invitation."

Jacks would have been lying to himself if he said it wasn't an appealing offer. He'd been drawn to the idea since the night he'd stumbled on Maarten's yacht, and Maarten had been giving him plenty of signals he'd like Jacks to stay on. Still, he didn't know if he could trust a werecat. He'd made that mistake with Benoit.

"Do you kill primmies?" he said.

Maarten chuckled mildly. "Such a humanitarian, you are. Well, I promise you, you'll fit right in. We couldn't be bothered to kill primmies."

Jacks studied Maarten, weighing his decision to make a

confession. "I felt the urge to kill. Not for the same reasons as the Glaring, but it's like this temptation. It came over me back in New York, when I was defending myself from a street gang. But I saw Benoit murder a defenseless man just because he had the bad luck to be in his territory, and I don't want to be like that."

"That killing instinct is part of you now. It's who we are." Maarten brought out his silver snuff box. "But there are ways to take the edge off. To redirect our nocturnal energies to other things."

He remembered the guys curled up together on the high-backed couch last night. Maarten went on. "We are plenty capable of defending ourselves, but there's no need to draw attention to our happy little pride by hunting human prey. We live and let live."

Jacks sat back in his seat with his arms outstretched on the back of his cushioned bench. He could be safe for the rest of his life on a luxury yacht with a group of guys who looked like international models. Maybe he could ask Farzan to join him. Then they would both be safe. Though Farzan would have to give up medical school. He would have to give up his family and his entire life. Was it even possible for Farzan to live among Maarten's pride?

"Your staff, they're human," Jacks said. "How does that work?"

"Annika handles them. There are background checks, legal documents, all that sort of thing."

"What happens when they leave?"

"They're bound to NDAs. We've never had a problem. They're paid well, and they know the consequences of indiscretion."

Jacks peered over at Willem, who was standing behind the bar. The young man's expression was even and attentive. He

200 ANDREW J. PETERS

didn't look to be nervous in any way about catering to half-wild, half-human creatures.

Maarten followed his look with a grin. "You're into primate trade?"

He fumbled to answer. That wasn't why he had been watching Willem, but there was some truth there. He liked Farzan.

"Anything can be arranged," Maarten said.

"No. Really. No."

Maarten laughed. It was contagious. Jacks realized he had just made his first werecat friend.

FARZAN STEPPED OUT to the front deck of his parents' cabin in the Catskills. The tall pine forest that surrounded the house was darkening at twilight. Raindrops thrummed on the tin eave above his head. Farzan's nephews and nieces were inside, playing board games. Baba and Sammy were watching some soccer tournament on the old fossil of a TV set in the living room while Maman washed the dinner dishes. He couldn't get interested in any of those activities. He just wanted to check his phone again, outside of the cabin, where he had gotten reception before.

The sight of the blank screen tore at him, for something like the hundredth time. No missed calls. No text messages. Farzan hunched in a corner of the deck, away from the front door, and he replayed the single voice mail Jacks had left him.

"Hey. My cell conked out, and I don't have my charger. I'm borrowing a phone from a friend. Just wanted to let you know I'm okay. I met up with some people, and I'm taking a trip off the island. I'll call you—"

The message fizzled into static, and then it cut out.

Farzan had played it over and over, studying every cadence

of Jacks's voice. He sounded so infuriatingly casual, but maybe there was more to his message that got eaten up by static and lost in the poor connection. Had Jacks tried to say how much he missed him? Had he bothered to ask if everything was okay back home? How could Jacks be so careless, so inconsiderate, leaving out without his cell phone charger after Farzan had been attacked by a wereleopard just the other night? There wasn't even a number for his "friend's" phone. The call came up with an ID block.

Farzan shoved the phone into the pocket of his track pants. What was he supposed to think? Jacks could be in trouble, but he didn't sound like he was in trouble. He was taking "a trip off the island," out and about with "people he met," enjoying himself.

Tears bled from Farzan's sinuses, and a rush of vertigo sent him swaying forward. He gripped the railing and clenched his eyes to stop himself from crying. He had to keep it together in front of his family. They thought Jacks was just away for a week, visiting his parents in Pennsylvania. Except for Sammy, they didn't know why Jacks needed to leave town. His family didn't know Jacks was Farzan's boyfriend. That would be an uncomfortable enough revelation without mentioning Jacks was embroiled in some uprising of feline shapeshifters. Especially now that stories were coming out about what had happened in New York City.

Seventy-eight people had been killed and ninety injured in big cat attacks throughout the five boroughs. The same night, similar attacks occurred in Boston, Philadelphia, and Washington, D.C. There had been press conferences with the mayor and the police commissioner and interviews with military spokespeople and wildlife experts.

No one had any reasonable explanation for the incidents. They were "exploring" some kind of terrorist plot. New York

City was under curfew while the National Guard took over the streets, and special military ops searched for the cats in parks. News stations showed reporters talking to residents, some of whom were disgruntled, but mostly they were spooked. Not a single animal had been found. The authorities didn't understand the creatures that were responsible could blend into the population.

The only good news was there had been no reports of attacks since the night he'd worked at the E.R. Maybe the werecats had left when they heard the military was being deployed. Or maybe they were gathering more numbers for a second wave.

Farzan stared out angrily at the dank forest with its light patter of rain and phantom sounds of pine boughs creaking under the precipitation. Cold fearlessness rose up in him. He wished one of the werecats would appear. There was an ax in the cabin for cutting wood, and he felt capable of taking one of the monsters down. Then, he would have proof to show his family, proof for the authorities. How else could he explain to people what was really happening? His father and his brothers fell silent and meandered away from the TV when their stupid soccer tournament was interrupted by the news bulletins. The mention of terrorism had switched them into denial mode. Farzan understood their fear. It didn't matter what was causing the attacks. Anyone resembling an Arab would be looked at with suspicion while terrorism was on people's minds.

He had to do something. The thought of going back into the cabin, pretending nothing was happening, sent needles working through his chest. It wasn't just his responsibility. Jacks was supposed to be figuring out how the Glaring worked, and how to call them off from their killing spree. These attacks were the work of his "people."

The cabin's screen door creaked open. Farzan saw Bella

coming out to the deck. He had been keeping her restricted to the cabin so she wouldn't run away, but he held back from scaring her back in. Bella sidled around the open space, surveying her surroundings. Did she know something about the Glaring? Did she know what happened to Jacks?

He spoke to her in a whisper. "Where's Jacks?"

She bent her ears back, and then she wandered over inscrutably. She rubbed her striped muzzle against his ankles.

Farzan scooped her up from under her forelegs and held her at eye level. They stared at each other, Bella dangling in his hands, as though they were playing a child's game to see who would look away first. Farzan concentrated and imagined he could penetrate her mind. *Is Jacks in trouble? Do we need to get down there to help him?*

The cat purred in his arms, never breaking eye contact, and her yellow-green eyes flashed. The answer was strong and sure in Farzan's heart, whether it had just needed time to gel or something more miraculous had occurred. Farzan gave Bella a peck on her furry head and set her down on the porch.

"I never thought I'd say this, but I'm starting to like you."

Farzan knew then what he needed to do. He would take his car and drive to the nearest airport. All the New York City airports had been shut down to control traffic into the city, but he could try getting a flight from Hartford or Albany and figure out an itinerary to Barbados. It might take a couple of days and a good amount of his savings, but he and Bella would find Jacks.

TWENTY

THEY DOCKED AT Port-of-Spain in Trinidad after midnight, and Jacks went into town with Maarten and his friends. The city center was a delightful cacophony of sounds and sights. Street performers beat tribal rhythms on goatskin drums. Reggae and Caribbean jazz blared from open air bars and restaurants. Indian ladies in yellow saris paraded down the main street, and, along its banks, dancers in bright, African-patterned costumes stomped and spun on makeshift wood board stages. Rowdy tourists clogged nearly every open space. The air felt charged and unstable, like at a Halloween parade.

Maarten's group caroused through it all, three and four astride, with their arms thrown over each other's shoulders, weaving, howling, and passing back and forth an earthen jug of milk-punch spiked with rum. The other guys had warmed up to him. How it had happened, Jacks wasn't sure. Some of them didn't speak English very well, which explained their standoff-ishness to an extent. Jacks was happy to be included now and didn't question it particularly.

Kwame and César shouldered Jacks along as they navigated

a route to some nightclub Maarten claimed was the best in town, though he seemed to take a new path at every intersection. They never found any posh nightclub and could have been retracing their steps in a maze of narrow streets and retail stalls. None of the guys really cared. They were all glad for the chance to roam on land. Whenever the someone broke out in laughter, Kwame explained the funny story to Jacks in English.

Jacks asked Kwame something that had been on his mind. "So, you all found each other." He fumbled with his wording. "Is there some connection between feline shapeshifters and gay men?"

Kwame and César exchanged an amused glance.

"It is said that eight out of ten werecats are male, and nine out of ten of them prefer males." Kwame gave Jacks a brotherly squeeze of his neck. "The feline god is good."

To be part of a community that both embraced its feline nature and its gayness was pretty amazing to Jacks "Why do you think that is?"

César chimed in. "It's the principle of moderation. If werecats were heterosexual, we'd be reproducing millions of our kind over time and overtaking every other species."

"So, it's like a natural selection, genetic thing?"

"Si, claro. The gay gene and the werecat gene are both on the Y chromosome."

"But not one hundred percent of the time." Jacks was thinking about Bernard, whose male scent repelled him, and Annika.

"Yes, it happens." César threw in some swagger. "Though I've never met a male werecat who wasn't open to fooling around with a little persuasion. It's the same way with wild cats."

Kwame regarded his friend reproachfully. "That's one theory, but there are others. Some say queer men are best suited to embody dual souls because we are born with the gift of shifting between worlds. The masculine and the feminine."

Jacks liked that theory. César, meanwhile, scowled. "You old vejestorios like to believe that. But science will prove that there's a genetic explanation."

The two bantered back and forth, both of them a bit tipsy. Jacks didn't know that much about their histories, but he remembered César bragging about his youth. He was curious about the generational differences among their kind.

The pathway in front of them emptied, and the city noise faded as they wandered farther from the center of town. Colorful boutiques and street vendors gave way to darkened lanes and boxy, tin-roofed homes. Maarten still insisted they were headed in the right direction. Jacks didn't know the city to question his judgment, though it seemed increasingly unlikely.

Mongrel dogs with their fur drawn tight over their ribs skirred away from them, stealing wary glances at the group. Kwame turned to one of the mutts, curled up his lip, and stretched his mouth into a terrifying lion's roar that sent the frightened thing scampering away with its tail between its legs. Everyone laughed, but as their laughter fell away, the neighborhood sharpened into focus.

Shed-like homes were tightly packed on tiny plots of dusty earth. Their yards were filled with garbage and stripped-down cars and unidentifiable mechanical equipment. It looked like an endless junkyard.

In the shadows, dark-skinned boys in soccer shirts stared at Maarten's entourage. Their designer graphic tees, expensive jeans, and fine leather sandals—things that Jacks himself had borrowed to wear— were worth more than the houses where the boys lived. At street corners, groups of men with their shirts stuffed into the backs of their pants swigged beer bottles in paper bags. Their conversations stopped when Maarten's group passed by. There were no women anywhere.

Jacks gained up on Maarten, who was leading their pack. "Hey, I think we should turn back."

Maarten chuckled. He was drunk on rum and high on his special snuff. "I'm telling you, it's just a little bit up ahead."

Jacks glanced at the Trinidadian men on the streetside. He could see in their faces a hardened sense of territoriality and disdain. If they tried something, the situation could easily spin out of control. "Let's try one of the bars we passed in town."

Maarten let out a plaintive huff. He deliberated with his friends in French. Meanwhile, Jacks noticed a cluster of boys who must have been following them down the street. They looked too young to be walking around unattended in this part of town, though the whole scene was unfamiliar to him. Jacks watched them nudge forward from their group a skinny kid with bulging eyes.

He barely filled out his striped soccer shirt and shorts, and he had knobby, dark-skinned legs. The boy sported an entrepreneurial grin beyond his years and approached Maarten.

"You American? Français? Deutsche? I show you around town. You like pretty girls? Caribbean rum? I show you all the best places."

Maarten snorted in amusement, and his friends fell out in laughter.

The boy kept smiling, undeterred. "I show you pretty boys too."

"We don't need anyone to help us find pretty boys," Maarten said.

"You like music? I take you to a very good club in town. All the best Caribbean music: steel drums, horns." The boy leaned in confidentially. "You like drugs? I find you some."

Maarten winced. The rest of the group scowled and muttered complaints to each other in French and Spanish. The guys from the neighborhood had a firm eye on the exchange, and they puffed out their chests, ready to intervene if something happened to one of their own. Jacks thought he had only seen five or six before, and now there were twice as many.

The boy kept trying with Maarten. "You like private parties?" The boy gestured to his friends on the side of the street. "You take your pick of all the best-looking Caribbean boys. They like European men." Ignored by Maarten, he turned to Somsuea. "These boys will do anything to show a handsome Chinaman a good time."

Somsuea was Thai, not Chinese. With sudden force, he shoved the boy in the chest. The boy stumbled backwards and fell down on his behind. Maarten and his friends erupted with laughter. Jacks glanced anxiously around. The Trinidadians had multiplied in numbers, and some of them hid in their hands what looked like switchblades.

Two packs of men closed in on them from either side. They spit out swear words and clenched their fists. It had probably been their plan all along to ambush the group, and now they had even more reason to do it. They didn't know who they were dealing with. They didn't know they would all be killed when Maarten and the others transformed.

The boy got up on his feet and shouted to the approaching mob. "You saw what these pervert foreigners tried to do? They wanted to take us home with them so they could drug us and do their nasty faggot business."

Three of the Trinidadians swaggered toward Somsuea. Their faces and chests were slick with sweat, and their eyes sparked red with malice. The front man brandished a box cutter. A low, collective growl rose up from Maarten's group. They were readying to strike out with claws and fangs.

Jacks rounded Somsuea in a hurry and did the only thing he could think of to intervene. He bore down mightily on the magical spot in his diaphragm. In a blink, he was a mountain lion, crouching on his hind legs.

He pounced on the guy at the fore of the attacking trio, knocking him down and pinning him to the street with his big paws on the guy's shoulders. He swept a ferocious glare around the mob and snarled.

The men held their hands in front of them and gingerly backed away. Jacks fixed in on one of the guys who was watching streetside, paralyzed, and he bared his teeth and drew out a sinister growl. The guy bolted into the backyard of a house, and then everyone scattered into the night, gasping and shouting like they had seen a demon.

Jacks stepped off the guy underfoot, and the man scrambled to his feet and scurried after the crowd. Maarten and his friends were quiet for a moment, and then they broke out in hysterics.

Jacks noticed Annika eyeing him peculiarly. He had lost track of her once again amid the livelier members of Maarten's crew, but their eyes locked for a moment. She appeared to be adding up things lost on the rest of the guys.

Maarten morphed into a hulking white lion with a downy mane, and the other guys reared up in lion shape and Somsuea burst into an orange and black-striped tiger. Maarten gazed over the group, and then he set off down the street at a gallop. Everyone followed, including Jacks and Annika at the rear, morphed into a lioness. They bounded through the deserted streets, accelerating, mouths open, huffing up freedom, an invulnerable pack laying claim to the night.

AFTER TRINIDAD, THEY stopped at the mountain-peaked island of Margarita. After Margarita, there was Bonaire, Caraçao, and Aruba. When Jacks casually mentioned he had always wanted to see the Panama Canal, Maarten told his crew to take them farther west, and they cruised through the lush, green-banked channel all the way to Panama City.

Every day began with a hearty brunch of freshly prepared raw meat and fish on the deck, and then there was sunbathing, and cold milk and rum over dominoes, and long, luxurious naps, which Jacks took alone while the other guys snuggled together in twos or threes or more. When the guys were feeling more ambitious, Jacks would join them for a dive off the stern deck to splash around or go snorkeling. At a sparkling coral reef off the coast of Belize, Kwame taught Jacks how to spearfish.

Nights were excursions at a new port, exploring little seaside towns, and finding beachside bars with local musicians. When everything in town closed for the night, Maarten's gang would prowl the deserted streets just stretching their legs and joking around. They would stay out until the rising sun washed away the shadows, and the chatter of birds filled the air. By morning light, they were back in the boat, snoozing until noon or later.

After the close call in Port-of-Spain, Jacks had worried about other confrontations while at port. Quickly, those worries fell away. Maarten and his friends were almost always groggy and agreeable, drunk or high on that substance in Maarten's coiled horn device. Unless they were pushed, as they were in Trinidad, none of them had any interest in violence.

In fact, their interest didn't seem to venture beyond their own exclusive group. At first, it fascinated Jacks how they could go from place to place so unaware, so uncaring about the existence of other people. Humans were merely objects to navigate around, or like their crew, interchangeable dealers in services:

the store clerks, the bartenders, the port wardens. No one got a hello, a thank you, or a tip. Jacks thought it was rude initially, but he caught on, it was more than that. For Maarten's pride, other people were just part of the scenery. No one would ever guess it, but some of the guys were a hundred or more years old. They had seen people come and invariably go. They were over it, and the only relationships that mattered were with each other. More and more, Jacks was feeling the same way. He was having the time of his life.

His only moments of unease came when they were away from land, cruising through the night. In the ground-floor cabin, Maarten would program whatever music he favored at the time — electronica or downbeat rap or ambient, always something with a hypnotic beat. The ship's crew would disappear to their quarters, and all the guys would gather in the lounge with its overhead red fluorescents and spectral chandelier, and sprawl out on the oversized couch. They would recline against each other, and gradually an open-mouthed kiss would pass from one to the other and another. That's when Jacks would make some excuse to call it a night, though part of him longed to participate.

Those were the nights when Jacks thought about Farzan and felt like a bastard. He remembered how happy Farzan was when they decided to be boyfriends. Jacks had been happy too. Farzan was so damn sweet and funny and cute *and* he'd saved Jacks's ass when he had nowhere to go. Though somehow Jacks hadn't been able to bring himself to call Farzan since the one time he had borrowed the boat phone to leave a voicemail. He always told himself he'd call him soon. He just didn't want to miss out on what the other guys were up to, and if he was honest with himself, he was shy about mentioning Farzan. His new friends might think it was weird and juvenile to have a human boyfriend.

Stepping away from the cuddle pile one night, Jacks caught the date on a digital wall clock. That call to Farzan had been over three weeks ago. He lost his stride, standing reefed at the foot of the stairs to the upper floor. He felt oddly apart from himself.

He'd never meant to be the kind of person who selfishly hurts someone they care about. Jacks still didn't want to believe he was that guy. The thing was, the past three weeks had been a revelation. He'd found his tribe, people who didn't fit into human society, and they didn't give a shit, which Farzan couldn't understand. He didn't want to blow off Farzan, he just didn't know how to explain things. His stomach burned. Probably, Farzan hated him now that he'd fucked things up so bad.

A voice roused Jacks from his thoughts. "Why is it that you're always leaving just when the fun begins?"

It was Maarten. He had crept up surprisingly near. His golden shoulders, chest, and stomach were laid bare by his discarded shirt, and his drawstring linen pants rode low, halfway down his hips. Jacks swiped his face, trying to pull himself together.

"I think I know what you're going through," Maarten said.

Jacks zoned in. He didn't know what he was going through himself. Outside opinions were entirely welcome.

Maarten clasped his shoulder with his big hand. "This must be a lot, being around your own kind for the first time in your life." A smile blazed across his face. "But it's wonderful Jacks, isn't it? There's a world for us, and we create the rules. There are no impossibilities, no limits. We are the present. The past doesn't matter. The future is whatever we want it to be."

"I was thinking about Farzan. I kind of shit all over him. He's probably worried sick that something happened to me."

"Do you want to call him?"

"I do. I just don't know what to say."

"When was the last time you spoke to him?"

Jacks glanced away. "About three weeks ago."

Maarten studied him with rare sobriety. "That should be telling you something."

"What do you mean?"

"It's not in your nature to be monogamous. You can have your favorites, but you can't deny what's inside here."

Maarten closed his hand over the spot below his diaphragm. It was a shockingly erotic sensation, warm pressure on the hidden place that enabled his feline transformation. Jacks eased away from Maarten, though not so far.

"I feel like such an asshole."

"That's because you're holding on to old ideas of who you are. Cats are wild, Jacks. We're at the apex of this world." Maarten stepped near again and fondly raked the scruff of his neck. "You won't believe how exquisite life can be when you accept that."

Maarten's scent was strong, beckoning, an odor in which Jacks could lose himself. The glands on his neck swelled and ached. They wanted to rub against skin and fur. He wanted to share his scent and have his body covered in the scents of other men.

Maarten brought out his silver horn snuff box from his pants pocket. He unclipped it and took a long sniff. The silver horn dangled in front of Jacks's face. "Try some. It will take that gloomy edge off of you."

Jacks took the horn in his hand. Maybe Maarten was right. He needed an escape. Holding the uncapped horn to one nostril, he took a snort.

A potent, otherworldly fragrance scorched his nasal cavities and permeated deeper, covering his brain like a luxurious carpet. The effect was nearly instantaneous and much more powerful than alcohol or marijuana. It was warm, groggy tentacles spreading through him, activating every cell in his body, making them happy, making them sing. His surroundings brightened, crisp and beautiful, everything unveiled, shimmering with life.

When he looked at Maarten, it felt as though he had never seen him in such an attractive light. Everything was just like Maarten had said—time standing still, being in the present. It was wonderful sharing this moment with Maarten, on his pleasure boat that had to be one of the most expensive and extravagant yachts in the world.

"How are you feeling?" Maarten said with a smirk.

"Good." Jacks took another snort.

Maarten threw his head back, and his roaring laughter thrummed through Jacks, enhancing the potency of the drug, making his head throb. Maarten retook his snuff box. His voice came back to Jacks, distant and echoing. "You should take it easy your first time." Maarten took another sniff for himself, closed the device, and hid it in his pocket.

Jacks reached for Maarten's bare shoulder. His hands wanted to touch. Skin was so smooth, soft, and delightfully tingly against his fingertips. Maarten's skin had so many vibrant shades of amber, ivory, and gold. Was there anything more perfect in nature? He discovered the silky hairs in Maarten's armpit. It was like they had been placed there just so Jacks could feel them.

"Why don't we see what the others are doing."

Jacks's face bloomed. The lounge. Kwame, César and all the other guys. Maarten led Jacks by the hand.

Jacks seemed to walk on air. The red fluorescent lights pulsed through him, and the chandelier was like a mobile, projecting shapes on the walls that took on the semblance of wild, shadowy animals roaming around the periphery. The cuddle pile called out to him, purring, chuffing like a family of cubs. Iridescent eyes flared and sparkled as Jacks approached.

He threw off his shirt and tripped his way into the tangle of bodies. They shredded his shorts and briefs. Mouths sealed over his lips and his neck. Jacks reached blindly, finding shaggy heads, firm and hairy limbs, sultry creases of flesh. Hands and tongues lapped over his sensuous achy skin. He was intoxicated by the haze of body heat and musk, and it was hard to tell where his body ended and another's began, as though they had become one organism, joined in a primordial way. He purred. *They* purred. Sexes were for sharing, filling mouths, rubbing against each other, rutting against thighs and into buttocks. Jacks plummeted into a deep psychic chasm, needing, feeling, gorging.

WAKING THE NEXT day, Jacks felt like he had been buried under the wreckage of a smoldering, multi-car collision. It hurt to open his eyes, so he kept them closed, and he squirmed to free his body. A giant, furry muzzle, snoring with hot wet breaths, pressed against his face. Lion-size limbs and haunches were thrown over him. Jacks tossed and twisted his big cat body. All of the guys must have transformed at some point last night. He didn't remember that part of the party, and he didn't care to. He just needed to break out of the tangle. It was boiling hot beneath all the fur, and he was thirsty, so goddamn thirsty he felt like he was going to die if he didn't get a drink of water.

He climbed out of the pile on his mountain lion fours. The cabin lurched at extreme angles. It was the aftermath of Maarten's catnip, which had charred his brain on a rotisserie. He opened his mouth, and shallow pants came out as he waited for the dizzy spell to pass. He had experienced hangovers before, but this was like being forcefully awakened from anesthesia in the middle of cranial surgery.

Jacks squinted around the dim cabin. He saw a puddle of sunlight at the far end, coming from the doorway to the stern deck, which meant it was morning. That's where the water was. At the bar. He bore down on his abdomen, retracting his matted golden fur, realigning his body, and returning to his human form.

He spotted a pair of camouflage athletic shorts tossed on the floor, and he stepped into them. They were too big, but they would do for getting him out of the cabin with a degree of modesty if he kept them hiked up by the waist with one hand. They probably belonged to Kwame or Jean-Luc, both of whom were sprawled out on their backs and sides, lion-mouths hanging open and sawing logs. They didn't look like they would miss a pair of shorts for a while. Jacks stumbled out to the deck.

Out in the daylight, he shielded his eyes from the sun while gripping the waistband of his shorts. It was blazing directly overhead, which meant it was later in the day than he had guessed. Fortunately, Willem was stationed behind the bar. Not so fortunately, Annika was sitting on a stool wearing a wide-brimmed straw hat and her usual judgmental face. The orange behemoth of a housecat was keeping her company on top of the counter. Jacks staggered over with his eyes stabbing at the bartender. "Two glasses of water, please. Lots of ice."

Willem scooped ice cubes into two tall tumblers and filled them with his beverage gun. Jacks reached for one of the glasses before Willem placed it in front of him, and he swallowed the water in one long, desperate gulp. Then he drank the second glass and banged it down on the counter.

"Keep 'em coming."

While Willem tended to the water, Annika and her cat

watched Jacks. His shoulders tensed up. He was too wrecked from last night to try to play nice.

"I get it, Annika. You don't like me."

Annika tapped her fingers on her smooth, brown knee, which was poking out of her black and white patterned sundress. "I haven't formed an opinion on you yet, but I know you don't belong here."

Jacks polished off his third glass of water and wiped his mouth with his hand. "Why's that? I'm not rich enough for you?"

Annika threw her head back with a supercilious grin. "That has nothing to do with it."

"Then what? You don't like Americans? You treated me like a disease the moment I knocked on the door."

Her orange tabby budged closer, pitting her gaze at Jacks.

"Initially, I thought you might be dangerous. But I'll admit, I couldn't have been more wrong about that." Her nose wrinkled as she looked him over. "Is this what you aspire to? To be another one of Maarten's playthings?"

"I play with who I want to." Jacks took a draw on his fourth glass of water. His body was replenishing, the joints in his body loosening up, the tightness in his head washing away.

"I knew Benoit," Annika said.

His attention returned to her.

"He wasn't like the others. When I heard he was your mate, I thought you would be more like him."

Jacks snorted. "If you knew Benoit like I did, I don't think you'd have such a high opinion of him."

"I *knew* Benoit." Annika's face was hard, defiant. "He was fierce with his emotions. He was self-made. He was a survivor."

"He also liked to kill innocent people. And he was a nightmare of a boyfriend. Had some pretty heavy control issues. Did he mention that?"

Annika's voice rose passionately. "Benoit was a scholar. He had a lifetime, several lifetimes, of education in history, philosophy, and mysticism. He was trying to understand the world. How our kind could live in modern times. Instead of running away from our problems like lobotomized cowards."

Her words penetrated a little, but Jacks didn't want to give her the satisfaction of letting it show. "The world's gone to shit. You don't need centuries of education to figure that out. Maybe it's been a long time since you've been out in the middle of it, but believe me it's not a lot of fun."

"Fun. Yes, that's all you toms care about."

Jacks drained the rest of his water. "Maybe you should try it sometime. Anyway, if you think it's such a cop-out, what's keeping you here?"

Annika stroked her orange tabby on the back, and it purred, luxuriating and gloating. "Someone has to look after Maarten."

"That sounds like a cop-out to me."

"You had the opportunity to learn from a master of weremagic, and you frittered it away."

"Benoit?"

"He reared you, didn't he?"

"Ye-ah." Her meaning eluded Jacks. Annika looked him in the eye.

"You understand the future of our kind depends on the rearing ritual? There are practically no weremagi left. We're a dying species."

He wasn't sure if she was being over-dramatic or trying to play with his head, but what she said was disturbing. Jacks remembered the violence of his conversion. Benoit slashing his chest, Benoit forcing Jacks to slash back at him, the commingling of the blood. "What are you talking about? All it takes is the mixing of blood, right? Anyone can do that."

Annika frowned at him contemptuously. "That's one element, but there's a lot more. Ancient invocations. Astrological conditions. It's sacred knowledge that is known by very few. That's why the Glaring has become so militant. They know our days are numbered. They want humankind to be extinct before we are."

Jacks leaned his elbow on the bar, propping up his face in one hand. The conversation was too heavy after last night's party. "What's the difference? Even if we can't procreate, werecats live forever."

"Werecats can live for three hundred years, four hundred in the best cases. We are not immortal."

"That's still a lot longer than humans. Ought to give us plenty of time to figure things out."

"Not if we're killing each other. Or spending all our time trying to destroy the human race." She wrinkled her nose again. "Or wasting our lives glutting on drugs and sex."

He yawned—not intentionally, but he wasn't displeased by the timing. "Benoit never mentioned any of these life-or-death, end-of-the-world scenarios. Are you sure we're talking about the same guy?"

"Maybe he didn't think it was worth sharing with you. Maybe he realized you were nothing special. Maybe he became susceptible to the weaknesses of the males of our kind. Taking advantage of quick opportunities rather than thinking about long-term sustainability."

"What exactly makes you so superior? What great, profound things are you accomplishing playing chaperone to a bunch of gay guys on vacation?"

Annika sharpened her glare. Before she could retort, Jacks went on. "I *was* special to Benoit. He shared everything with me. It was more than sex, but since you mentioned it, yeah, we had sex a lot. You should try it sometime."

"So predictable. A female disagrees with you, and she must be frigid and sexually frustrated."

"I didn't mean it like that." An amusing thought occurred to Jacks, and he couldn't help himself from snickering. "But you have to admit, it's a little sad. You're spending your life on a luxury cruise with gorgeous guys, and you might as well be invisible."

Annika turned from him and stared out to the sea. In the silence, guilty feelings gained up on Jacks. A sigh heaved out of him. "Alright. That was a little harsh. I'm sorry."

"Your insults mean nothing. You don't know anything about me."

"You're right. I don't know about you. And you don't know anything about me."

She sucked her teeth. Jacks continued. "All these problems werecats are having, you make it sound like it's my responsibility. I've been a werecat for all of five months. Yeah, I was with Benoit, but if he was working on preserving our species like you say, he kept a real low profile about it. He stayed at youth hostels and slept in abandoned buildings. The only things that interested him were having sex and protecting his hunting territory."

"Of course he kept a low profile. Did it never occur to you why?"

Jacks said nothing. Benoit had been paranoid about being discovered both by humans and werecats. Jacks hadn't considered he might have reasons for that beyond an instinctual aversion to people and other toms.

"You were his downfall," Annika said. "You exposed his vulnerabilities, and then you killed him."

"I exposed his vulnerabilities?" Jacks took a slug of water, but it didn't cool him down. "He pursued me. It wasn't the other way around. Are you fucking kidding me? I was terrified of him at the end, so don't fucking pretend you know anything about our relationship. You got that?"

Annika was quiet for a moment. Maybe his words had brought about some empathy. She'd been a feline-human hybrid for a while and had to understand how brutal their relationships could be. She came back at him in a more measured tone.

"I'm sorry Benoit was cruel to you. So, you never knew about his holdings in Barbados?"

"No," Jacks snapped. "I was never interested in his money. If I get it, I'll give it to charity."

"What about his safety deposit box? Where he kept his magi knowledge."

Jacks shivered. He hadn't thought about the safety deposit box in quite some time. Secrets to werecat magic...that's what Bernard had been after?

"Whatever Benoit has locked up in that box—journals, books, or artifacts—the Glaring is salivating to use it. They'll destroy humankind. And if humans get hold of Benoit's stash, they could use it to destroy us."

The safety deposit key was sitting on the bedside table in his room, wasn't it? Jacks had a sudden urge to run up and check on it, then hide it someplace where it wouldn't be discovered. He also needed to get his damn phone charged. Mrs. James from the bank could have tried to call him, and her message would be in voicemail. It would be irretrievable until his phone was working and he could catch a signal.

Jacks stood up from his stool. "I've got to go to the bathroom."

INSIDE THE CABIN, Jacks started toward the bathroom on the main deck, and then he swerved for the stairs at the quickest shuffle he could manage wearing shorts that kept sliding down his behind. He glanced at the cuddle pile before climbing the stairs. They were snoring, and their tails swung lazily, with particles of fur hovering around them in a messy cloud. Jacks hurried up to his room on the second floor and quietly shut the door behind him.

On the bedside table, he found some loose change, his watch, his dead cell phone, and his travel documents. He rifled through the stuff, and he spotted the flat, silver-plated key.

He heaved a sigh of relief and sat down on the bed. He had to be more careful. He'd been such a flake, leaving the key lying around for anyone to take it. He peered over at his alarm clock. August 27th. One day before Benoit's accounts were supposed to be released to him. He couldn't believe he had lost track of time completely.

Someone knocked. Jacks put the key in his shorts pocket and stood.

"Who is it?"

"Your invisible friend."

He started toward the door and stopped. He had no idea what to do.

Annika called out, "We prefer our guests to use the water closet rather than peeing in the ice buckets, if that's what you're doing. But somehow, I think you're up to something else."

Jacks glared at the door.

"Open up, Jacks. I've come to play nice. I don't want to burst in uninvited, though you may have noticed there's no lock."

He went for the doorknob and pulled it open. Annika stood in the hallway with a smart-alecky look on her face. She had brought a newspaper, rolled up under one arm, and her orange cat sidled up beside her.

"What do you want?" Jacks said, looking from one visitor to the other.

"I want to see the key."

"Why?"

"So you can prove you really have it."

He studied her. "You sure you don't want it for yourself?"

"What good would that do? You're the only one who can get into the bank and use it. Show it to me, and then we can talk about what you're going to do."

She could also take the key and storm the bank as a lioness to get the contents of the box, though that didn't seem too likely. He stepped aside to let her and her overfed tabby in, and he closed the door behind them.

Annika looked at him expectantly. Jacks invited her to sit down on his armchair. Her cat went straight for the bedside table. She did a half-leap from the floor, and then she made a bumbling, clawing effort to scale the table. As soon as she pulled herself all the way up, she sniffed through his things.

"What's she doing?"

Annika shrugged. "Getting familiar with you."

He watched the tabby nosing over his phone and passport. Her loyalty was obviously to Annika, and she would share whatever information she found with her mistress — the lingering scents of Farzan and Bella, the forged travel documents. Jacks would have shared them voluntarily anyway, so he let the cat have her fun. He stood in front of Annika, dug into his pocket, and held out the key in the palm of his hand.

Annika's eyes flared. Jacks replaced the key in his shorts.

"So now what? I suppose if you wanted to steal it from me, you could have done it a long time ago."

"I also could have let that wereleopard kill you to get the key for the Glaring."

Jacks rolled his eyes. He could've handled the wereleopard by himself. "Okay. So, if you're right about what's in the box, what am I supposed to do with it?"

"I *am* right about what's in the box. When Benoit stayed with us, we talked for hours while Maarten and his friends were partying late into the night. Benoit mentioned an ancient text called The Báalam-Tet. He acquired the book through his travels. It's filled with knowledge about spirit-summoning and power that can be unlocked through astral rites. He was working on translating the passages into a journal. Whatever is in his safety deposit box must be kept safe. From both werecats and humans."

Jacks thought on it. "Then maybe it's best to leave it at the bank."

"It's too late, Jacks. You already led them to the bank. They'll be waiting for you to get in there, and if you don't, they'll find their own means."

He fingered the key in his pocket. "It would be safe here."

"Sure, tell that to Maarten."

"Maarten said I could stay here as long as I like. He said we didn't have to worry about the Glaring."

"That's when you were a minor liability. With Benoit's stash, that risk increases a thousand fold. We'd be fighting off a pack of big cats at every port. That's not a lifestyle my brother would abide."

"You're saying he'll kick me out?"

Annika didn't reply.

Jacks scoffed. "I'll talk to him. We'll go back to Barbados. He's not going to leave me to fend for myself."

"You think you know my brother so well after a couple of

weeks? You think you'd be the first person he's cut out of his life?"

The force of her anger left a wake of silence in the room. He glanced at her, shocked and alert. Annika shifted in the armchair.

"Maarten and I were out of place in the world long before we discovered our feline souls. Our mother had an affair with a Black man when she was very young, and we were our family's dirty secret. We were raised as Afrikaners and sent abroad to a Dutch boarding school. We had half-brothers and sisters after our mother married a proper white man, and we were told our father had been a French-Algerian military officer who was killed during the Basque conflict. It was a respectable enough story to keep most people's mouths shut when they wondered about our darker skin and thicker hair."

Jacks worked through the details to place Annika and Maarten's ages. The Basque conflict was in the '60s and '70s. That meant the two were somewhere in their forties. He was curious to know when they had been reared, but he sat down on the bed across from her and let Annika continue.

"Maarten had just finished his final term of boarding school when our birth father came looking for us. Our mother broke down. She explained everything that had been hidden from us. Though our stepfather didn't like it, she convinced him we were old enough to make our own choices. Maarten and I started to spend time with our father. He was a good man. He had a family, and he introduced us to a whole new set of half-siblings at their home in a Zulu township. We had never been greeted so warmly. Our father told us times were changing. The Bothe government was falling apart, and soon we could all be together. He loved Maarten. That was quite profound for my brother. He had always been an awkward, quiet boy who was treated awfully at school and kept at a distance by our stepfather because of his skin color. Everything seemed perfect that summer after Maarten's graduation. I still had a year to finish school, but we talked about going to university together in Cape Town so we would be close to our father's side of our family." Annika looked away from Jacks and said nothing for a while.

"Then the accident happened," she continued. "Maarten was driving us home from the township. It was dusk, and we were on a remote road through the bush. The headlights of our car caught a white lion in our path. White lions are rare and sacred to the Zulu. They say they're bearers of prophecy from the divine. Maarten swerved onto the shoulder. But he was driving too fast, and we spun out of control and hit a tree. The car was undriveable, and when we ventured out, we realized the animal had been laying a trap. He was a werelion, and he attacked us both."

The memory of the rearing ritual came back to Jacks, horrifying and tantalizing. *Cats are wild*, Maarten had said. There was a quiver in Annika's eyes, a tacit acknowledgement that the event both she and Jacks had been through, brutal as it was, had been an exquisite, carnal awakening.

"I woke up in the hospital, convinced it must have been a dream," she said. "Maarten remembered. He showed me the extraordinary things we could do. My brother felt strong and confident for the first time in his life, and for a while, the only thing that mattered to him was finding the white werelion who chose to give us the gift. He decided not to go to college so he could explore the backcountry and Zulu villages. He spent less and less time with our father's family, hardly any time with people at all. Something changed in him. Maybe it was discovering white lions were being poached to extinction by fur traders. Maybe he found out our maker had been killed. He never spoke to me about it. When I came home from school on holiday, he had a new group of friends, all two-spirit werelions, wereleopards, and weretigers. His only interest was buying expensive things and partying. He said both sides of our family were a sham—our mother who never wanted to raise us and our father who abandoned us. I tried to tell him our father was making up for the past, but Maarten refused to hear it. He scolded me for spending time with him."

Annika broke off for a moment. Her complexion darkened. "Then the riots in the townships worsened. The police were killing people nearly every day. South Africa was a spectacle watched around the world, and Afrikaners were being likened to Nazi Germans. Our stepfather arranged to emigrate abroad and manage his businesses in Cape Town from Australia, and he encouraged me and Maarten to come along. Many mixed-race people were leaving the country. Others joined the liberation movement. Maarten said it was a waste of time. He didn't believe political change was possible. He said human selfishness would always win out. He proved that theory himself. Our father, brothers, and sisters risked their lives to fight for a new South Africa. Maarten bought a yacht to sail around the world. A few months later, we found out from a dear cousin on my father's side that our father and two of our brothers had been killed by a riot squad."

"That's awful," Jacks said. Annika stared grimly at a corner of the room, avoiding his sympathy. He tried to offer it anyway, albeit in an awkward meter. "Do you feel like a traitor? I mean, you shouldn't. I don't think. If you had stayed, you could've been killed, too."

Annika returned to him sharply. "Yes, I wanted to stay, but I didn't. For a million cowardly reasons. I was a girl. I didn't think I could make a difference. I was afraid of rubber bullets and tear gas, and even more of what would happen if someone discovered I was a hybrid creature. Maarten was my older brother. We had always relied on each other, having no one else to understand what it was like to be neither black nor white. Then, we shared a new outsider status as werecats."

She stared beyond Jacks, wistfully. "I thought someday we would make a difference. Return to South Africa and establish some sort of charity to help the people in the townships. Days stretched into months, then years. Maarten's antics became more of a worry. He was picking up all sorts of werecat drifters on his travels. He needed looking after so he wouldn't get taken advantage of, or worse."

Annika's hard, combative exterior seemed to melt away before his eyes. He had thought her bitter edges came from deciding to tag along with her brother for all these years. But he realized she held inside something much more painful, and that sorrow penetrated Jacks. Would he ever truly be part of a "family?" Was it possible to live a meaningful life as a hybrid being?

Annika had shared so many personal things with him, it must have been because she saw him as someone who would understand. He remembered her curious glance at him the night he had prevented the street fight in Port-of-Spain. She did see him as different from Maarten's other friends, and it was in a good way, a way that made him feel proud.

"You could still go back to South Africa," he said.

"We left twenty-five years ago. There's no place for me there."

Jacks wasn't sure he agreed.

"The world has changed," Annika said. "There's nothing to be done about the past. But we, *you* can do something about the present."

"I don't understand. Benoit's journal, The Báalam-Tet—I have no idea how to use those things. What good is it going to do for me to retrieve them?"

"So they'll be in your hands rather than the hands of genocidal extremists."

Jacks stood and paced. "You said the Glaring will be watching the bank. That I'm basically a goner if I go back there."

"You'll need help."

"How long does it take to raise a werecat army?" Jacks said with a smirk. He paced around some more. "What if I went in and took photos of everything and left the originals at the bank? Then they'd be safe, at least for a while, and we can find someone who understands them in the meantime."

"There isn't time. The Glaring has already begun to strike out."

She brought out the newspaper she'd set aside. She uncurled it and passed it to Jacks.

It was a newspaper from their last port, Grand Cayman, several days old. A headline caught Jacks like a hard slap in the face.

"New York Survivor Tells Story of Panther Attack But No Clues Yet Into Bizarre Night of Terror."

Jacks sped through the article, and then he read it again, and then a third time. His thoughts tripped over themselves. The attack happened three weeks ago, with others in Boston, Philadelphia, and Washington, D.C.. At least three hundred fatalities in total. Jacks had been cocooned from the world on Maarten's yacht. No one had turned on a TV or had mobile devices with push notifications for breaking news stories. He felt so selfish, and terrified something could have happened to Farzan.

"Attacks from The Glaring have never been this organized," Annika said. "In the past, they've accomplished a single assassination here or there, but this widespread strike shows they are more united than ever. They'll keep doing it to draw you out."

He had to get back to Barbados. He had to call Farzan. If Farzan or anyone in his family was hurt, he would never forgive himself.

"Will you help me?"

"I've seen genocide before, and I won't be a bystander this time. So yes. You won't be alone, Jacks."

TWENTY-ONE

ANNIKA INSISTED ON talking to Maarten alone, so Jacks didn't know what she said to her brother to convince him to sail back to Barbados. He could tell Maarten wasn't happy about it, though. He heard raised voices from conversations in private parts of the yacht, and whenever their paths crossed, Maarten swept by without a look. He was freezing Jacks out, and the other guys fell in step. Except for Kwame. He joined Jacks for breakfast one morning at his lonely spot at the bar. Neither of them broached the subject of what was happening, but Jacks was grateful for the company.

He tried calling Farzan from Willem's cell phone, but he couldn't get a connection on the open sea. The ship's Wi-Fi was spotty, and Jacks couldn't send an SMS email out from the captain's laptop cither or surf the web for news from New York. He tried to bridge a psychic connection with Bella and came up empty.

By the time they anchored at Port St. Charles marina, Annika had put together a plan. She would scout the island for the Glaring with her two tabbies. They would find out what the strays on the island knew, while Jacks returned to his guest house to get his travel bag, charge his phone, and check on the status of Benoit's bank accounts. Under a willful glare from Annika, Maarten offered to accompany Jacks. Kwame, Nicolas, Jean-Luc, Somsuea, César, Lars, and Thierry would stay back and rendezvous at the bank in Bridgetown when it opened the following morning.

Jacks was finally alone with Maarten in the taxi from the marina to the guest house. Maarten's vibe was ice cold. Jacks didn't feel great about dragging him into a dangerous situation, but they were friends, weren't they?

"I appreciate you doing this," Jacks said.

Maarten avoided his gaze.

"You didn't have to, and I get why you wouldn't. I just wanted to say, I know I owe you big time. When it's over, if there's anything I can do to make it up to you—"

"You haven't anything to make up to me. I agreed to help because Annika asked me to."

Jacks wrung his frigid hands. "I get that. It just means a lot that you took me in. I brought my mess into your life. I didn't even understand how messy it was when we first met. I know you didn't either."

"Yes. If I could go back in time, I would have left you at the dock at Port Saint-Charles. Annika will tell you, I have a weakness for charity cases. But when this is over, you'll make your own way."

That stung Jacks. "I'm sorry. It's a lot, this mission we're doing. But I guess Annika convinced you it was worth it."

"Annika convinced me of nothing. We're putting a bounty on our heads by getting involved in matters that are none of our business. I told Annika I was only helping out of family obligation."

"So, I guess if I had asked, the answer would've been no."

Maarten chuckled dryly.

Jacks stared out the window for a moment. "It doesn't bother you that if the Glaring gets Benoit's book, they could potentially wipe out humankind? I thought your motto was live and let live."

"Precisely."

"There won't be any humans left to *let live*."

"The world goes through cycles. Peace. Revolution. War. I don't subscribe to my sister's alarmist view that the Glaring will ever have the power to annihilate humankind. Not entirely. No genocide in history has succeeded in doing that."

"You heard what happened in the States?"

"I read her newspaper. Three hundred fatalities. There are seven billion humans on the planet. The Glaring has a long way to go."

Heat rose up his neck. "One of them is my friend. Farzan. I don't even know if he survived."

"Well. Then you can dedicate this mission to him." Maarten brought out his snuff box and took a long snort.

"Don't you think it would help to stay a little more alert? There could be Glaring hunters waiting for us at the guesthouse."

Maarten pocketed the box. "It helps me to stay alert."

"I guess if you're high all the time, it doesn't make much of a difference."

"How many kills have you made?"

Jacks thought on it. There were Benoit and Bernard, though he had shot Benoit with a gun while he was in human form, so Bernard was the only one that counted, he supposed.

"Not many, is it?" Maarten said. "Stick to what you know. Don't question things you don't understand."

"Why did you leave South Africa?"

His question briefly silenced Maarten. "I gather Annika has told you all sorts of horrible things about me."

Jacks studied him. He wanted there to be some reason why Maarten had become so cold. Even lions in the wild fought to protect members of their pride.

"I made the decision to leave, that's all."

"Were you scared?"

Maarten clucked his tongue. "I was never scared. I just couldn't be bothered with nonsense."

"You could have helped your father and brothers. You could have taken them with you."

"What do you know? My family never gave me anything. I take no responsibility for them."

Jacks knew about being let down by family. But Maarten's situation was different. If Jacks had had a father who really wanted to be in his life, he'd never have abandoned him to fight a war alone. "You really don't care about anyone, do you? Besides yourself."

"Now you're starting to understand."

"I think that's sad."

"Does it make you teary, Jacks, to realize the world is cold and uncaring?"

Jacks returned to staring out the window. Maarten's true character had been revealed, and it did hurt. He had pretended Jacks was special. That he belonged in his "pride." But it was all surface level, just Maarten acquiring party buddies to entertain him in his bubble from the real world. Jacks was angry at himself for believing he had found his tribe. In the meantime, he'd let down the people who actually cared about him, Farzan and Bella.

It was torture being stuck in the back seat of the cab with Maarten while feelings stormed inside him. They'd never see eye-to-eye, and he was tired of being mocked for whatever he said.

As the taxi zipped along the last bend to the guesthouse, he told Maarten, "Soon as we're done at the bank, I'll give you the money for paying up my hotel room and whatever else I owe you for the past three weeks." Jacks anticipated a snobby reply from Maarten. "I don't care if it's a drop in the bucket for you. It means something to me. We part ways the same as we met: We owe each other nothing."

AS THE CAB pulled into the guesthouse driveway, Jacks's nose twitched from a familiar scent. It was impossible. He rolled down his window to confirm it. That scent was strong and glorious. He could visualize it on a straight line to the back of the guesthouse.

While Maarten paid the driver, Jacks threw open the door and ran for the stairs to the porch. He jabbed at the doorbell repeatedly to get the night attendant to open up, peering through the door with his nose against the glass panel.

A young man emerged and let him in. Jacks fished out his passport from his pants to prove he had a rented room and staggered through the hallway to the back of the house. His nose led him to Room 107, which was adjacent to the one he'd been renting. He rapped his knuckles on the door. Sweat ran down his face in rivulets. He heard the springs of a cheap bed — someone getting up all of a sudden. There was a mewl and then the door flew open.

Farzan stood in the doorway in a T-shirt and his sleeping boxers, and Bella came out of the room and wove around Jacks's legs flirtatiously.

He pounced on Farzan with an enormous hug. Farzan slowly closed his arms around him. Jacks nuzzled against

Farzan's head, luxuriating in the rich, natural odors of his sleep-tousled hair. He never wanted to let go of him again.

Farzan's body went still, and his arms came down to his sides. Jacks took a half-step back. Farzan had a wide, accusatory glare on his face.

"Where the hell have you been?"

He scooped his cell phone out of the white linen pants he had borrowed from César. He showed Farzan the dead display screen. "You don't even know. I tried calling you a million times. My battery died, and nobody had a charger. I borrowed phones to call you whenever I could, but we were out of range a lot and the Wi-Fi was spotty. It was driving me insane."

Jacks was suddenly aware he hardly looked the part of someone wracked with worry. He had thrown on Somsuea's trendy, chest-hugging, graphic tank-top that morning and a pair of Gucci sandals. Lars had cut his hair a few days ago in a tapered undercut and shown Jacks how to zhuzh it up with product. He was also wearing bracelets, a multi-strand red coral necklace, and a blingy stud in his ear. Farzan's upper lip ticked. He left Jacks by the doorway and wandered into the darkness of the room.

Jacks closed the door and followed him. Farzan clicked on the bedside lamp and sat down on the bed with his face buried in his hands. Jacks took a seat next to him. He was suddenly breathless.

"What's wrong?"

"What's *wrong*? You disappear for an entire month. I thought you were dead." His voice rose sharply. "But you're not. And unless you were trafficked into a ring of circuit party rent-boys, you've obviously been having the time of your life while my whole world has gone to shit."

"I was worried about you, too." He rubbed Farzan's shoulder. "I didn't know what happened in New York until yesterday. I came back here as soon as I could. I've been calling you all day."

Farzan picked his phone up from the bedside table. Jacks could see it was fully charged, and there were no missed calls on display.

"The signal's really bad here," Jacks said.

Farzan snorted out a weary breath.

"You think I'm lying?"

"They told me your room is paid up for the month, but no one has seen you for weeks. What am I supposed to think? You've been traveling in a dead zone day and night, all this time? You never once had the opportunity to use a landline?"

Jacks edged up closer and reached his arm around Farzan. "Baby, listen, you can't even imagine how glad I am to see you—"

Farzan pulled away from him.

"How's your family? Is everyone all right?"

Gradually, Farzan nodded.

"I can't believe you came down all this way. What about med school?"

"I took a leave of absence."

Jacks's insides sank. Becoming a doctor meant everything to Farzan. Jacks clasped his hand over Farzan's, which was resting lifelessly on his knee. Farzan finally spoke, quietly, with his head angled to the side. "It was probably the biggest mistake I've ever made."

"You didn't have to—"

Farzan shot up from the bed. "I *wanted* to." He took a few steps with his back turned to Jacks and snorted out a bitter laugh. "I used up most of my savings. I left my family and very possibly screwed up my scholarship at school. I didn't think twice about it because I thought you were in danger or worse.

I've been to every hospital, every police station, the US embassy."

No one had ever cared about Jacks that much, which amazed him at first, but then that high receded, laying bare his guilt. When he started to speak, tears rose up to his throat. "I'm sorry. I should have tried harder to reach you." He went to Farzan and embraced him back to chest.

"Just tell me. Am I a fool for coming down here?"

"No. God no. I fucked up." Tears sprouted from his eyes. "I met some people who I thought were my friends, and I just... got lost in that for a while." Jacks wiped his face. "And I know that's a shitty excuse, but I swear, when I caught your scent outside, I *knew*. You mean everything to me."

Farzan pulled away from Jacks and pressed his fists into his eyes. "I thought you were dead, Jacks. You left me with no other explanation."

He took Farzan in his arms again and nudged him to meet his gaze. "I really need you to forgive me. I screwed up. Big time. But I came back, didn't I?" Farzan tried to move away from him, but Jacks held him steady. "Hey. I promise, I'll never do that to you again."

"You say that, but you've lied to me so many times."

"When did I lie?"

Farzan threw up his hands and wrangled himself free. "You lied about everything. About who you are. What happened with Benoit." Farzan looked at Jacks fiercely. "Everything you've been doing down here."

"You're talking about the past. I explained that all to you. And as for what I've been doing, I told you I was joining some people for a cruise. I didn't know it would be for so long."

"Listen to yourself, Jacks. You went on a cruise when you knew werecats were staking out my apartment."

Jacks turned away. "I know. It was stupid and selfish. I

thought I'd found people like me. Good people, I mean. Who could help us."

Farzan was silent for a moment. "Werecats?"

Jacks stepped over to sit down on the bed. He was suddenly mentally exhausted.

"How did you have money for a cruise?" Farzan asked.

"I didn't. It was a private yacht. One of them owns it."

"Werecats," Farzan repeated. "Like the ones who murdered three hundred people earlier this month."

"They're not like that."

"I suppose I wouldn't know. The only ones I met wanted to kill me. Or you."

"Those are the Glaring."

"I see. And how do I know, how did *you* know they weren't man-hating killers?"

He looked up. "Because I knew." He shook his head. "*I'm* a werecat, Farzan. Do you think I'm a man-hating killer? I mean, if that's what you think, why did you even want to be with me?"

Farzan came at him. "No, you don't get to turn this around like I did something wrong. You left me for a month. I was in the ER when it was overcapacity with people dying from maulings."

Jacks gulped back a wave of tears that was threatening to come back. "So, you get to be mad at me for that." He nodded. "I don't know what to say, but if that's the way you feel."

Farzan sat down next to him. "I'm not saying it's your fault." While Jacks was hunched over, rocking a bit, Farzan rubbed his back. "I thought I lost you. I'm trying to process things."

Jacks gripped his hand. "Just tell me when you get to the part where you forgive me and trust me again."

"That may never happen at the rate we're going." Farzan

watched Jacks withdraw his hand like a wounded boy. It made Farzan grin for the first time since they'd started the conversation. "It's going to take more than a couple of minutes. This situation would be difficult to accept even for a person who didn't have massive trust issues."

"Yeah. That goes both ways." Jacks looked Farzan in the eyes. "Babe, I'm sorry for hurting you. I know it looks bad, but I really am trying the best I can." Before Farzan could respond, Jacks held his face and kissed him, open-mouthed. It felt perfect for a moment, reaffirming how much they cared about each other. Then Farzan gently broke off their embrace.

"You're infuriating, you know that?"

"How am I infuriating?"

"You make me want to believe you, but what sane person would?"

Jacks held Farzan's thigh. "I wish we had more time to talk through it."

"How do you mean, you wish we had more time? You're leaving again?"

"No. But I found out more about the Glaring. There's a lot to explain."

Farzan straddled Jacks's legs and folded his arms around his shoulders. "How 'bout we leave that for the morning?"

Make-up sex was awfully appealing, but someone knocked on the door. Farzan shifted, startled. Jacks eyed him steadily. It was too soon for them to be interrupted when they'd finally gotten back to a good place.

A second series of knocks broke out.

"Who could that be?" Farzan said.

Jacks smelled a musky, jasmine scent.

Farzan maneuvered off of Jacks. Bella was by the door, on her haunches, staring with suspicion.

"Should I?" Farzan started to say.

Jacks nodded without looking up.

Farzan swung open the door, revealing Maarten, standing at the threshold with his dirty schoolboy smirk.

"Hello. I'm sorry to bother you, but I think my friend came by this way."

"Who are you?" Farzan said.

Maarten craned his neck to look past him. His glance landed on Jacks like a laser pointer, and his smirk broadened into a toothy grin. He held out his hand to Farzan.

"Maarten. Jacks and I have been traveling companions for the last few weeks."

FARZAN AND MAARTEN handled each other with their respective brands of contempt. Farzan kept a sidelong, dubious watch on Maarten. Maarten seemed to forget Farzan existed.

Jacks tried to moderate the situation, firmly introducing Farzan as his boyfriend and explaining to him that Maarten and his family and friends had helped when the Asian wereleopard tried to kill him. Neither party seemed moderated. Farzan was already piqued by Maarten's arrogance, while Maarten listened with coyly piqued attention, ready to spring open like a jack-in-the-box with details Jacks wasn't ready to share.

It helped a bit when he used Farzan's phone to make an outgoing call, which joggled the phone's voicemail and its missed call history. He showed Farzan his eleven calls from Maarten's yacht. Jacks plugged his cell into Farzan's charger.

Meanwhile, Bella was enamored of Maarten. She purred at his feet while he sat on the bed. When Maarten reached down to rub her chin, she exalted in a stretch on the floor, inviting a full body grooming.

Farzan watched their interaction with mounting indignation. He said to Jacks, "If Bella was able to warn you about the wereleopard, why didn't you know what was happening in New York?"

Jacks stared at the cat. He'd wondered the same thing. She returned his glance blandly.

"I don't know. I left her with you to protect you from The Glaring. Maybe she was focused on that."

"But she's been connected to you the whole time," Farzan said. "She *wanted* to come down to Barbados to find you." He told Jacks about the uncanny moment with Bella back in the Catskills.

Maarten interrupted. "A cat is loyal to her master." He batted Bella's sides playfully. "It's obvious, really. She knew if she told Jacks about the attack in New York, he'd return and fall right into the Glaring's hands. She knew he was safer thousands of miles away."

Jacks eyed Bella reproachfully. It was hard to think of her as just a cat, unconcerned with his feelings for Farzan. If Maarten was right, Bella had withheld information in a manipulative way, after Jacks had entrusted her to keep a lookout for trouble, certainly without deference to her "master." He stomped toward Bella.

"You should have let me know."

Farzan swept in front of him and stooped down to gather Bella from the floor. He cradled her. "Don't take it out on Bella. She risked her life to protect me twice."

He told Jacks about the second visit from the Glaring, the werejaguar he and Bella had subdued with the help of his IKEA bookcase. Bella's ears pinched back as he spoke, and Jacks looked from her to Farzan, confounded. He had wanted Farzan to warm up to Bella, but now, between Bella's defiance and Farzan's lingering bitterness, he felt like the odd man out.

He went over to his charging cell phone. There was a

recent missed call from a local number and a voicemail waiting for him. He crouched by the bedside table so he could listen to the message while the phone was on a short cord to the outlet.

It was Mrs. James. Everything was in order for the transfer of Benoit's accounts. He just needed to fill out some paperwork at the bank.

Everyone was looking at him when he set down the phone.

"It's ready." He explained to Farzan about Benoit's documents and the urgency of keeping them from the Glaring.

"It's a fool's errand," Maarten said.

"No one asked for your opinion," Farzan said.

Jacks told Maarten, "Annika is going to help me interpret Benoit's journal."

"You need a werecat mage, not my sister," Maarten said. "Annika thinks because she spent a few hours talking to Benoit, she's qualified to use some archaic text."

"She knows more about it than me or you," Jacks said.

Maarten laughed at that. "That's not much of a recommendation. Besides, Annika won't be sticking around. She stays with the pride, and we're pushing out to sea as soon as you finish your business at the bank."

"Don't you think that's her decision to make?"

"Annika knows her place. She's not going to run off with a stranger we picked up on a whim."

Sparks of anger scored Jacks's insides, urging him to transform and gnash and claw at Maarten. He wanted to teach Maarten a lesson about fucking with the wrong person. But remembering the seriousness of their situation, he guarded those impulses. Annika had given him her word about helping, and he couldn't screw that up by starting a fight with her brother.

Maarten reclined on Farzan's bed with his shirt riding up

244 ANDREW J. PETERS

his flat stomach. He glanced at Jacks and then Farzan, with other things on his mind as usual.

"What are you doing here?" Farzan demanded.

Maarten shrugged. "My job was to deliver Jacks safely to his guesthouse."

"You've done that. You can leave."

Jacks stood in front of Farzan. "He and his friends are going to come with me to the bank."

Before they could fight about that, Bella scurried to the room's single window with the back of her fur puffed out. Annika's orange tabby climbed over the windowsill from outside, and then her black cat leapt up and pulled its large body over and into the room.

Two giant, downy paws appeared at the sill, followed by the enormous head of a lioness, scouting the scene. Annika lifted herself up and plunged into the room on all fours. Her magnificent feline presence made the space feel like very tight quarters. Farzan backed against the opposite wall.

Annika morphed into her human self, and Jacks made awkward introductions. Taking Annika aside, he told her about the message from the bank. He glanced at the time on his cell phone. It was nearly three in the morning.

"The bank opens at nine," he said.

"Glaring hunters have been scouting the island," Annika said. "They left to try to track you through the southern Caribbean, according to the strays. But the strays know you're here, and they can't be trusted. They'll be channeling the information to the nearest hunters to try to stop us."

Bella recoiled and hissed at Annika's tabbies. It was too many cats in one room for Bella, and too many for Farzan surely. Annika seemed to understand. She asked for the key to Jacks's room so that she, Maarten, and the housecats would be close by. She and Maarten would be a perilous surprise for any hunters looking for Jacks. They said their goodnights.

When they were all out the door, Farzan collapsed on the bed. He looked like he had gone through a long spin in a centrifuge.

Jacks sat down next to him and held his hand. "You stay here tomorrow morning. If something happens, I'll let Bella know. The two of you head straight for the airport and back to New York, okay?"

"I'm coming with you."

Jacks smiled and squeezed Farzan's hand. "You're my brave man. But I can't let you do that."

"You think this is up for discussion? I'm not sitting on the sidelines when you could get torn to pieces."

"It's too dangerous."

"I'm in this, too. I was there for the attacks in New York. One of those hunters tried to kill me. If there's a way to take down the Glaring, I want to be part of it."

Jacks lay down beside Farzan with his head on his shoulder. He could tell Farzan wasn't going to budge on the issue. Though his instinct was to protect him, Farzan made an inarguable point. When Jacks had left him in New York, Farzan had still faced danger. It was safer to keep him close.

Neither of them were going to get much sleep, but it felt good to lie together. Farzan stroked Jacks's head. Jacks closed his eyes, imagining the waves of anxiety inside him rolling out to sea. He curled closer to Farzan, and their bodies molded together, like pack-mates conserving the warmth, the way that felt right, the way it should be.

TWENTY-TWO

THE BEECHFIELD BANK looked to be deserted at nine o'clock the next morning. Jacks and Farzan had taken a cab and gotten there a few minutes before it opened, so they walked around the block, trying not to look too suspicious. Once the security guard opened the doors, they approached the bank at a measured stroll. The dragon-headed insignia loomed above them like some dark rune of foreboding. The sky was bright and cloudless. The calm before the storm? Jacks wondered. He and Farzan entered the bank through its glass double-doors.

The plan was for Annika and Maarten to come in shortly thereafter, impersonating a young couple looking to open an account in case the Glaring showed up. Kwame, Jean-Luc, Nicolas, César, Somsuea, Lars, and Thierry were keeping watch at points outside the bank. Bella and Annika's domestics waited at Maarten's yacht and would send a warning if any hunters showed up there.

The balding, middle-aged bank officer from the last visit greeted Jacks, and Jacks introduced Farzan as his boyfriend. Mr. Applewhite smiled in a way that said he wasn't sure what to do with that information, then he walked them upstairs to Mrs. James's office.

Glancing over the second-floor railing to the gallery below, Jacks reconfirmed it was just a single security guard and two bank tellers behind the counter down there. He wasn't picking up any scent of werecats, only humans with their curious body odors dowsed with even more curious perfumes and colognes.

Mrs. James waved Jacks and Farzan into her office with much more exuberance than when she had first met Jacks.

"There's my favorite customer." She added with a scolding frown: "Who doesn't believe in calling ahead."

Like her bank officer, she didn't seem to know what to make of Farzan, but she gave him a little grin and a handshake. He and Farzan sat down in front of her desk.

They exchanged and signed documents. After a call to Sammy earlier that morning, Farzan had gotten a pair of forged reference letters emailed and printed out at the guesthouse. Jacks presented the letters to Mrs. James.

"I decided to set up an account here," Jacks said. "And I'd like to make a withdrawal and to retrieve the contents of the safety deposit box." The last part made a bubble of nervousness float up his chest. He elaborated, "I promised to return some items to Mr. Guichard's friends."

Mrs. James handled everything routinely and efficiently. There was a withdrawal slip, and a signature card to fill out for the security box. While Jacks completed the forms with one of her gold-plated pens, she tapped some numbers and letters on her keyboard. "We can post the cash withdrawal against Mr. Guichard's savings account. The other funds will remain restricted for now, but you have options for drawing down a percentage of the balances based on local and international policies."

He exchanged a glance with Farzan, who was fighting to

keep his eyes off of the withdrawal slip. Jacks had written fifteen thousand dollars.

"Have you enjoyed your stay in Barbados, Mr. Heathcliff?"

"Oh, yes."

"I hope you will be coming back."

Jacks scratched his ear. "Maybe we will."

"My sister is a real estate agent. She could show you the island's finest properties if you're interested in an investment or a vacation home."

"That sounds interesting."

"Or maybe you prefer the climate in Manitoba?" Mrs. James let out a shrieking laugh.

Jacks grinned nervously as he remembered his lie about biking with Benoit in Canada. She was a bit like an alcoholic aunt you tried to steer company away from when they met your family. Jacks didn't know if Farzan, who wore every one of his emotions on his face, could hold back his bewilderment.

Her printer clanged and whirred. Mrs. James swiveled around in her executive chair, retrieved some pages, and handed Jacks a transfer statement.

She stood. "I'll walk you downstairs for the transaction."

When they returned to the first floor, Maarten and Annika had appropriated the chairs in front of Mr. Applewhite's desk, though the bank officer had disappeared. Jacks took account of the rest of the gallery. The security guard was at his post, yawning. The bank tellers were busying themselves with work at their computer monitors. No customers to be seen.

Mrs. James called over one of the young ladies behind the counter. They held a quiet conversation, and Mrs. James passed over the paperwork. The teller gave Jacks a friendly grin and tapped away at her computer station to bring up the savings account.

That bubble of nervousness lifted into his throat. Fifteen

thousand dollars was more money than he had ever owned and certainly more cash than he had ever seen. It was dangerous traveling with so much money, but he would need it to get around as well as to pay back Maarten.

"How would you like it?" the teller asked.

He hesitated. Farzan broke in. "Hundreds, and the last five hundred in twenties." It sounded reasonable enough to Jacks. How would they break thousand dollar bills while traveling? The teller brought out bills from a drawer and counted everything out twice. She placed the money in a legal-size envelope. Jacks stuffed it in his messenger bag.

Mrs. James looked at Jacks expectantly. "Would you like to see the safety deposit box?"

Jacks nodded, and he followed her toward the back rooms of the bank, along with Farzan. Mrs. James glanced over her shoulder. "I'm sorry, but we only allow the owner in the security box area."

As many things as he and Farzan had talked about in planning the visit, Jacks hadn't expected this. The policy made sense, but he didn't like the idea of leaving Farzan alone outside. He looked a little worried himself.

"I'll be right back," Jacks said.

He watched Farzan wander over to the display of bank brochures in the middle of the floor. Then he followed Mrs. James through a doorway and down a corridor.

They approached a chamber closed off by a metal gate. Mrs. James swiped her ID card through an electronic reader mounted on the wall, and the gate rolled up by a hydraulic mechanism. She stepped inside and waved Jacks along.

The chamber wasn't much bigger than his room at the guesthouse and much more claustrophobic with its windowless walls encased in metal-plated safety deposit boxes. There was a narrow counter in the middle of the room for the customers to examine their boxes. Jacks noticed an adjoining space through a single doorway that looked to be a second safety deposit chamber.

"The key, Mr. Heathcliff?" Mrs. James said. He rummaged in his pocket and brought out the silver-plated key. He handed it to Mrs. James. She went over to the left side of the room and fit the key into a compartment at the level of her shoulders. Jacks noticed the number. 1309.

With a noisy scrape, Mrs. James pulled out a long metal box and set it on the counter. The contents were covered by a vinyl privacy sheet.

"When you're finished, you just replace the box in its compartment and lock it. I'll leave you to go through your things." She stepped out of the room.

Jacks stood in front of the box, momentarily paralyzed. He knew what he needed to do and how important it was. But it was eerie, exposing things that belonged to a dead man.

He glanced around the empty room. A human scent had wafted to his nose. It was vaguely familiar — an old-fashioned men's cologne — but Jacks was too nervous to focus on it. He figured it was a bank employee down the hall. Meanwhile, he spotted security cameras on the ceiling, recording his dealings. He needed to shake off his hesitation and make things look routine. He lifted the box's vinyl privacy sheet. With all the anxious energy thrumming through him, it took a moment to focus.

He noticed first a pair of old-fashioned photographs. They were faded and on paper with scalloped trim—antiques from the nineteenth century, it appeared. They weren't what Jacks was looking for, but he couldn't resist examining them.

The first was a portrait of a bearded man with a top hat, a coat and vest, and a wide cravat. Despite the costume, the resemblance to Benoit was uncanny. It had to be Benoit's father. The other photograph was a portrait of the man with a teenaged boy in a similar three-piece suit. Father and son. Benoit had said his father had a thriving fur trading business. They looked like the perfect nineteenth century family, genteel and proud.

Jacks put the pictures aside and picked up a leather-bound journal. He fanned the pages. They were filled with writing in tidy cursive, and as Jacks looked closer, it was all in French, Benoit's native language. That would be another obstacle. How was he going to get it translated into English?

Beneath the journal, he found something that looked like a rudimentary book. Two wood covers held its pages together with fibrous straps. There were cuneiform symbols that had dulled or eroded on its covers. It was hard to tell whether they had been written in ink or carved. The book certainly looked ancient. It had to be The Báalam-Tet. The covers were softer than they appeared at first, and Jacks deciphered that they must have been encased in a very fine skin, like an animal intestine. It smelled putrid.

He had plenty of time to study the book later. Farzan was waiting for him. He slid the strap of his messenger bag off his shoulder to shove the stuff into the bag. That scent from before, that presence, made his nose twitch. It was a person, and the spicy cologne suddenly connected with a memory. Jacks heard movement behind him.

A blunt object pummeled the back of his head. Sparks ate up his vision, and an enervating pain claimed his body. His legs gave out, and everything went black.

FARZAN UNFOLDED A glossy brochure on home refinancing. The colorful text and photos blurred in and out of focus while his chest constricted and his mouth went dry. He kept staring at the brochure, trying to keep himself anchored to something. The sweat from his hands smudged and blurred the text of the pamphlet, and he wondered how suspicious he was going to look walking out of the bank with ink stains on his fingers.

Maarten and Annika were steps away on a pair of sofa chairs in front of a bank officer's desk. Farzan had to pretend he didn't know them. He had to act like everything was casual. Acting casual was not something Farzan was good at. He was good at taking charge and being in the middle of things and managing messy situations to get them under control. In this situation, he had to admit, he was nearly useless, and that made him even more antsy and nervous. Idling in the bank, just waiting for Jacks to come back from the security box vault, he felt like he was dangling in midair, fifty stories above the ground.

He noticed Mrs. James come out from the back end of the bank. That meant she had left Jacks to retrieve Benoit's archaic items. Farzan prayed Jacks would be quick about it. Things had gone smoothly so far, but every extra minute they spent in the place was time for things to go hurtling out of control.

He heard Maarten call Mrs. James over to the bank officer's desk. Farzan turned his back to them, pretending not to listen to a conversation in easy earshot.

In an entitled, peevish tone, Maarten asked Mrs. James about the whereabouts of the bank officer. Mrs. James was warm and placating. Maarten, whether he was playing up a distraction or just being his naturally bossy and rude self, wasn't having it.

"This is outrageous. My wife and I have been waiting for nearly half an hour. It's not as though you have a rush of customers here. If you can't provide someone to assist us, we'll take our business elsewhere."

Mrs. James responded in the steadying tone of a woman well-acquainted with the demands of young, rich tourists. "Good gracious, we wouldn't want that. If you and your wife have a moment to spare, I'll just run back and check on Mr. Applewhite. Would you like a cup of coffee or tea in the meantime?"

She called over one of the pretty tellers from behind the counter to get them something to drink. Maarten huffed and muttered a complaint in Dutch to his sister. The tension in the air thickened like a noxious fog.

Gradually, Farzan noticed it was more than the tension between Maarten and Mrs. James that had changed the climate of the high-ceilinged bank. His lungs shrunk, and he had the horrible hypnagogic sensation of being smothered. The daylight seemed to flutter as though a horde of demon angels was closing in around the building. Farzan couldn't say how he knew it, but he knew. They were all trapped.

He looked up at the decorative moldings along the perimeter of the ceiling. He couldn't see the intruders, but they were out there, watching, menacing. He had to warn Jacks.

The bank's double glass doors flew open, and a posse of men morphed into a snarling cyclone of muscled hide and fur. Maarten and Annika burst out of their seats as roaring lions. The girl who had come out to bring them coffee and tea dropped her tray and screamed. Mrs. James clutched the girl's arm, trying to steady her, while she looked for her other bank teller. She'd disappeared beneath the counter. Hopefully, she was sounding an alarm.

Farzan stooped low to the ground behind the brochure display. It was a flimsy barrier, but he needed to keep an eye on things. Warning Jacks was one matter, but there were the two women who were scared out of their minds. They needed help to make it safely behind the counter to the back room where they could lock the door behind them.

His attention turned as two more big cats bounded into the bank. He counted five spotted jaguars and now two lions gnashing and tumbling over each other. Jacks had explained those lions were the good guys. They were friends of Maarten, guarding the bank. But the Glaring had come with numbers. Two jaguars rolled over one of the lions, and they clamped their jaws down on its meaty haunches.

Farzan winced. Maarten and Annika, lion and lioness, cantered forward, gauging an approach to intervene. In the midst of it all, the security guard pivoted around with his gun raised in his hand. He was completely overwhelmed.

A bestial brawl exploded overhead. Farzan looked to the balustrade and shuddered. More big cats had burst into the building. They must have come through the second floor windows. There were striped ones and mottled ones, and at least one other tawny-maned lion trying to hold them off.

One of the spotted monsters hunched over the railing and zoned in on the entrance to the backrooms of the bank. Farzan's heart leapt from his chest. They must know Jacks was back there retrieving Benoit's magical book.

Before Farzan could make a break for the counter and onward to Jacks, everything went berserk. One by one, leopards and jaguars dove down from the balustrade, laying claim to the bank. Their dander rained through the building, and their wild animal musk seemed to choke the oxygen from the air. Some of the big cats snarled and clambered toward the fray by the front of the bank. Some of them closed in on the back end.

A spotted jaguar skulked toward Mrs. James and the bank teller. The two ladies stared at the 200-pound beast, holding on to each other and moaning. The jaguar's gaze was unbreakable and murderous.

Farzan whirred around the brochure case to get the two women out of the way. There was no time for them to make it through the swinging door of the bank counter, but he could pull them out from the open where they were sitting ducks.

He caught the arm of the teller and tugged at her to bring her along with him behind a desk. The jaguar pounced. Mrs. James screamed. She was buried by its clawed forelimbs and spotted heft. The girl sprang away and clung to Farzan.

Farzan moved her along quickly. Mrs. James was lost, and the jaguar would turn to the two of them in seconds. He raced for a desk at the far end of the room, nearly dragging the young teller, and he pushed her toward the space beneath it. He crouched low on the floor. Cold sweat beaded his face. His eyes clenched shut at the sound of gunshots, and then the room was filled with a human cry for mercy and the savage brawl of dozens of feline monsters. What could he do? Would the were-lions be able to hold off the attack? Was there a chance that anyone would make it out of the bank alive?

FROM A WOUND-UP panicky place inside Jacks, he fought to resurface from a black hole of unconsciousness. His skull felt like it had been pulverized. His eyelids had shuttered to blanket himself from the pain. He had to open his eyes so he could find a way to escape from his attacker. Someone had been waiting to ambush him. The strike to the back of his head had been meant to kill.

He couldn't pick up the scent of his attacker. His senses had been drained by the blow. He opened his eyes, and the room's overhead lights stabbed into his brain. An unearthly gravity pounded down on him, and nausea gripped his stomach hard.

He tried to breathe. He had to make sure that Benoit's book

and journal were safe. Jacks willed his feeble arms to push up from the floor, and he lumbered drunkenly to his hands and knees.

Just steps away, the bank officer was at the counter rifling through his messenger bag. Mr. Applewhite. His crude and brutal weapon, a galvanized steel pipe, was sitting on the counter.

A growl gurgled up Jacks's throat.

Applewhite grabbed the pipe, took one stride toward Jacks, and bashed him hard on the shoulder. Jacks collapsed to the floor again, grasping weakly to protect his wound. Tears bled from his eyes. A strobe light of pain throbbed through his body.

"Stay down there this time."

Jacks struggled to see him. He was a ragdoll from the bludgeoning, but he managed to spit out words.

"Why are you doing this?"

"That's none of your concern." Applewhite put the journal and the book in his attaché and

clipped its bronze spring clasps shut.

"Are you going to give those to the Glaring?"

"Good guess."

"Why?"

He shot a crooked glance at Jacks. He was completely unmasked of his mild-mannered, bank officer persona. In fact, he looked older, bonier, and more desperate than Jacks had noticed—a middle-aged, middle manager who hated himself and the world. He wasn't a werecat. Jacks would have sensed that before.

"Because it pays better than working for the bitch who stole the job that belonged to me."

Jacks wondered how long Mr. Applewhite had been in collusion with the Glaring, poisoned by his petty gripe, and lured into an opportunity to make some fast cash. It was an unbelievably dark agreement. He had to know what the Glaring was capable of. The murder spree in New York must have made news headlines around the world.

He pieced things together bit by bit. The local strays must have relayed to the Glaring that he had come down to Barbados. The Asian wereleopard had been the first on the scene, tipped off by Bella so he wouldn't bother Farzan, while his brethren pulled off their attack in New York. Since then, they must've scoped the island, seen the public notice about Benoit's estate, and discovered a good strategy in Applewhite.

Maybe Applewhite didn't have authorization to get into Benoit's safety deposit box. Maybe the Glaring had wanted to play it sly rather than storming the place. So, they waited until Jacks returned to open the box for them, and they were using him to grab the contents.

Jacks felt like an idiot. He had bumbled his job epically. He wondered if there was some hope with Maarten, Annika and the others stationed around the bank. If he could delay Applewhite and create some kind of commotion, they might still have a chance of stopping the Glaring's plan.

"What did they promise you for the book?"

"You think you can make me a better offer?"

"You think they'll reward you when you give them what they want? They'll take that book and butcher you like prey."

He grasped the pipe again. "Why don't we see what we can do about shutting your mouth for good." He came at Jacks with his weapon raised.

Jacks slid away from him on the floor. Applewhite towered over him, a sadistic gleam sparking from his eyes. He looked over Jacks as he might consider a cattle for slaughter, gauging a spot for a finishing blow.

Human screams and a bestial commotion erupted from beyond the chamber. The outburst distracted both Jacks and his assailant. Alarms and lights blared from the ceiling, and the gate to the security box chamber slammed down. When Applewhite turned his head to the gate, Jacks summoned his feline transformation. His weakened limbs morphed into fighting legs and claws.

He tackled Applewhite too quickly for him to put up a fight. Jacks sunk his jaws into a death grip, savoring the convulsions of his victim. Warm blood saturated the fur of his muzzle. When Applewhite's heart stopped beating, he dropped him, lapping the blood from his muzzle in wide, luxuriant swaths.

He swiveled his ears toward the gated door. A battle was going on out there. He could hear snarls, excruciating yelps of pain, and frantic shouts for mercy. The Glaring must have been staking out the bank and discovered Jacks had come with back-up. Farzan was out there, helpless. Jacks had to get to him. He transformed back to his human self, went for Applewhite's attaché case, and transferred Benoit's journal and the Báalam-Tet into his messenger bag.

He ached a bit from being bashed by the pipe, but his self-healing powers worked quickly, amped up by the urgency of the situation. He rooted through Applewhite's pants pockets, searching for a magnetic card like the one Mrs. James had used to open the gates. He found it and hiked his messenger bag up on his good shoulder. Jacks staggered to the gate, swiped the card, and the gates lifted up.

He drew up by one side of the door to the teller counter and peeked out to the bank gallery. It was barely recognizable as the place he'd left just minutes ago. Desks, chairs, and computers had been thrown helter-skelter, and papers and brochures were scattered across the floor. The industrial carpeting was gouged and buckled in places. From one corner to another, the bank had been transformed into a battlefield.

He spotted two wildcat skirmishes going on at the front of

the bank and another closer to the stairs to the second floor. A bloody, metallic taste filled his mouth. People had been gored. He couldn't see the bodies on the floor from his position, but he smelled their damp desperation, sweat pooling on their brows and chests as they sputtered and convulsed, grasping for life.

Where was Farzan?

Jacks turned to the backroom corridor and spotted a rolling freight cart against one wall. He quietly stashed his messenger bag behind there. He needed to go out into the war zone as a mountain lion to face the hunters. He had glimpsed six or seven leopards and jaguars. There could be more he hadn't caught during his quick scan. He bore down on his diaphragm once again.

He skulked out from the backroom into the teller booth. The bank teller who had given Jacks his cash lay mauled and motionless beneath her station. Beside her was a naked stranger with his neck ripped apart. He must have made the kill and then been taken out by Maarten and Annika's crew. Jacks put his front paws up on the counter and stood on his hind legs to snoop out at the gallery.

Two werelions, Jean-Luc and César, were holding off a trio of wildcats at the far end of the bank. Annika was finishing off a spotted leopard with her jaws planted in his neck. Maarten and Somsuea stood off three jaguars and an ocelot by the stairs. Mauled corpses were everywhere, some of them in uniforms. Policemen must have arrived on the scene, responding to the alarm, and been ripped apart by the big cats.

Jacks recognized the body of the security guard farther down the floor toward the front doors. The young man lay tangled and bleeding. He saw many unfamiliar naked men and women, members of the Glaring that Maarten's pride had killed.

As he stole through the swinging door of the teller booth,

he froze mid-step and his breath caught in his throat. Thierry and Lars both lay dead by the brochure display. How many of the Glaring must have shown up to overtake a pride of lions? Was anyone else dead?

He couldn't see Farzan anywhere, but as he pivoted around, he heard a whimper and a familiar, whispering voice.

"Shh. Just stay still. It's going to be all right."

He focused in on a spot on one side of the bank's bay of desks. The voice was coming from behind one of the few desks that hadn't been overturned. His olfactory senses told him the other bank teller and Farzan were hiding there.

Jacks crept toward that desk, steady and low to the ground, keeping a gauge on anyone watching his movements. He passed by the slaughtered body of Mrs. James. His stomach lurched with grief and nausea, but he swallowed it back. He had to focus on getting to Farzan and bringing him safely into the back area of the bank where they would find an exit. Skulking step by step, he came up behind the desk. The bank teller looked at Jacks with trembling brown eyes. Farzan slid away on his behind. His frightened expression softened with relief as he recognized Jacks. But the girl was still terrified by the sight of him as a mountain lion. She screamed.

Farzan tried to shush her. It was too late. All of the big cats, both the werelions and the werejaguars honed in on the outburst. The hunters would have to get past Jean-Luc, César, Maarten, and Somsuea if they wanted to attack Farzan and the girl. But overhead, on the second floor colonnade, Jacks noticed a big jaguar with a black and orange mottled muzzle had locked in on them, quivering in anticipation.

He gazed at Farzan intently and nudged his head toward the back of the bank. Their best chance was to make a break for that corridor where they had better places to hide while he held off the jaguar.

Farzan read the message. He took the girl's hand. "We run. We stay together. We'll be okay."

A noisy scramble came from the stairs. The four big cats Maarten and Somsuea had been holding off had figured things out. They were finding positions from higher ground to make a strike at Jacks.

Farzan touched the side of Jacks's muzzle. "You stay alive, okay?"

He nudged reassuringly at Farzan's hand. Then he pointed his eyes to the back of the bank.

Farzan and the bank teller raced for the back corridor. The mottled jaguar leapt down to chase them. Jacks bounded into the jaguar from the side, and they went tumbling together and wiping out on the floor. Jacks righted himself and glanced at the back end of the bank. It was clear. Farzan and the teller must have made it through the counter.

The jaguar quickly got up on his fours. The two of them circled each other with hateful snarls.

The other four cats lunged down from the second floor railing. They approached him at measured angles and were closing the space rapidly. He kept his eyes on his opponent. The jaguar was longer and bulkier and could easily wrangle him down if he found the right advantage. His glare glinted bloody red. Jacks stared back at him unimpressed. Cat fights were as much about confidence as strength. He had to make the jaguar believe he could easily destroy him and then take on the other four cats.

A roar and a bustle of motion broke out. He caught in his peripheral vision Somsuea burying the ocelot with his hulking tiger weight and ripping into its neck. Nicolas leapt out from a felled desk and ambushed one of the jaguars. Then Maarten launched forward at one of the leopards and chased it across the bank. A piteous yelp told the rest of the story. Maarten must have caught the leopard and made the kill.

Jacks saw a flash of worry in the jaguar's eyes now. Its pack was down to two, and there were three big cats plus Jacks to deal with. Then he noticed Annika stalking toward them. Then Kwame, the biggest lion of them all, trotted down the stairs. His golden muzzle was smeared with the crimson blood of a kill.

The jaguar backed away from Jacks, slyly gauging a route for his retreat. Jacks swaggered toward him. He wanted the kill.

Sirens wailed outside of the bank. In the space of heart-beats, tires screeched and a stampede of people sounded from outside. It had to be a local riot squad. Broken glass crunched and scattered underfoot. A team of men in uniforms and bullet-proof vests stormed in with rifles at their shoulders.

As soon as the first bullet was fired, the jaguar sprang for the back corridor. Jacks stampeded after him. Rounds of bullets sprayed through the bank gallery. He worried about Annika, Maarten, and the others. But the jaguar was headed the way Farzan had gone, and he had to stop that first.

Hurtling through the backroom corridor, Jacks caught the jaguar by his thick mottled hide. His claws tore through fur and flesh. The jaguar kept moving, but he was struggling. Once a cat acknowledged fear, his only instinct was to flee, no matter if he had bigger jaws or more powerful limbs. Jacks used the weight of his upper body to bring his quarry down. The jaguar flailed, but Jacks braced his claws into the floor. Then, he lunged for the back of the neck, twisting the jaguar's head, severing cartilage and sinking his teeth deep. The jaguar convulsed beneath him. He didn't let go until his whole body was still.

Farzan peeked out of the door to a back office. His face was grim and glazed with sweat. "The cops...there's an exit...we've got to go."

Jacks drew back into his human form. He remembered his messenger bag by the freight cart and went for it. César came clambering around the corner of the corridor. Then Somsuea, Nicolas, and Maarten, who was limping with a bullet wound to one of his haunches, and finally massive Kwame, also injured with bullet gouges in his sides seeping blood. The hail of ammunition in the gallery slowly tapered off into single shots as the riot squad spread through the bank making finishing kills. Jacks stared at Maarten as he went through his transformation, cringing from the shot to his upper leg. *What about Annika? And Jean-Luc and Thierry? Should we go back for them?*

Maarten glared at Jacks coldly. His voice stabbed into Jacks's brain. *They're lost. Thanks to you.*

Farzan explained the way to a loading dock where they could slip out to the street. He had gotten the keys to the bank teller's car, which they could pile into and make their way through backcountry roads to Maarten's yacht at Port St. James. The girl remained in the back office, clutching herself. She would be fine when the police discovered her.

Maarten peglegged briskly past Jacks in the direction of the loading dock. César, Somsuea, Nicolas, and Kwame retracted their feline bodies and followed him. Jacks stumbled along in a daze. He couldn't believe Annika was gone. Farzan nudged him down the corridor. There was no time to think about anything. The riot squad would be coming into the back rooms of the bank with their guns at any moment.

TWENTY-THREE

SITTING AT A chaise lounge on the stern deck, with his knees drawn up to his chest, Jacks stared out at the endless, gray sea in the waning light of dusk. Screams of bloody torture echoed from the cabin of Maarten's yacht. He had listened to Maarten and César's agonized complaints for over an hour while Farzan tended to their wounds. The latest desperate scream sounded like it was from Kwame. The werelions' bodies would repair themselves, but they couldn't expel bullets. They were lucky Farzan was on board.

The noise was an awful reminder of the carnage at the Beechfield Bank, but what haunted Jacks more, now that they had clipped out to sea, was the absence of Annika, Jean-Luc, Thierry, and Lars. They were gone, and they would never return. Their bodies wouldn't receive the dignity of being claimed by the people who cared about them.

Annika had championed their mission, and the others had volunteered to help, but Jacks couldn't shake off the feeling that their deaths were *his* fault. If he had been quicker retrieving the books in the security box vault, they all might have gotten out of the bank before the Glaring arrived and then the riot squad. If he hadn't drawn them into the plan in the first place, they'd all still be alive.

Bella purred at his feet, trying to nudge out an invitation to nestle next to him. He rubbed her between the ears. All she cared about was that he and Farzan were safe. He couldn't blame her. He understood that living fully as a cat, she relied on her allies of the moment and couldn't afford to be sentimental about anything else. And she'd been through her own ordeal with the werecats in New York and traveling to a strange place.

Farzan emerged from the cabin with a gory bib over his T-shirt.

"I'm done," he declared. "They can take their chances with lead poisoning. I've had more gracious patients come into the E.R. for a leg amputation. What do they expect? I'm working with kitchen tongs and a paring knife for a scalpel. There's hardly any alcohol left to sterilize the equipment anyway."

Jacks glanced at him. He knew Farzan wouldn't really give up. He was already checking out the bar on the deck, which was fully stocked with liquor.

"Take a break."

"This wouldn't be an easy job for anyone," Farzan went on. "A fully-trained trauma surgeon *or* a veterinarian."

"I know." Jacks scooted over in his chaise to make room. "Sit down." Farzan wandered over, still distracted. He caught sight of the swollen, yellow-purplish bruise on Jacks's shoulder and flinched.

"You're supposed to be icing that. What happened to the pack I made for you?"

Jacks glanced at a terrycloth hand towel lying in a puddle on the deck beside his chair. "It melted."

Farzan frowned. Jacks could see the deliberations going on

in his head. Before he could run to the kitchen freezer to prepare another pack, he clasped Farzan's arm to gently pull him closer. "It barely hurts anymore. Just sit with me for a little while, okay?"

Farzan sat down, untied his bib, and placed it on the side. Jacks reached around Farzan's waist and kissed his neck. "You've been amazing." Farzan usually melted at his touch, but he was wooden.

"I feel like if I don't keep doing something, this is all going to hit me."

Jacks heaved a breath. "I'm sorry. You shouldn't have been involved." His vision dimmed. "All of those people...y'know, I'm responsible."

"This is bigger than you, Jacks."

"It didn't have to be."

Farzan turned to him. "I saw, *you* saw what the Glaring is like. They'll do anything to wipe out humankind. Whatever is in that book of Benoit's might be the only thing that can stop them."

Jacks sank in his seat. "I should have gone in alone. I can't stop thinking about all the people who died. Annika was a really good person. Thierry, Jean-Luc, Lars — they didn't have to be there. Mrs. James. The bank teller and security guard. They're all dead because of me."

Farzan took his hand and squeezed it. "I'm sorry, Jacks. Maybe I can't understand what you're going through. For me, it's a miracle any of us made it out alive. And if we can do something now to stop the Glaring from killing more people, that's what we have to focus on. So that all the casualties meant something."

His words floated in Jacks's head, gradually neutralizing the guilt. Farzan and Bella had both survived. It *was* a miracle. He had to believe there was a reason for that. That they could still, together, figure out a way to end the Glaring's plan to destroy the human race.

The messenger bag was sitting at the foot of the chaise lounge. He hadn't opened it since they had returned to the yacht. "We're going to need a lot of help. Annika was the only person who had some knowledge of the book, the Báalam-Tet. And Benoit's notes are in French."

"I took three years of French in high school," Farzan said. "But I don't think we want to rely on that to figure out whatever is in that book."

"We need a werecat mage like Maarten said."

Having said the words, Jacks remembered Benoit talking about visiting Zapotec mystics in the Yucatán. Maybe one of them could help. He had to somehow put the Glaring's feud to rest. That brought Jacks to the man who Maarten had mentioned, Tepe, the Glaring's capitán. Could he be reasoned with or paid off by Benoit's fortune?

Maarten came out of the cabin in a plush bathrobe. He was still favoring one leg. Maarten took a brief notice of the two of them, and then he went to the bar, poured some rum into a tumbler, and tossed it back in a single gulp. Willem quickly materialized, swept behind the bar, and refilled his master's drink.

Farzan gazed at Jacks forbiddingly, but Jacks got up from his chair and approached Maarten at the bar.

"I'm really sorry about Annika. And Jean-Luc, Thierry, and Lars."

Maarten looked stricken for a moment, and then he turned his back to Jacks and downed another rum.

"You blame me, probably."

Maarten answered in a low voice. "The only person I blame is myself."

Jacks came up on him, an arm's length away. Maarten's

body was tight, ready to spring out like a coil. Still, Jacks felt he had to say something to him. "You shouldn't. You did everything you could."

When Maarten spoke, he seemed to be talking things out to himself more than addressing Jacks in particular. "We'll return to Bridgetown in a few days. Annika's cats will know where to find them. Annika would want to return to South Africa, where we were born."

"I know."

Maarten swung around. "You don't know anything. I *blame* myself for bringing you on board. I blame myself for indulging your stupid plan to go back to the bank." He roared at Jacks. "I blame myself for not ripping out your throat the first night we met."

Farzan shot up from his chair, ready to get between them. Jacks didn't budge. He wanted to take the full force of Maarten's anger and grief, for both Maarten's sake and his own. In the awkward interim, Kwame lumbered out to the deck, weakened by his injuries, but still a commanding presence in his belted bathrobe. César, Somsuea, and Nicolas followed him.

"I'd be honored to help bring back their bodies," Jacks told Maarten.

Maarten's eyes blazed. "We're dumping you at Caracas. We're setting sail there to get the ship prepared for the journey to Cape Town, which you will not be part of."

"I know you never wanted to have anything to do with the Báalam-Tet or the Glaring. But it doesn't have to end like this, Maarten. I cared about Annika and your friends too. We're on the same side."

"I was never on any side. I allowed my sister's misguided compassion to pull us into a war that is none of our business."

Maarten's face was ashy and hard. "Annika's dead. You have no friends here."

Farzan burst out. "Obviously, you don't care that the Glaring is killing humans. But doesn't it bother you they killed your friends?"

Maarten looked over him and Bella and sneered at Jacks. "You ought to keep your underlings in line. It's several days' sail to Venezuela, and they could make for a lovely, savory meal."

Farzan blurted out something, but Jacks cut him off. "Let it go." Farzan stormed off down the deck. When it seemed like he had traveled a safe distance away to cool down, Jacks tried with Maarten again.

"I was wrong about you. You do care about other people. I get it now. You left South Africa because you wanted to protect your sister. Maybe she resented you for it. But you were always her big brother. You were everything to her."

Maarten turned away from him, tight-shouldered. Jacks wasn't sure what to make of it, but his words felt right, and it was really the only thing he could think to say. The tumbler of rum wobbled out of Maarten's hand onto the bar. His friends inched up on him with concern. For a moment, Maarten looked like he was breaking down, and his legs might give out beneath him. Then, he headed toward the cabin, his strides growing more confident along the way, and he disappeared inside.

Jacks looked out at the deck. Farzan had found a place at the far end, overlooking the railing. He was no doubt simmering over what Maarten said. Meanwhile, Kwame drew up beside him.

"Maarten just needs some time. That was his grief speaking."

Jacks nodded grimly. "I know. Anyway, I guess it'll be safer for everyone if I don't return to Bridgetown. Thank you for all you've done."

"We all battled bravely. It was a righteous cause."

He was glad Kwame saw it that way.

"What will you do now?" Kwame glanced over to Farzan. "You, your boyfriend, and your tabby will have a hard time on your own."

"Ye-ah..." Jacks raked his hand through his hair.

"Would you like some company?"

He looked at Kwame in disbelief.

"I heard the journal is written in French," Kwame went on. "It's my native language. And I can help you get around South America. I spent some time there before I met Maarten."

"Kwame, I couldn't ask you to."

"Maarten has help for when he returns to Barbados." Kwame glanced at César, Somsuea, and Nicolas. "We talked about it. Someday we will all join up again. Now, we must use Benoit's book to avenge the deaths of Annika, Thierry, Lars, and Jean-Luc."

Jacks's heart swelled from Kwame's generosity. There was no doubt having someone to translate the journal would be a huge asset, not to mention Kwame's intimidating size and strength. He caught a glance from Farzan who seemed to be adding things up.

"Thank you," Jacks said.

Kwame nodded somberly, and then he stepped away with his three friends.

Jacks fetched Bella from the deck and walked over to Farzan. He was lost in a scowl, leaning on the rail. Beyond, the night sky was thickening, melding with the sea.

"We can't get to Caracas soon enough," Farzan said.

Jacks sidled up close so that their shoulders were touching while Bella curled into his chest. "Maarten didn't mean what he said."

Farzan didn't look particularly impressed by the comment, but he kept his thoughts to himself.

"Kwame is going to help us."

"What if the Glaring attacks New York again? How am I supposed to keep my family safe?"

Jacks didn't know what to say. They were headed to South America, and logically, the Glaring would focus on finding him to get the Baalem-Tet, though it was possible they could strike out anywhere. He couldn't give Farzan any guarantees, but he didn't want Farzan to go back to New York. He needed him by his side. Jacks wasn't sure if that was selfish to say.

"I wish I could protect them," he said.

"The only thing we have is that journal and that book." Farzan turned to Jacks and dropped his head on Jacks's good shoulder. Jacks encircled him with his arms, gently, since Bella was between them. Farzan had to be beside himself worrying about his family. He had left them to be with Jacks. He had given up everything and been dragged into this brutal nightmare. Jacks wondered if he regretted it.

"If you want to go back to New York, I'd understand."

Farzan looked up at Jacks. "Is that what you want?"

"What am I supposed to say? You've got your family and medical school."

"Tell me how you honestly feel."

He hesitated. "I want you here with me. But not if you're going to regret it. I can't say how long it will take to figure out what's in the Báalam-Tet and how to use it as a defense against the Glaring. It'll be dangerous, and you won't be able to see your family for a long time."

A silence ensued. Jacks was split in half. He'd be devastated if Farzan left, but at least he'd be safe.

"I can't think of anything more important than saving the human race," Farzan said. "Considering the alternative, it would be pointless to have a medical degree, don't you think?" He gripped Jacks's side, and Bella jumped down to give the two men their moment. "You're not getting rid of me so easily, Jackson Dowd."

Jacks kissed the side of his face. Then he whimpered from the emotions swelling inside him. "Thank you. And you know what? I love you."

Farzan held him tight. "It only took three months, four wild cat attacks, and giving up on medical school to get you to say that?"

Jacks laughed tearily, and Farzan joined in. Their path ahead was deeply uncertain, terrifying really, but they were able to share a moment of amusement.

"I love you, too," Farzan said. "Because you're beautiful and brave–"

"You're braver," Jacks interrupted.

"I'll take that." Farzan's face drew up in a thoughtful frown. "But it can't be that hard uncovering the secrets of werecat magic while an army of jaguars tries to track us down."

"You're right. It'll be a piece of cake."

They held each other, staring out at the night-shrouded sea, minding their own thoughts. Somehow, a little optimism perked up inside Jacks. They'd foiled the Glaring once now. They had the Báalam-Tet and leads on a wereshaman and Tepe. Most importantly, they had each other.

ABOUT THE AUTHOR

Author Andrew J. Peters is the third most famous Andrew J. Peters on the internet after the disgraced former mayor of Boston and a very honorable concert organist. He's an award-winning author, an educator, and a cat lover. His passion is writing fantasy inspired from ancient world mythologies, and he also loves retelling classic stories from a queer point of view. Andrew lives in New York City with his husband and their cat Hugo. For more about him and his writing:

Website: https://andrewjpeterswrites.com

Facebook: https://www.facebook.com/andrewjpeterswrites

Goodreads: https://www.goodreads.com/author/show/6908025.Andrew_J_Peters

Bluesky: @ajpeterswrites.bsky.social